A DREAM TO FOLLOW

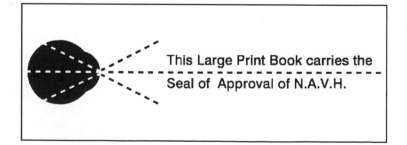

This Large Print Book carries the
Seal of Approval of N.A.V.H.

A DREAM TO FOLLOW

LAURAINE SNELLING

THORNDIKE PRESS

A part of Gale, Cengage Learning

Detroit • New York • San Francisco • New Haven, Conn • Waterville, Maine • London

Copyright © 2001 by Lauraine Snelling.
Return to Red River Series #1
Thorndike Press, a part of Gale, Cengage Learning.

LIBRARY OF CONGRESS CATALOGING-IN-PUBLICATION DATA

Snelling, Lauraine.
    A dream to follow / by Lauraine Snelling.
        p. cm. — (Return to Red River series ; #1) (Thorndike Press
    large print Christian historical fiction)
    ISBN-13: 978-1-4104-0902-7 (hardcover : alk. paper)
    ISBN-10: 1-4104-0902-3 (hardcover : alk. paper)
    1. Red River of the North — Fiction. 2. Frontier and pioneer
life — Fiction. 3. Norwegian Americans — Fiction. 4. Dakota
Territory — Fiction. 5. Large type books. 6. Christian fiction. 7.
Domestic fiction. I. Title.
PS3569.N39D7 2008
813'.54—dc22   2008017963

Published in 2008 by arrangement with Bethany House Publishers.

Printed in the United States of America
1 2 3 4 5 6 7 12 11 10 09 08

DEDICATION

To Cecile, who has made my life
so much easier, and to
Eagle One, who made it richer.

Bjorklund Family Tree

Soren Jarlsberg
(1847—)

— 1869 —

Johann Bjorklund
(1844—)

Anna Knutson
(1851—1878)

— 1874 —

Thorliff Bjorklund
(1875—)

Roald Bjorklund
(1846—1882)

— 1879 —

Carl (Andrew)
Bjorklund
(1882—)

Ingeborg Strand
(1858—)

— 1884 —

Astrid Bjorklund
(1885—)

Haakan Howard
Bjorklund
(1854—)

Augusta Bjorklund
(1857—)

1890

Gustaf Bjorklund
(1822—1884)

1842

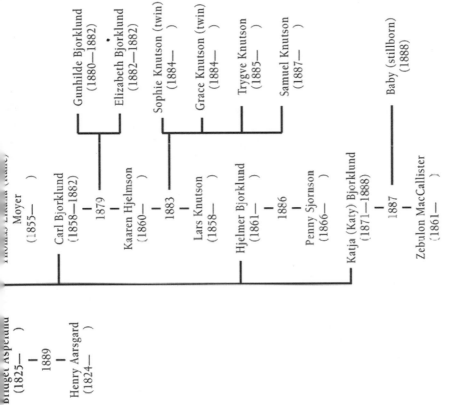

CHAPTER ONE:
BLESSING, NORTH DAKOTA
SPRING 1893

"I'm afraid to open it."

Ingeborg Bjorklund stared at the letter her tall, sometimes awkward son laid on the table. "Looking at it won't make it change, Thorliff."

"I know, but . . ." At seventeen years of age Thorliff Bjorklund had yet to fill out the shoulders of his full-sleeved white shirt. The sweater vest in shades of natural wool, knit by his grandmother, hugged a chest that promised breadth. He sighed. Bjorklund blue eyes stared at the envelope as if afraid it might bite.

"Open it, son. It could be wonderful news." Ingeborg, enveloped by a white apron, gripped the back of the handmade oak chair.

But what if they don't like my story? It won't be the first time, but . . . Taking his pocket-knife from his pocket, Thorliff opened the blade before reaching for the envelope. The hiss of sharp knife through paper sounded loud in the kitchen that also seemed to be holding its breath. The crackle of papers extricated from a paper womb and then unfolded filled the silence. Thorliff closed his eyes, sighed again, and opened them to read the letter. His hands quivered, shaking the missive like a breeze rattling cottonwood leaves. He read, stopped to glance at his mother, then read swiftly to the end, his breathing keeping pace with his eyes.

He clutched the letter to his chest, his face shining like after the first summer sunburn. "They like it."

Ingeborg pulled out the chair and sank onto it. "Read it aloud."

" 'Dear Mr. Bjorklund . . .' " Thorliff paused and grinned at his mother. "They called me mister, can you believe that?" At her nod he continued.

"We are pleased to inform you that we would like to publish your story, *The Long Winter Night,* in an upcoming issue of *Harper's Magazine.* Your attention to detail and evocative wording made us wonder if perhaps this event had happened to you, since you hail from North Dakota. We will be pleased to pay you the sum of ten dollars upon publication of your story. Please keep us in mind for any further submissions.

Sincerely,
Michael Smith, Editor
Harper's Magazine . . ."

Thorliff's voice trailed off at the end.

"I knew that one day someone would like your stories. I always have."

Thorliff could feel the embarrassing heat start in his neck. "But you're my mor. You *have* to like my stories."

"True. But some I like better than others, and this one was the very best you have ever written."

"Mange takk." Thorliff scanned through the letter again. "Ten dollars." The awe came through in his voice.

"Tante Kaaren is done with classes now, and since she was the heroine of your story . . ." Ingeborg's voice trailed off as she remembered that frightful event. "Uff da. Such a freak blizzard that was, and it could have been so tragic if you all hadn't stayed at the school." She shuddered. "By the grace of God, it wasn't." She paused, caught in the memory before continuing. "I know how much Tante Kaaren would love to hear your good news right away." Ingeborg clasped her hands on the red-and-white checkered tablecloth. "Perhaps this will help your far understand how important it is for you to go to college in the fall."

Thorliff made a sound deep in his throat. His going to college might be important, but the past years of drought had them all tightening their belts. They hoped that was over, but everything depended on the harvest. Some of the Bonanza farmers had given up and sold their land. Nils Haugen, south of town, had sold out and gone back to Norway.

It would take more than one little story being published to change his stepfather's mind. Thorliff had replayed their last discussion over and over in his head until he had every word and gesture burned on his brain. Haakan Bjorklund believed clear down to his bootstrings that his sons should stay home and help with the farming, especially the eldest son. With the added acres and the new addition to the cheese house, they needed every hand they could get. After all, farmland was the reason they'd emigrated from Norway. When his sons married, they would build another house on the land and, please God, if they could afford it, buy more land. Always it was buy more land. Think land, not college.

How do I make him understand that Andrew

12

is the one who loves the farm? Just because he's not the eldest should have nothing to do with it. Thorliff refolded the paper and inserted it back in the envelope, taking care to see no corner was bent. He placed it in his shirt pocket, covering the pocket with one hand.

"I'll cut you some bread and cheese to eat on the way." Ingeborg stood and, rounding the table, laid a hand on his shoulder. "If it is God's will that you go to St. Olaf, you will go."

But what if it isn't? And I want to go so desperately. Thorliff sighed and nodded. Sometimes understanding God's will took more time than he believed he had or wanted to spend waiting.

Ingeborg lifted a towel off freshly baked loaves of bread and sliced off the heel and another slice of one. Lifting the glass dome from over the cheese, she cut thick slabs of their own cheddar and layered the pieces between the bread. She poured a cup of buttermilk from the crock and handed cup and sandwich to her son. "You go on now. Kaaren will be so excited."

"Andrew and Astrid are bringing the wagon. I left school early to run an errand for Pastor Solberg and then ran all the way home. I couldn't wait." He glugged the buttermilk and set the cup on the drainboard by the dry sink. "Mange takk." Ripping a bite off the sandwich, he strode out the door, the screen door banging behind him.

Looking off to the west, he could see his stepfather, Haakan, riding the sulky plow behind three across of their heavier horses. To the north his uncle Lars used the same. They would expect him to yoke up two span of oxen and take out the third plow as soon as he came home from school. With the early warmth of spring, fieldwork had started early also.

Father God, if you can find it in your will to let me go to college, I promise I'll work so hard all summer that they won't miss me so bad come fall. He set off at a fast jog to the house on the other side of the short pasture. The wing added on to his aunt Kaaren and uncle Lars's house to make a school for the deaf made it look as big as many barns. That, along with the extra barn for the horses, the machine sheds, and the granaries — now nearly empty — took up better than an acre. Thorliff had heard people around say if you wanted to see a couple of prosperous farms, go by the Bjorklunds'.

The two brothers, Roald and Carl, had immigrated to the area in 1880 with their families. But both had died one terrible

14

winter — Carl in a flu epidemic and Roald in a fierce blizzard. Thorliff remembered some of those days, since he'd been through it all.

He stuck his head in the back door of the house and called, "Tante Kaaren?" When no answer floated back, he headed for the school entrance. This time when he called her name, she answered from the classroom on the first floor. Upstairs, the dormitories housed fifteen students ranging in age from ten to twenty. He paid no attention to the living room, taking the hall to where he could hear people talking.

Aunt Kaaren, her golden hair worn in a braid wrapped around her head like a crown, stood talking with Ilse Gustafson, another immigrant and orphan, who had become her assistant in teaching sign language to the deaf students. "Thorliff, is something wrong?" Aunt Kaaren asked.

"No. Why?"

"You've been running."

"Oh no. I have good news." He pulled the letter from his pocket and waved it as he crossed the floorboards painted a deep blue. "Here, you read it."

"Can't you just tell me?" Kaaren stared at the return address. "*Harper's Magazine.* They bought your story?"

Thorliff could feel his face about to crack from the width of his grin. "Read it."

Ilse stepped closer to peer over Kaaren's shoulder. "You sold your story about the night we all spent at the schoolhouse in the blizzard?"

"Ja, that's the one." Thorliff drew closer to Kaaren's other side. Kaaren smiled up at him and read the letter again.

"This is the most wonderful news. Thanks be to God, others see your talent besides us." She reached up to pat his cheek. "I am so proud of you, I could just burst." She waved the paper. "And to think, ten dollars. That can help you buy books at college. What else do you have out to publishers?"

"Not much. I got three others returned in the last couple of weeks."

"So you must send them out again." Kaaren folded the letter and handed it back to Thorliff. "Have you told Haakan yet? And Pastor Solberg?" She glanced at the clock on the wall. "And how come you are home so early? Teacher get mad at you?" The three of them laughed. If anyone got sent home, it was Andrew for fighting, and always at the behest of someone less fortunate. Pastor Solberg, who doubled as teacher of the one-room schoolhouse, had been forced to discipline Thorliff's younger brother more

16

than once for using his fists before using his mind.

"I must get out in the field. I will show this to Pastor in the morning." Thorliff tucked the envelope back in his pocket and, once out the door, leaped the three stairs to the ground. While he'd earned money working for neighbors at times in the past, this was his first money from his writing. And to think it was for a story he almost didn't write. Another thing to be thankful to Pastor Solberg for. And Anji Baard.

The thought of Anji slowed his feet. Ah, if only he could run back across the fields and tell her. She would dance around the room, laughing and calling out the good news to her entire family. Anji never could keep a secret. Somehow in the last year they'd taken to walking home together from church and school rather than riding in the buckboards with their families. The Baards, who had homesteaded soon after the Bjorklunds, lived only one section over. If Thorliff worked until dusk, maybe he could run over there before supper.

Once back home he bounded up the stairs to change into his work clothes, carefully hanging his school clothes on the pegs along the wall. He tucked the precious envelope into the collection of Dickens' stories he'd

17

received for his seventeenth birthday, clattered back down the steep stairs, and with a wave to Ingeborg, who was now folding clothes out at the clothesline, he whistled for Paws. Paws, their caramel-colored watchdog, had been a member of the family since their second year in the new country and was now getting up in years.

Plowing to a stop, Thorliff turned around. "Mor, where's Paws?"

"He must be out with your far. Haakan said he waits for the mice to run out of the furrows and then tries to catch them."

"Has he gotten any?"

"I don't know." She snapped a sheet to get the folds even. "But I've not known him to bring any home."

A meadowlark sang from the fields and another answered. Thorliff cupped his hands around his mouth and whistled again. Paws had gotten hard of hearing lately too. It looked as if he'd have to round up the oxen by himself. He flipped the bail off the gate by the barn, swung the three-pole gate open just enough to slip through, and headed across the pasture. The sun felt warm on his face and shoulders, not like the sun of winter that glistened so bright on the snow it hurt your eyes but had no warmth for the body. Green shoots spread a haze across the

18

land, poking up through the brown leftovers of last year's grass and reaching for the sun. Dandelion and plantain leaves spread broad enough for harvesting, if only he had time. He'd tell Mor about them so Astrid could come picking. Fresh greens cooked with bacon would taste mighty good after all the canned food of winter.

By the time he'd reached the oxen lying down chewing their cud, Paws caught up with him, leaping and yipping as if apologizing for his tardiness. Thorliff reached down and ruffled the dog's ears, then thumped him on the ribs and back. "Good dog, even if you are a bit slow." He waved his arm in an arc. "Go get 'em, boy."

Paws barked and darted at the animals. General, the red-and-white lead ox, hoisted his rump in the air with no show of hurry, then unfolded his front legs and rose, arching his back and stretching, tail curled around his haunches. When he'd finished to his satisfaction, he turned and ambled toward the barn, the others repeating his actions and falling into line. The milk cows grazed in another pasture, where it would be Astrid's job to bring them in for milking.

By the time Thorliff had the oxen yoked and harnessed to the plow, the wagon arrived with the schoolchildren. One of

Kaaren's deaf students drove the wagon and waved at Thorliff.

"How come you got home early?" Andrew, six years younger and a shade blonder, leaped from the tailgate and charged across to where his brother was just climbing on the plow.

"I'll tell you later. Tell Astrid there are greens ready for picking in the pasture."

"I wanted to go fishing, but I'll be out in the field with the other team as soon as I can."

Thorliff shrugged. "See you." He slapped the reins on the oxen backs and headed for the field. With the days getting longer, he might get a couple hours of plowing in before dusk.

While the oxen were slower than the horses, he didn't mind. The fragrance of rich dirt, the earth curling over alongside two straight furrows behind him, the sun on his shoulders, the grunt of the brown ox behind General, a crow cawing from a willow in the boggy section of the pasture — all announced the arrival of spring. Andrew wanted to go fishing, but he'd rather be hunting — or writing. Baptiste was most likely already down at the river with fishing pole and rifle both at his side.

Thorliff turned the oxen, slowing them

enough to keep the furrows even on the turn. The fields needed to be tilled, then disked and harrowed so wheat could be sown. The better the harvest, the more chance there would be money for his schooling. Unless the railroad raised their shipping rates again. Over the winter, there'd been heated discussions of how to keep the rates within reason.

His hands burned by the time he followed his father's team into the barnyard. Like a fool he'd forgotten to take his gloves. Winter hands, that's what he had. Soft and white, or red in this case. Blisters squished in the palm. He'd have to take a needle to them tonight so they'd drain.

"You got out there mighty early." Haakan helped him raise the yokes off the oxen's necks.

"I know." It was all he could do to keep from blurting out his surprise. "Pastor sent me on an errand and said I didn't have to go back today."

"You that far ahead?"

"Ja. I usually help some of the others." He hefted the yoke and heaved it up onto the peg rack built into the barn wall just for that purpose.

Haakan followed him and draped the horse harness over its pegs. By the time all the animals were unharnessed and let loose in the pasture, peeper frogs were singing their evening medley, and a lamp glowed in the kitchen window. Haakan and Thorliff, with Andrew right behind them, headed for the milking barn, where two of the deaf students, along with Astrid, were sitting on three-legged stools, their foreheads leaning into cow flanks and milk streaming into buckets.

Haakan nodded to the students as he passed them and stopped by Astrid. "How many yet to go?"

"Four. The milk cans are nearly full." Astrid nodded over her shoulder. Three cans, one with a strainer atop it, sat among an eager assortment of cats, some cleaning, some crying, and some pacing. "I fed the cats, but I think they want more."

"Looks like it. I'll take the next one. Thorliff, you take the Holstein. When you're finished, bring in another can."

Thorliff grabbed the handle of a bucket, flinching at the cold metal against the blisters on his palm. Milking was going to take real strength of character tonight. "Easy, boss." He settled his stool, brushed the grass off the cow's udder, and set his bucket in place. Hands on the two front teats, he squeezed and pulled in the ancient rhythm that drew milk from a cow, setting his hands to screaming. Thorliff bit his lip but kept on milking.

The cow swished her tail, the coarse fibers catching him on the side of the face. "Hold it. You got no flies to swat now." *Fool critter.* He blinked his eyes, fighting the watering, grateful he didn't need to see to keep milking. When the last drops hit the foam, he lifted the bucket off to the side where the cow couldn't kick it over and rose, one knee cracking as he did so.

"I'll let 'em out. You boys go on up to the house." Haakan poured his full bucket through the strainer and slopped the last of the milk into the flat pan for the cats.

Thorliff sighed in relief. "Mange takk, Pa."

"And get Mor to take care of your hands." Haakan took the bucket his son had filled and poured the milk into the strainer.

"H-how'd you know?"

Haakan clapped a hand on his son's shoulder. "No gloves when you drove in. You won't forget 'em next time, you know?"

"I know."

The deaf students and Astrid had already left when Andrew stripped the last cow and poured his bucket into the strainer. Haakan slammed the lids on the cans, and Andrew took the wagon handle to pull the rig over to the cheese house. In spite of what Haakan had said, Thorliff started lifting the drop boards that held the stanchions closed at one end of the barn while Haakan did the other. One by one the cows backed up, turned, and followed one another out of the barn and into the star-studded night.

"I got a surprise up at the house."

Haakan slung an arm around his son's shoulder. "What?"

"I'll show you."

Thorliff ignored the burning hands and took the stairs to his bedroom two at a time, gasping for breath at the top of the steep stairs. He grabbed his letter and, hands bracing on the narrow walls, clattered back down. Back in the kitchen, he handed his father the letter.

Haakan cocked an eyebrow as he took the envelope.

"Hurry, Pa." Andrew stopped at Haakan's side.

Haakan tapped the edge of the letter on his finger. "Good news, right?"

Thorliff sketched a nod. *Hurry.* He glanced from the letter to catch the smile dancing in Haakan's eyes.

"Haakan, don't tease the boys so." Ingeborg joined the trio. Her smile widened in the lamplight, her hand settling on Thorliff's shoulder.

Haakan slid the paper from the envelope and unfolded it. He nodded as he read. "Good. Very good." He looked from the letter to his elder son, who had shifted from foot to foot the whole reading while. "It will be a pleasure to read your story in a magazine. And to think you will be paid for it." He handed the letter to Andrew.

"Ten dollars!" Andrew's jaw hit his chest.

"Ja."

"I think that when the money comes, Thorliff should put it into his college fund." Ingeborg raised her gaze to meet her husband's.

"Thorliff doesn't need college to farm. You know how I feel about that." Haakan turned away, a mask dropping into place as he did so. "Let's get washed for supper."

Thorliff closed his eyes. Far certainly hadn't changed his mind, no matter what anyone said. But Thorliff knew so much depended on the harvest. Already they were praying for a good harvest this year.

CHAPTER TWO

Morning chores of milking cows, slopping hogs, and feeding cattle and horses took time.

Thorliff glanced at the clock. Instead of being early as he'd wanted, he was running late. And he knew he smelled like pig. But there was no time to wash again, so he'd changed clothes and scrubbed his boots.

"Thorliff and Anji sitting in a tree, k-i-s-s-i-n-g." Astrid chanted the words around the piece of toast she chewed. The *s*'s came out more like *th* since she was missing two front teeth.

"Astrid, don't talk with your mouth full." Thorliff clenched his hands in his lap so he wouldn't reach over and pinch his little sister. He could feel the heat clear up to his ears.

"Astrid Bjorklund, where do you learn such things?" Ingeborg turned from the stove where she was scrambling eggs. "You apologize to your brother this instant."

"Sorry." But anyone looking at her knew she was not in the least bit sorry. The laughter dancing in eyes that matched the blue of her two brothers gave her away.

Ingeborg set the plate, mounded with fluffy eggs mixed with cream and bacon pieces, in front of her eldest. At the look on his face she laid a hand on his shoulder. "You have to eat in order to think well."

He sighed and scooped up a loaded fork, grateful this wasn't a meal where he had to chew a lot. Foot tapping, he gulped down the food.

"Here comes the wagon for school." Andrew, who'd already eaten, grabbed his lard pail and headed out the door.

"Just a minute." Ingeborg snagged him by the arm. "You didn't comb your hair."

"Mo-orr." But Andrew went to the sink, took the comb off the shelf, dipped it in water, and in front of the wavy glass mirror placed there for Haakan to use when he shaved, ran the comb through hair that waved back nicely when his mother combed it. For Andrew it flopped forward. With a quick glance to see if she was watching, he pitched the comb back in the general direction of the shelf and darted out the door.

"Ma, where's my slate?" Astrid shoved her

arms into her sweater sleeves.

"I do not know. Where did you use it last?"

"Don't know."

"Look in the parlor." Thorliff pushed his chair back. "Wish I had saddled Jack." The mule was seldom used any longer for heavy fieldwork because he was getting up in years.

"What is wrong with the wagon?"

"I wanted to be early to talk with Pastor Solberg." Thorliff motioned to the letter in his pocket.

"That is all?" Ingeborg's raised eyebrow said she was teasing.

"Mor!" He could feel his ears flaming.

Her gentle smile made him grin back.

"I can't find it." The wail from the parlor made them both shake their heads.

"She couldn't find her way out of a gunnysack." Thorliff rolled his eyes and turned back to the arched doorway to the parlor. He reached under an afghan on the horsehair sofa and pulled out the missing slate. "You have to look, little sister."

"Tusen takk." Astrid smiled up at her big brother and, with slate in one hand, took his with her other.

"You are more than welcome." He gave her a push. "Now hurry. They are waiting for you."

"Aren't you coming?"

"I'm going to run. Faster that way." Besides, he could cut across the fields, the distance being much shorter as the crow flies.

"To see Anji?" Laughter floated back over her shoulder as Astrid kissed her mother good-bye, grabbed her lunch bucket, and ran out the door, her thick braids bouncing on her back.

Ingeborg handed Thorliff his lunch pail and reached up to kiss his cheek. "You are a good brother, my son. Go with God."

Thorliff leaped down the steps, caught up with the wagon before it cleared the yard, handed Andrew the lunch bucket, and headed out across the field toward the Baard house. The laughter of the children in the wagon rippled like birdsong on the breeze. Spring in North Dakota burst on the plains, redeeming the land after the long hard winter. Dandelions glowed like miniature suns, sprouting up from deep-green serrated leaves, mounds of richness begging to be harvested. Tiny purple violets managed to bloom right next to recalcitrant snowdrifts, like their cohorts the snowdrops. Spears of grass grew fast enough to be measurable each day.

Thorliff's long legs covered the ground like a racing Thoroughbred. He snatched the porkpie hat off his head before it could be blown away and, arms pumping, ran on. He leaped a drainage ditch, the act of flying releasing a shout he could not contain. The air he sucked in no longer cut like daggers as did the winter air but filled him with joy that bubbled like the root beer they'd capped last fall.

He slowed to a jog when he reached the Baards' yard and waved to Knute, who had gladly given up school several years earlier so he could help his father on the farm. Neither he nor his older brother Swen had much tolerance for sitting in a classroom.

"If ya come for Anji, she's helping Ma hang clothes on the line." Knute clucked his four span of mules forward to hitch them to the plow.

"Thanks." Thorliff headed on around the house to the lines stretched between two posts, each with a crossbar at the top and set into the ground. Sheets flapped in the breeze, nearly hiding the girl fastening them in place with clothespins. Hair the rich brown of a beaver pelt and braided for a crown was all he could see of her until he ducked under the line. Her smile caught him in the chest. Never sure when the childhood friendship had deepened, his reactions to her still surprised him. Wild roses blossomed on her cheeks, and chunks of summer sky filled her wide-set eyes. But her smile — how could her smile make him warm all over?

"Why, Thorliff, I didn't hear the wagon," she said, stepping away from the clothesline.

"No, I ran." He removed the letter from his pocket with trembling fingers and held it out to her, all the while his gaze swimming with hers.

"What . . . ?" She took the letter and read the return address. "Oh, Thorliff." Her whisper of his name was all the approbation he coveted.

"Read it." His feet, not yet tired of running, shifted so he had to order them to stand firm. He sucked in a breath, feeling beads of sweat trickle down behind his ear.

She read the short letter and, throwing her arms wide, threw herself at his chest. He caught her and swung her in a circle as if they were dancing the Pols. When he set her down, she stepped back, her face as red as he knew was his own.

She patted her chest. "Oh my." The words hung between them, caught on the moment like feathers on a breath. They'd danced together often. Why was today different? But this embrace *was* different, and they both knew it.

Anji broke the silence first. "Your story will be in *Harper's Magazine.*" She shook her head slowly, as if she knew it to be true but still could scarcely believe it. "How wonderful." She read the letter again. "And they will pay you."

"Ja, I now can say I am a writer."

"Nei, you've been a writer for years. Who else has written all our Christmas programs and the play we did last year? Who else writes the lines for the Fourth of July celebration? The first graders learn to read from some of your stories." Her gaze dropped to the letter in her hand, then curtained by dark lashes, rose to meet his again. "Who else has sent me poetry?"

Thorliff clenched his hands together to keep from reaching for her. Her words strangled any response, no matter how he tried to force them out.

A dog barking shattered the moment. He could hear it fall like shards of glass at their feet. "I need to show this to Pastor Solberg before all the others get to school. Can you come with me?"

Anji glanced down at her apron and reached behind to untie it in the same motion. "Of course. I'll tell Ma." She flipped her apron over the clothesline and started toward the house. "You start out, and I'll catch you."

Instead, he followed after her and waited at the door, watching teams plowing the fields — the three Baard rigs and off in the distance Haakan and Uncle Lars. Much as he loved school, today was a day to be spent out of doors and riding a sulky plow behind the heavy rumps of a good team. Or hunting or fishing, of course.

The wagonload of schoolchildren was turning into the yard when they trotted down the lane to the schoolhouse, which stood right next to the steeple-topped white church the community of Blessing had built years before. The soddy that had started as a church and became a school was now used for storage. The wood-framed building had replaced it two years earlier.

Just as Pastor Solberg drove his wagon carrying his adopted nieces, Manda and Deborah, into the shed built to shelter the horse and to hold coal and firewood, the two young people dropped, panting, to the three front steps of the one-room schoolhouse. Like other buildings in the area, the structure was several feet off the ground to allow for flooding in the spring when the Red River often overran its banks due to the still-frozen mouth up north at Lake Winnipeg.

Thorliff watched as Manda, who also was graduating, unhitched the horse, took off his bridle, and tied him to the manger. He and everyone else had learned through trial and error not to offer to help her. Not unless they wanted to be told off in no uncertain terms. Even Pastor Solberg let her have her way in this while he and Deborah carried things to the schoolhouse.

"Good morning. You two look like you're about to bust with something. Care to let me in on the secret?"

Thorliff grinned over his shoulder at Anji, then pulled the letter from his pocket and held it out. "This came yesterday." He crammed his hands into his pockets to keep them still.

Pastor Solberg tipped his dark fedora back with one finger. "Well, I'll be a monkey's uncle." Smiling up at Thorliff, who now topped him by half a head, he pulled the letter from the envelope.

"What is it?" Deborah, now a sixth grader, danced in place at his side, trying to peer over his arm. She switched to Thorliff. "What is it? Who's the letter from? Come on, tell me, please?" At a gentle look from her uncle she sighed and rolled her eyes.

Solberg nodded, a smile tugging at the corners of his mouth and slightly lifting his

34

well-trimmed mustache. "So you've done it, young man." He reached out to shake Thorliff's hand. "Let me congratulate you. I know you've had many nays on the pieces you've sent out." His gaze returned to the letter, nodding all the while.

"Who? What?" Deborah peered from one face to the other.

"Thorliff has sold one of his stories to *Harper's,* a rather famous magazine back East." Anji laid a hand on the dancing girl's shoulder.

"Does that make Thorliff famous?" Deborah looked up with questioning eyes.

"Not yet, but maybe someday." Anji smiled at Manda, who'd just joined them. "Thorliff has sold his story about all of us being trapped in the schoolhouse during that blizzard."

Manda nodded. "Good. He should sell some of his other stories too. That one about Andrew being lost in the tall grass is really good."

Thorliff gave Manda a raised eyebrow look. He'd not heard her string that many words together at one time ever since she came to town.

"Well, you are good." Her chin came out in its usual fashion, and her lips thinned. She squared her shoulders as if waiting for him to take the first punch.

"Mange t-takk, tusen takk." Thorliff stuttered in his surprise, reverting to Norwegian as he sometimes did when caught by surprise or shock.

"We better get ready for the day." Pastor Solberg handed the letter back to Thorliff and clapped him on the shoulder. "You want to share that with the whole school, or . . ."

"Ja, I do." Thorliff fingered the envelope. "But . . . but would you read it?"

"To be sure." Solberg opened the door to the cloakroom. "How about raising the windows and letting that warm spring air come in? We don't need a fire today. Manda, you want to fill the water bucket?"

Anji and Thorliff pushed up the three windows on each side of the long room. The floors had been swept and the blackboard washed the night before, so there was little to do since they didn't need to light the stove or bring in wood. Laughter and shouts floated in as children of all ages arrived by foot or wagon or even on horseback, as did the two who lived way south of the small town of Blessing. Dinner buckets clattered on the shelf, and their owners pounded back outside to get in one game of Red Rover before the bell rang.

Pastor Solberg came to stand beside Thorliff as he stared out the open window. "I imagine your ma and pa are right proud of you."

Thorliff nodded. "Tante Kaaren too." He heard his teacher take in a deep breath and let it out.

"Was there any mention of college?"

"Ja, Mor said I should save the money to use for books at school in the fall."

"And Haakan?"

"I don't need college to farm. Then he left the room, but his face said it all. He believes I should stay home and work on the farm. As he's said in the past, there's no need for more schooling to be a good farmer." Thorliff shook his head, his shoulders slumped. "He . . . he might be right, but I don't care that I'm the oldest and the farm will be mine one day. Andrew wants the farm, not me."

"I know. Andrew is a natural-born farmer, with his love of all things growing."

"Do . . . do you think you could talk with Pa?" Thorliff studied his finger.

"Your pa is a fine man, and I believe he will come to agree with you in time. I can speak with him, but you know we've talked about this before. If God wills for you to go away to college, and I hope it will be St.

37

Olaf, then He will change Haakan's mind. Our job is to pray for that and for the money to be there for you to go."

"If it is God's will." Thorliff clamped his teeth against the rush of frustration he could feel trying to swamp him. "How . . . how am I to know if this is God's will? Why would He — I mean, if it isn't His will, why do I love to write like this?" *Does God play games with us? Hold out a prize on the end of a stick and then jerk it away if we get too close?* But no matter how much he treasured his pastor as a friend, he didn't dare voice the last questions.

"I have learned there are many paths to a goal, and when God bars one, He swings wide the gate on another. Remember, if God be for us, who can stand against us?"

"But my pa thinks God is on his side."

Pastor Solberg nodded slowly. "That is true. Children are to obey their parents, but you are soon to be a man, and honor is given in many ways. You have plenty of time before fall. Now go ring the bell. We are late in starting class today."

"But what about applying for school?" Thorliff crossed to the desk and picked up the brass handbell, holding the clanger silent with his other hand.

"One thing I have learned. After praying,

you go down the path you see before you until a gate closes in front of you. God guides us when we are moving."

"Yes, sir." Thorliff strode outside and rang the bell as if the schoolchildren were a mile away instead of running to take their places in line in front of him.

CHAPTER THREE

"You think Tante Penny's going to have a baby?"

"Andrew, you know better than to ask questions like that." Thorliff glared at his brother lying in the wide bed beside him, his arms clasped behind his head. "That's not proper."

"Well, she's gotten fat only in her middle, and Ma is knitting baby things again. I heard her and Bestemor talking about a baby, so what do you think?"

"I think you better go to sleep. Morning comes awful soon." Thorliff reached over and blew down the lamp chimney, putting out the flame. The smell of smoke and burning kerosene curled into the air.

"I hope she does. She's been wanting a baby for a long time."

"How do you know?" Thorliff felt his brother's shrug.

"I listen." The rafters creaked as the house

settled for the night. Their breathing sounded loud in the stillness until Paws barked from the back porch. Coyotes yipped and sang their wild free song somewhere down by the river. The peeper chorus rose and fell with the breeze.

"You going to marry up with Anji?"

Thorliff reared up on his elbows. "Andrew Bjorklund, would you hush up and go to sleep? Now!" Thorliff flopped back down. "Besides, like the other, that is none of your business."

"Sure it is. You are my brother, so she would be my sister-in-law." Andrew's voice cracked on the last word, as it had a tendency to do lately. "I'm going to marry up with Ellie as soon as we get out of school. You want to help me build a house across the field?"

"I want you to go to sleep so that I can too. If you aren't tired, go sit somewhere else."

"I'm tired." Andrew yawned wide enough that his cracking jaw could be heard. "See? But sometimes my mind won't be quiet. Just keeps on asking questions."

"Well, hold 'em until tomorrow." Thorliff rolled to his side facing away from his brother in the hopes that would cut off the chatter. But now his mind took up the

41

chase. What would happen? Would he go to St. Olaf? Would Far be mad at him? Would Anji wait for him? Did he want to marry her? Did she want to marry him? Round and round the questions teased, but with no answers. He heard Andrew slip into the even breathing of sleep.

Paws yipped again. Through the half-open window night sounds floated in, one of the gifts spring brought. He rolled over to his other side, left hand underneath his pillow. *Father God, please believe that I truly want to do your will, but that is hard when I don't know what it is. Forgive my doubts. But do you mind if I ask questions?* He waited, wishing and hoping for an answer. *Maybe you could answer in a burning bush as when you spoke to Moses. We've got bushes around here you could use.* Lassitude stole up from the bottoms of his feet, bringing with it warmth and a fuzzy mind. Thorliff sighed and fell asleep like a candle being snuffed out.

Saturday morning they took out four rigs with Haakan on the disc. This was Andrew's second season helping with spring fieldwork. The women and younger children took over the milking and home chores so the men could spend every minute getting the fields ready to seed.

42

Midmorning Astrid brought out to the field jars of coffee and sandwiches, her basket on her arm as she jumped from one furrow to another. Crows and blackbirds rose in a cloud behind the plows, rushing to feast on the upturned bugs and worms.

When Thorliff stopped for his turn to eat, he looked up to see two V's of geese honking their way north. Astrid looked up too.

"You think Baptiste is off hunting?"

"Lucky dog. Of course he is." Thorliff swallowed his mouthful of bread and cheese. "Mor isn't threatening to take out the rifle, is she?"

Astrid shrugged. "She said to ask if you would turn the garden after dinner. She says her green thumb is aching to dig in the dirt." Astrid held up a thumb. "Don't look green to me."

"It's just a saying." Thorliff took another swig of the tepid coffee. "Next time bring buttermilk, please."

"Trygve or one of the twins will bring it out this afternoon. I'm going to help Bestemor at the boardinghouse." Bridget Bjorklund had joined her family in America after her husband passed away in Norway. Seeing the need for accommodations for folks arriving on the train, she opened a boardinghouse in Blessing.

Thorliff handed the jug back to his sister. "Mange takk." He slapped the reins on the horses' rumps and set the plowshares back down with a pull on the lever. Turning to look over his shoulder at the curl of black dirt, he saw Astrid leaping from one flat surface to another, her braids flying with each leap. His mind went back to the story he'd been cogitating on. If only he could stay awake long enough tonight to write it down.

"Pastor Solberg and Mary Martha are coming for dinner with Manda and Deborah," Ingeborg announced in the wagon on the way home from church the next morning. "I thought since it is so warm we could have a picnic."

"Down at the river?" Andrew glanced up from watching the lines his dragging stick made behind the wagon. He, Thorliff, and Trygve had claimed the tailgate, leaving the girls to chatter, with both mouths and hands, in the wagon bed. Now that there were so many pupils at the deaf school, they had to take three wagons to church.

"No, I was thinking of the south side of the house, by the cottonwood trees. That one we planted when we built the house is big enough to make real shade this year."

44

"Tante Penny and Onkel Hjelmer coming too?" Andrew asked over his shoulder.

Thorliff elbowed him.

"No, just Kaaren and Lars with the schoolchildren." While the two families used to share most meals, now with all the students at the deaf school, Ilse and Kaaren did most of their own cooking there. Students helped with the cooking as well as the cleaning and farm chores. Part of the program was to help the deaf learn to live normally like everybody else. Too many people figured that if someone couldn't hear, they couldn't think or see or do much else. Grace and Sophie changed lots of people's minds as they talked with their hands, a skill all the local students and many adults had learned in the regular school too, now taught by Pastor Solberg but started by Kaaren after Grace was born deaf.

And I thought I could spend the afternoon writing. Thorliff sighed. Perhaps he would be able to sneak off for a bit, but he'd be expected to help entertain the young ones. Of course with the diamond already laid out in the short pasture, everybody would be out to play baseball, even the men and women. He watched the furrow carved in the dust by Andrew's stick. That's the way he felt at times, like the stick or the furrow,

45

not the one holding it.

"We'll have enough for two teams." Andrew poked his big brother. "Won't we?"

"More than enough."

"Not if we don't let the girls play." Trygve hunched his shoulders.

"You're just jealous 'cause Astrid hits better than you." Now Andrew poked his cousin.

"No, I ain't." Trygve pushed back.

"Are too."

"Not."

"Are." The two nearly fell off the tailgate, pushing and shoving.

"All right you two back there, jump off and walk." Haakan looked over his shoulder.

The two boys leaped to the ground and raced up the road.

"Oh, to have that kind of energy." Ingeborg shook her head.

"I'll put 'em to chopping wood. That oughta take care of the push and shoves." Haakan tipped back his fedora. Already he'd been out in the sun enough that he wore the telltale sign of a farmer — a tanned face and a white forehead.

"If we weren't having company, I'd take the shotgun out this afternoon." Ingeborg looked up at the V of ducks flying over. "A couple of geese would taste mighty good."

"I heard Baptiste's gun this morning. He might have got a deer. They sure aren't as plentiful as they used to be."

"Pa!" Andrew came running back. "That sow's farrowing."

"You go watch her. Don't let her lie on the babies."

Andrew tore off again.

"Change your clothes first," Ingeborg hollered after him. A raised hand said he heard her.

Haakan clucked the horses into a faster trot. "At least she isn't having them in the snow like she did last year." The sow had chosen to farrow outside, and a freak snowfall had them carrying baby pigs to the house to warm on the oven door to keep them alive. All in all she'd lost only three, but Haakan often remarked she wasn't the smartest sow in the herd.

"I should have stayed home. I knew she was making her nest." Haakan stopped the team by the back door of the house.

"Andrew asked, and I told him no." Ingeborg laid a hand on her husband's arm. "I'll get a warming box ready."

By the time the others arrived for dinner, they had thirteen baby pigs, two in the warming box behind the stove. Andrew refused to leave his post, sitting in the corner of the box stall where they had nailed boards across the corners for the baby pigs to be able to get away when their mother lay down.

Thorliff leaned on the stall door, watching his brother make sure that each piglet had a chance to nurse. "How many teats does she have?"

"Eleven good ones. Pa says to knock the runt on the head, but I won't." Andrew held the smallest baby to a nipple. "Come on. You can suck," Andrew urged. "I'll keep the others away."

The sow grunted, lying flat on her side so her brood could nurse.

"She been up to drink yet?"

"Once. I put molasses in the warm water. She likes that just fine."

"You want me to make up some warm mash?"

"If you want." Andrew moved one of the more aggressive babies away from the runt.

"You can't stay out here all night, you know."

"I know, but he has to have a chance." Andrew looked up. "You think Tante Kaaren might take him for a pet for one of the school kids?"

Thorliff shrugged. "Maybe, if you ask her nice."

"If I can get him to nurse good a couple of times, he'll have a better chance."

"She'd still have twelve."

"I know."

Thorliff headed for the feed bin where they kept the hog mash they'd run through the grinder. He scooped out enough for half a bucket and took it to the house for hot water and whey from the last cheese pressing.

"How is she?" Ingeborg dipped water from the reservoir into his bucket.

"So far all the babies are alive. That sow doesn't dare lie on them with Andrew there." He stirred the mash with a wooden spoon. "But you know he won't leave her."

"Not even for a baseball game?" Kaaren turned from where she was slicing bread on the sideboard.

"Not even." Thorliff headed back out, waving at the others as he passed. Haakan had told the other children not to bother the sow right now, so they all stayed away. The women were carrying food outside to the tables, and the men stood in a circle by the coffeepot simmering over a low fire. *I should have snuck upstairs and gotten my tablet. I could have stayed with Andrew in the barn.* Thorliff shook his head as his stomach rumbled. Maybe he could take Andrew a

49

plate of food and still do that. Anything for some writing time.

"Hurry up for grace," his mother called.

Thorliff poured the warm mash into the trough, and the sow surged to her feet, baby pigs flying in all directions. Andrew scrambled to pull them back before she stepped on any, and he gently herded them under the cross board in one of the corners. A gunnysack hung over the board from the wall above to trap heat, and if it got too cold, they would put jars of hot water along the wall to keep the piglets warm.

"You want I should stay?"

Andrew shook his head. "They learn fast."

Thorliff joined the group of men just in time to hear his uncle Lars mention his story.

"He really did sell it," Haakan said, thumb and forefinger cradling the bowl of his pipe. "Going to get paid too."

"I always told you he was a fine writer." Pastor Solberg added, "Don't know what we'll do for Christmas programs with him gone."

"Just because he's graduating don't mean he'll be gone." Tension sang in Haakan's reply.

"No, but he'll be a man, and who knows

50

if he'll want to write school programs. After all . . ."

Haakan cleared his throat. "You know how I feel about him going away to school, John. We need him here."

"I understand. He'll be a big help on the threshing crew this year, but . . ."

"No *buts.* He wants to keep writing — that's fine — but he can do that in the evening like he always has. Me 'n Ingeborg, we built this farm so our sons would have this land. We have a good life here. Why would anyone want to leave it?"

"Farming isn't for everyone, my friend."

"Dinner's ready. Would you lead us in grace, Pastor?" Ingeborg broke into the circle.

Thorliff watched his father's face. The tight jawline spoke of Haakan's displeasure as he knocked his pipe against the heel of his boot to dislodge the used tobacco. Changing his far's mind would border on the miraculous.

Bowing his head, he joined in praying the age-old Norwegian words. "I Jesu navn, går vi til bords . . ." As he stood even with Haakan's shoulder, the thought of leaving this place and these people struck Thorliff like an arrow. He glanced down, half expecting to see a shaft quivering in his chest. At the

51

amen, he looked around, studying the faces of all those who meant so much to him. Tante Kaaren, who had instilled in him a love of reading and first told him that he wrote well. Far, who had come to them across the prairies the year after his real father died in the blizzard. Mor, who always said he could do anything he set his mind to. Uncle Lars, so quiet until he figured he had something important to say like "Do your best. That's all the good Lord and I expect of you." The twins — Grace who couldn't hear and Sophie who loved to tease. Astrid, his baby sister, who made him feel as if he stood ten feet tall. Mrs. Solberg, who helped him rewrite, then pushed him to send his stories to magazines, as did Pastor. If it hadn't been for Pastor Solberg, Thorliff wouldn't have a solid knowledge of Greek and Latin, of the classics and the great philosophers, of his Bible and Bible history. Did he really want to leave them? Was going away to college necessary, or could he continue to learn and to write here at home as Haakan insisted?

CHAPTER FOUR: NORTHFIELD, MINNESOTA MAY 1893

"I don't think you want my father to know about this, do you?"

"Probably not." Hans raised his head. "But it's not my fault you're so pretty and all. I just lost my head there for a minute."

Elizabeth Rogers gave a decidedly unladylike snort. "Hans, you been at the still or something?" She took out a handkerchief and, turning to the side, wiped her mouth. If that's what kisses from the male species felt like, she wanted none of it. Not that Hans's lips had quite made it to her mouth, but . . . She rubbed her cheek too, her handkerchief coming away with the black stain of ink. "Oh, my word."

"Now what?"

"Do I have ink on my face?"

When Hans stepped closer to peer at her cheek in the dim light, she forced herself to hold still and not flinch. Her heart still thudded some after his advance. She could hardly call it an attack, and yet that's what it felt like.

"Yep."

"Bother." She stuffed her handkerchief back in the heavy duck apron she wore to protect her clothes and turned on her heel. "See that you get that ad set in type. I'll be back in a minute."

"But Eliza — er, Miss Rogers, you know you pick type faster'n I do."

"Too bad," she muttered as she stormed down the hall. "You should have thought of that before . . . before . . ." She swung open the door and turned up the gaslight by the mirror. Sure enough, there was a black smear on her right cheek. "Ugh." She dampened a cloth from the pitcher, rubbed it over the soap bar, and scrubbed at her cheek. Printer's ink was near to indelible if not washed off right away. Her father's hands were mute testimony to that, with ink under his nails and cuticles no matter how hard or how often he scrubbed with lye soap and a stiff-bristled brush.

With a curl of hair dangling toward her eyes, she whipped off the kerchief she'd tied over her hair to keep it out of the way and, tucking the errant lock back in a comb, re-tied the kerchief. Her glance in the mirror spoke the lie she'd heard from her father's employee's lips. According to her, her gray eyes lacked color, her nose was too upturned for fashion, and calling her chin firm or decisive didn't begin to describe it. Stubborn and mule-headed were terms she'd heard more than once. Her unruly hair — the closest description came to dishwater brown shot with red flames — was best kept tied or braided back out of the way. Not that her description made much sense. Her legs were long enough to do what they were destined to do, but her hands, now that was where a hint of vanity came in. While her mother called them hands for a piano to entertain thousands, she saw them handling doctors' instruments to save lives.

But then she and her mother never had agreed on much. Or rather she and her stepmother. Her real mother was a distant memory of soft voice, gentle hands, and a face growing paler day by day as she succumbed to the ravages of the babe growing within her. Neither she nor the baby survived, like so many other women who died in childbirth or shortly thereafter.

Elizabeth Rogers wanted to change what men took for granted. Women did not need to die giving birth to babies. No matter that the Bible said women would have travail in the birthing, it didn't say so many of them needed to die.

She turned the lamp back to low, rinsed out the cloth, hung it on the bar near the sink, and returned to the pressroom where Hans had only half of the display ad set. *Tarnation, how can he possibly be so slow? Surely there are other men or boys Father could hire.*

"Look, Hans, you set to sweeping up, and I'll finish the ad. Otherwise we will be here all night, and I have homework to do." Thinking of the stack of books waiting made her fingers fly faster. Besides, she'd rather study than work at the newspaper any time. But the ads needed setting, and her father had a meeting that night. As a member of the Northfield town council, Phillip Rogers served the city in two ways. First, by keeping the council from spending money they did not have, and second, by taking notes for the next article he would write on what the town fathers were planning and doing. He also printed letters from citizens venting their opinions on the decisions made by the governing body. The people of Northfield held strong opinions. Having two colleges in town, St. Olaf on the hill and Carleton downtown, most likely had something to do with that.

With the ads set and the paper ready to

be put to bed, Elizabeth locked the door behind her and walked with Hans to the corner, where she said good-night. Two blocks farther on she turned right and walked down a block to the two-story brick house she'd lived in since the day she was born. Letting herself in the front door, she hung her sweater on the hall tree.

"Mother, I'm home," she called.

"That's good, dear. Your supper is in the warming oven." The voice floated down the curved walnut stairs. As usual when her husband was out, Annabelle Rogers, Elizabeth's stepmother, had already retired. She loved to read in bed as much as Elizabeth did, but when Phillip was home, he expected her to sit with him in the parlor while he read, so she would work on her needlepoint then.

Elizabeth detested needlepoint or any other kind of handwork unless it involved sewing up an injury. She'd practiced on her dolls, cats, dogs — anything that needed suturing. Somehow that word appealed to her more than sewing, though the principles were the same. She'd been in her element the day her cousin split his knee open when they were out on a picnic. Elizabeth just happened to have her surgery kit along and sutured the wound as if she'd been doing so all her born days. There had hardly been a scar.

Elizabeth traversed the long hall, not bothering to turn on the gas jets. Jehoshaphat, her golden tiger cat, met her halfway, winding his way around her legs so she'd trip if she didn't stop to pick him up. Cuddling the monstrous cat under her chin and rubbing his ears until he set to purring so loudly she could hear nothing else, she bumped the kitchen door open with her hip and dropped the cat onto his chair by the stove.

"Now you stay there while I eat, and then we'll go upstairs."

The cat set to cleaning himself, carefully licking each paw and wiping it over his ears and head.

Elizabeth picked up a potholder and, opening the warming oven on the top of the cast-iron wood stove, took out her plate and set it on the table. Her place had already been set, including her napkin in a silver ring, sliced bread under a glass dome, and butter under another one. She filled her glass with milk and moved the teakettle to the warmer part of the stove. "A cup of tea would be nice, don't you think?"

Jehoshaphat mewled an answer and continued his bath, his tongue rasping over the fur on his chest.

Before she sat down, Elizabeth fetched a book from the study and, opening to the correct chapter, began studying biology. She read from the text she'd purchased at the Carleton College bookstore and ate at the same time, stopping her fork hand to take notes on the pad of paper beside her plate, underlining and jotting notations on the book pages also. The teapot whistled, and she dropped a pat on the cat's head as she retrieved the tea tin from a glass-fronted cupboard.

Muttering the phyla for vertebrates, she dumped tea leaves into the china pot, poured in the hot water, and set the teapot on the table, reaching for the knitted cozy as she passed the counter. With the tea steeping, she read on, fork mechanically lifting food without her paying attention.

She glanced up, mumbling the list again.

Jehoshaphat chirped again, but with no answer leaped to the floor and crossed to twine himself about her ankles. When that elicited no response, he put both front paws on her thigh and whined plaintively.

She left off eating and stroked his head with one hand, never giving him a glance. She even managed to pour her tea in between words. She'd just lifted her teacup to her mouth with her right hand when the cat leaped into her lap, banging her elbow and sending tea splattering everywhere.

"Bad cat!" With a yowl, he jumped back to the floor and scooted under the table. "What do you think you're doing?" She brushed the drops off her hand with her napkin, then scrubbed the marks off her textbook before cleaning her skirt. "Stupid animal."

"Meow."

"Too bad. You could see I was busy." She caught herself, reviewing what she'd said. "As if you know what I'm saying." Shaking her head, she laid the book face down on the table and, lifting the cutwork linen tablecloth, stuck her face under the edge. "Jehoshaphat, come here, boy. I'm sorry." She made comforting noises, but the cat was having none of it. Tail in the air, he padded out from his hideout, stalked over to his chair, and leaped up. Without looking at her, he proceeded to clean again.

"Serves you right." Elizabeth poured herself another cup of tea and continued reading. Later, when she cleared the table, she saw the tea stains. "Oh no. Mother will be after me now." She glanced over to see the empty chair. Jehoshaphat had scrammed. "Always one more thing. What's wrong with being allowed to study without interruptions?" All the while she lifted the cloth from the table and set it to soak in cold water. Perhaps the stain would just disappear. Perhaps the sun would rise in the west too.

When the page blurred and rubbing her eyes no longer helped, she climbed the stairs to her bedroom. Had her father come in without stopping to talk? Or had he stopped all right, but not at home?

She paused beside the closed dark oak door to her parents' bedroom, listening for her father's floor-shaking snore. Nothing. He'd not come home yet. Morning would be stiff again with her mother hardly talking, and if he did make it to church, he'd fall asleep during the sermon. She was grateful she sang in the choir so she didn't have to sit with them.

Sometimes she hated council meetings. Or wherever else he'd been.

The next morning church passed as she'd thought it would. She kept her gaze off the slumped figure in the third row on the right. You'd have thought at least her parents would have had the decency to sit in the back. But no matter, third pew on the right belonged to the Rogers family, as much as

61

if they'd paid for it. Relief surged through her when the pastor pronounced the benediction and the choir stood for the closing hymn. If her salvation depended on what she'd learned in church this morning, she'd be heading the other way. As Pastor Mueller made his way to the narthex to greet people as they filed out, she and the other choir members exited to the choir room to divest themselves of their robes.

"Went right well," Dr. Gaskin, lead baritone, pronounced. The fact that he said the same whenever he made it to church made no difference. Everyone nodded and wished each other a good week.

"Miss Rogers?"

Elizabeth turned. "Yes?"

"I'm thinking Mrs. Sidney might be going into labor today. If you want to come along, you be ready."

"Oh, thank you. I will." Elizabeth followed the others out the side door of the brick church, complete with bell tower and white window trim. She shaded her eyes with her gloved hand. Her mother and father waited in the buggy. New leaves, still tight to the branches, furred the oak trees that lined the hitching posts where members of the congregation tied up their horses. When she reached the buggy, she looked up at her father.

"I think I'll walk home. It's such a beautiful day."

"We'll be eating right away. Your father says he has to go back down to the paper."

"Oh." Elizabeth climbed into the rear seat of the buggy. Since this was the cook's day off, she knew she'd be expected to help put dinner on the table. And if her father had to wait, he'd turn into a grumbling bear. "I thought you weren't going to work on Sundays anymore."

"That's what he always says." Annabelle clasped her hands on her watered-silk dress, nodded to an acquaintance, and shot her husband a look compounded with equal parts sadness and disdain.

The ride home passed in silence, matching that on the drive over.

They'd just finished dinner when the doorbell clanged.

"I'll get it." Elizabeth wiped her mouth with her napkin and pushed her chair back. "That was delicious, as always, Mother. Thank you."

"Won't you be having dessert? Cook made a canned peach pie."

Elizabeth left the dining room and, like a

diver coming up for air, paused to take a deep breath and let it all out. Now her step regained its usual bounce, and a smile returned. "I'm coming," she answered to another knock. She opened the door. "Oh, Dr. Gaskin, so soon?"

"Told you to be ready. You coming or not?"

"I'm coming. Let me tell Mother and get my apron. Should I bring anything else? Like peach pie?"

"We'll get that later. This baby's in a hurry."

Elizabeth flew back down the hall, called to her mother as to what she was doing, grabbed her apron and a shawl in case they were late, and was out the door before the doctor had finished climbing into his buggy.

"Whew. Oh, I forgot my hat." She paused before sitting down.

"Too late." The buggy was already in motion, causing her an abrupt connection with the leather seat. He clucked the horse to a fast trot and headed south of town. "How's school coming?"

"Near to the end of the term. I've been studying like mad for my biology exams. The lab class takes a lot of time, memorizing and dissecting. Going to Carleton for science classes is not really convenient."

"You think that's hard, wait till you get to med school. You have to memorize every bone, muscle, nerve — every part of the human body. But with a mind as good as yours, that won't be hard."

"If they let me in."

"Don't borrow trouble. The Lord says to let the day's own trouble be sufficient for the day."

"I know."

"Now tell me the steps for a delivery."

Elizabeth listed them, using her fingers to count on for memory.

"What if the baby doesn't start to breathe?"

"Then rub the chest, raise the arms over the head, and if all else fails, smack the buttocks."

"Sometimes breathing in the face helps or compressing the chest real gentlelike. Remember to check the throat and nose for any obstructions."

"I read in a book that swishing the baby in warm water can help too." Elizabeth turned sideways to look at her mentor and friend.

"Hmm, not surprised. After all, the baby's been swimming in warm water for nine months." He turned the team into a long lane that led to a white two-story farmhouse. A dog ran out to bark at the wheels. A man stepped down off the porch as soon as they reached the gate to a picket fence.

"I'll take care of your horse. You better hurry."

"You got the water boiling?"

"Yup. And clean towels and sheets and things for the baby. Martha's been prepared for days now. Go straight through the kitchen. She's in our bedroom."

"Think I don't know the way? Third baby in less than three years — going to wear her plumb out." The doctor muttered his way into the bedroom, where shades were drawn over the windows.

"Howdy, Miz Sidney. Looks like that baby's in some kind of hurry."

The woman on the bed arched with another contraction, this one lifting her clear off the bed. "In . . . a . . . hurry, but . . ." She sighed and sank back down, panting as though she'd been running. "Can't seem to go no farther."

"All right. Let me get scrubbed up here and see what we can see." He turned to Elizabeth. "You scrub too. If it's what I think, those small hands of yours are going to come in plenty handy."

Elizabeth did as she was told, flinching at the groan that came from the bed. This was

66

her third delivery. She should be used to the agony that preceded the ecstasy of a baby to hold. She watched as the doctor examined the woman, shaking his head, humming a little tune all the while.

"Now, Miz Sidney, I think what we have here is a breech. I'm going to have Elizabeth help turn the baby when I give her the signal. First, let's help you up onto your hands and knees."

"Doctor, you got —" She huffed a couple of times as another contraction hit, then groaned deeply.

"All right, dear, ride with it. That's right." When she relaxed again, Dr. Gaskin nodded for Elizabeth to wipe her face. "Now roll this way." He pulled the woman by the shoulder. "That's right. Hands and knees. See, this takes the pressure off the baby and lets it relax for a minute."

He nodded to Elizabeth. "Now you see if you can help that baby turn around, just like they do with lambs and calves."

Elizabeth swallowed hard, her hands shaking so badly she was afraid they wouldn't do what was needed.

"Now, this is going to hurt some, Miz Sidney, but bear with us."

Oh, God, please help me. I don't know what I'm doing. But at the doctor's insistent nod, she did as told.

"What do you feel?"

"A foot, I think."

"Okay, now with the next contraction, turn that baby."

As Mrs. Sidney let out a scream that could be heard clear to town, Elizabeth pushed the foot back while the doctor manipulated the hanging belly. Elizabeth gritted her teeth, closed her eyes, and concentrated on what her hand was feeling. The baby was moving.

Mrs. Sidney screamed again — long, drawn out, tapering off as if she had nothing left to scream with.

"You're doing fine. You got to stay with us," Dr. Gaskin said.

"It turned. I have the head." Elizabeth removed her hand, tears streaming down her cheeks. "It turned, Doctor."

"I know, dear." He beckoned to Elizabeth again. "Now, I'll hold her while you help ease the baby out. Turn the shoulders gently as soon as the head presents." He looked down at his sobbing patient. "We did it, Miz Sidney. Just a couple more contractions, and we'll be done here."

"Yess." The voice hissed on another contraction.

"The head. I can see it." Elizabeth touched

the crown with a tender finger. On the next pain the baby slipped right into her hands, squalling as soon as she felt the air. "She was tired of being cooped up like that," Elizabeth murmured. *Oh, dear God, look what you've done here. A beautiful baby girl.* Elizabeth held up the squirming baby for the doctor to see.

"Good. Lay her here on her mother's belly so the two of them can finally get acquainted face-to-face."

Elizabeth did as told, blinking back her tears so she could see better. With the baby in place she picked up a corner of her apron and wiped her eyes. "Have you ever seen anything so beautiful in your whole life?"

"And it never changes. Birthing a baby is about the most wonderful act of worship I know of."

The woman in the bed cupped her daughter's head with a hand full of love. "Thank you."

"You are most welcome." Dr. Gaskin cut and tied the cord, then turned to his helper. "Let's get back to work. You clean up the baby, and I'll take care of the rest here."

Elizabeth washed the baby, gently wiping her eyes and nose with a soft cloth. When she'd dried the red little body, she pinned a folded diaper in place and wrapped the baby in a cotton blanket before laying her in the crook of her mother's arm. Then she wiped the mother's face and brushed the soaked hair back from her forehead. After sliding a fresh sheet under Mrs. Sidney, she stood and looked down at the two, both now sleeping soundly.

"That was close," Dr. Gaskin said. "Might not have had this happy picture if it hadn't been for you."

Elizabeth stared down at her hands. Yes, this was what they were designed for. She looked up at the doctor. "I *must* get into medical school. But what if I'm not accepted?"

CHAPTER FIVE: BLESSING, NORTH DAKOTA

Plowing until past dark left precious little time for schoolwork, let alone for writing.

Thorliff dragged his tired body up the stairs to the room he and Andrew shared and flung himself across the bed. While the full moon was beautiful, it only meant longer hours behind the teams.

"Another one of the baby pigs died." Andrew sat on the bed to unlace his boots.

"Sorry."

"Pa says that's just the way of pigs. That's why they have so many, but there must be ways to keep them from being stepped and laid on. That dumb sow."

"Some are sure more careful than others." Thorliff levered himself upright. Today Pastor Solberg had given him the forms to fill out for application to St. Olaf. Now the big question came. Would he be going against his father's orders if he just filled out the papers? Pa hadn't said not to fill out the papers. He'd said Thorliff should stay on the farm. *What do I do, God? If you are working on changing Far's mind, I sure don't see it.* He thought to the verse Pastor Solberg had had the whole school memorize. *"Faith is the substance of things hoped for, the evidence of things not seen." So does that mean I'm to have faith that you are changing Far's mind and proceed as if you have?*

"Why do things have to be so difficult?" He slammed his fist against the pillow and stood.

"I don't know. I'm going back out to check on them." Andrew tied his laces around his ankles and clomped back down the stairs, leaving Thorliff to stare after him. Things were so simple for Andrew. Go to school. Do the chores. All he cared about was what happened on the farm, in school, and in their town of Blessing. He wouldn't mind leaving school, but when he'd suggested so, Mor had given him a big piece of her mind. Andrew hadn't asked again.

Thorliff took his books and papers back downstairs to work at the kitchen table where the light was better. The paper he'd been assigned — to compare the teachings of the apostle Paul and the teachings of Aristotle — was taking longer than he'd planned. Reading the writings of each in Greek slowed him down some, but writing his paper in English slowed him even more. He flipped both books open to the pages he was reading and started in again.

The forms for St. Olaf stayed out of sight in the back of the leather case his father had made him for Christmas.

With four students graduating from Blessing School, the first class ever, Pastor Solberg had asked all of the graduates to write a commencement speech as well as a paper on what they felt the school had done for them. He then called a meeting one afternoon after the bell rang.

"So then, how are your themes coming?" He looked at each one of them directly.

"I'm finished." Anji held up her pages.

Thorliff sighed and gave her a rolled-eye look. Anji always had things finished ahead of time. "I'm about halfway done," he said. "The longer the daylight, the less time I have."

"I understand that." Solberg looked to Manda.

She shrugged and shook her head. "I hate writing stuff like this." She gave her scribbled pages a shove, then scrambled to keep them from fluttering to the floor.

"I know." He nodded to Jacob, the eldest

73

son of a family new to the area. "How about you?"

"I wrote it all right in Norwegian, but uff da, saying it in English . . ." The slender boy who walked with a limp shrugged. "I am working on it."

"Good. Now I'd like to talk about the graduation exercises. Of course, your final exams come first, but the actual graduation ceremony will be held in the church. Hjelmer has gone to the trouble of having a photographer come, so we will have pictures of you for both the church and your families. He looked to the two boys. "If you could borrow a suit or if you have one, that would look very nice."

Thorliff had an idea his grandmother and his mother and Aunt Kaaren were sewing him a suit on their Singer sewing machines. Mor had measured his arms and chest and down his legs. When he'd asked what it was all for, she'd tapped his arm and said, "None of your business, young man." He shared a grin with Anji.

"If there is any way I can help you, please don't hesitate to ask."

"You could write this paper for me," Manda muttered loud enough for only Thorliff to hear. He knew she'd rather be out training horses than staying in school,

74

but Pastor had insisted she finish. Thorliff kept a chuckle from going further than his mind. Here he wanted nothing more than to go to school, and she'd rather farm.

The discussion continued with Pastor Solberg outlining how graduation would go, what papers he expected before exams, and how he would run the final exams. "I just want to make sure we've met all the state requirements." He glanced at each of them again. "Are there any questions?"

"If there is nothing else, sir, I need to get home," Thorliff said.

"You want a ride?"

"No. I can run it faster than the team. Thank you, anyway." Thorliff rose. "See you tomorrow." Once out the door, he hit the ground running. He burst through the kitchen door and, seeing no one around, leaped up the stairs to his bedroom to change clothes. Back downstairs he cut off a chunk of cheese, sliced a hunk of bread, and chewing them both, headed for the barn. Andrew already had the team harnessed. As they lifted the yokes over the necks of the oxen, one of the beasts shifted and stepped on Thorliff's foot.

"Ouch." He gave the animal a shove. "Get off."

"I think he does that on purpose." Andrew

tried to keep from laughing. "General would rather stay in the pasture."

"Dumb beast." Thorliff bent down to push the bow up through the holes in the yoke. His hat fell off when the same critter nosed it. "Now see what you did?" He pushed the pegs through the hoops and reached down for his hat, only to get a nose swipe from Paws. Thorliff came up wiping his nose and glaring at his brother, who'd lost his skirmish against laughter.

Paws leaped from one boy to the other, yipping his delight at having them home again.

"You'd think he was still a pup the way he carries on." Thorliff thumped the dog on the ribs and settled his hat back on his head. "You want the horses or the oxen?"

"I'll take the oxen. Pa said for you to go on over to Onkel Lars's section."

"All right." Thorliff backed the horses on either side of the sulky and hooked the traces. "See you later." He started to cluck the team forward but looked over his shoulder to Andrew instead. "You seen Baptiste lately?"

"No, but Metiz was on her way to the store when we came home from school. Mor is at the boardinghouse."

Metiz, who was old when the Bjorklunds

met her soon after they located land to homestead, was half Lakota Sioux and half French Canadian. Her grandson, Baptiste, had grown up with Thorliff, the two fast friends. Baptiste had learned what he needed and left school as soon as he could.

Thorliff nodded. Tonight he'd suggest Pa hire Baptiste to help plow during the day. Although why they hadn't already done that was beyond him. Or Sam from the blacksmith, if he wasn't working for someone else.

Burning the midnight oil took on new meaning for Thorliff as he struggled to finish his commitments to school, keep up with his share of work on the Bjorklund farm, and eke out a bit of writing. He collapsed into bed long after the rest of the family slept and woke up tired.

"What time did you blow out the lamp last night?" Ingeborg asked as she set a plate of ham and eggs in front of him.

"I don't know." He rubbed his eyes and scrubbed a hand over his hair. "I'll be glad when school is over. That is all." He shoveled in the food and pushed back his chair. "Mange takk."

Ingeborg walked with him down the steps.

"Have you filled out the forms for St. Olaf yet?"

"No. No time. Besides, I know we can't afford that, and you know how Far feels. How can I go against him?"

"You let me deal with your far. You fill out the papers and send them in. Somehow this will all work out."

That afternoon Thorliff stayed after school long enough to finish the forms he'd started to fill out during the day. From there he ran over to the store and handed his envelope to Mr. Valders, who helped his aunt Penny in the store when she needed to be gone.

"All the womenfolk are over at the boardinghouse." Mr. Valders reached for the letter. "That'll be two cents for the stamp."

Thorliff dug in his pocket and laid a nickel on the counter. "The mail hasn't gone yet, has it?"

"Didja hear the train come?" Mr. Valders asked, handing Thorliff his change.

Thorliff shrugged. "Sometimes I don't pay no attention."

"Well, it should be here right soon. Your mor need anything?"

"Not that I know. Thanks." Thorliff headed back out the door and broke into a run, leaping off the porch, hanging on to his porkpie hat with one hand until he snatched it off his head and pelted down the lane. Fields awaited him.

"Thorliff, wake up." Andrew shook his brother's shoulder the next day in class.

Thorliff raised his head from his arms. He blinked, then shot upright. "Sorry." He could feel his face flaming as one of the other students giggled. He'd fallen asleep at school, his head on the desk. He glanced up to see Pastor Solberg shaking his head.

"You have been burning the candle at both ends and the middle too, I'm afraid."

Thorliff could do nothing but nod. Of course he was right, but what else could he do?

That night when Andrew blabbed about the incident at the supper table, Thorliff wanted to reach over and smack him. "Hush!" He put as much authority into a whisper as possible.

Haakan studied his eldest son. "Are you behind in your schoolwork?"

"No, sir, but . . ." Thorliff thought of his hours ahead. "Just have a lot to get done before graduation."

"I see." Haakan and Ingeborg exchanged a look. "Then I suggest you take the next afternoons and finish before you fall asleep on the plow and fall off. You can get hurt right bad thataway."

Thorliff nodded. "Thank you."

"And tonight, get to bed early."

"Yes, sir." Thorliff took another bite of his bread. "What about hiring Baptiste?"

"Good idea. I'll talk to him tomorrow. Since he's been providing much of the meat for the boardinghouse, he's not had much free time."

The next afternoon Thorliff arrived home to see his team already out in the field. Ignoring the guilt that thrashed him about the head and shoulders, he helped Andrew yoke up the oxen, then set to his books. With the extra sleep he'd been able to accomplish more during school too, so when Haakan blew out the lamp, Thorliff closed his books and headed up the stairs.

"Thanks again, Pa."

"You're welcome. There's some letters to go in the mail tomorrow if you'd take them with you in the morning."

"Of course. Good night." Thorliff stumbled on the top stair and caught himself on the doorframe. Was he really that tired? He crawled into bed without disturbing the sleeping Andrew and rolled onto his side so he could look out the window. Sayings from the apostle Paul and from Aristotle chased each other through the maze of his mind, as if the two were debating. But when they both began speaking in Norwegian, he pulled the pillow over his head. *Run the race.* He repeated the words in both English and Norwegian. *God, what is the race you have set before me? How can I run it if I don't know?*

When he woke in the morning to the sound of Haakan calling his name, he felt as if he'd been running all night.

The following Sunday, graduation day dawned clear and sunny like all the days preceding. Thorliff knelt by the windowsill to watch the flaming orange disc break clear of the horizon. Shouldn't there be fireworks or something spectacular to herald this day?

"Lord God, beginning and ending, how can one thing be both?" He whispered the words so as not to wake Andrew. He needed every moment of rest possible, just like his older brother. But sleep had been hard to come by the night before, and Thorliff had risen before the rooster crowed, when the sunrise was only a promise of narrow silver.

If only I knew for sure what I am going to do. He rested his chin on his crossed hands and listened to the wrens twitting their morning song, the cheery notes seeming to promise good things ahead.

"Thorliff, Andrew, cows to milk." Inge-

81

borg's voice floated up the stairs at the same time Haakan's whistle told Paws to round up the cows. Most of them would already be lined up at the back barn door, patiently waiting to trail inside.

Andrew stirred in the bed, then his feet hit the floor. "You all right?"

"Ja." Thorliff stood, his knee creaking a protest after kneeling on the hard floor for so long. They shrugged into their overalls and headed for the barn.

"Ready for the big day?" Ingeborg called after him. Thorliff didn't answer. Didn't matter if he was ready or not, the day was here and would go on in spite of him. The thought brought up his coming commencement speech. Now he had a whole flock of butterflies chasing around in his middle. All the while his hands pulled milk from the cows, his mind repeated his speech. How come the other day it sounded just fine, and now it seemed like barley chaff to blow away on the wind?

"You ready, Thorliff?" Astrid greeted him with a grin after the men had washed up at the outside bench.

"I guess." He rubbed his middle.

"Hungry, son? Let's get seated and say grace." Ingeborg set a platter of sliced ham on the table. When they were all seated,

Haakan waited for silence. After the normal I Jesu navn, he paused before the amen. "And, Lord, give our son a calm spirit this day as he prepares to give his speech. We all know he will do a fine job, now please calm him inside and out." He raised his gaze to wink at his son. "Amen."

Never had Thorliff spoken a more heartfelt amen.

"Thorliff, you are handsome." Astrid stared openmouthed at her big brother, dressed now in his new brown tweed suit, sewn with love by his mother, grandmother, and aunt Kaaren.

He could feel his ears flaming at her unabashed delight. "Mange tusen takk." He resisted the urge to pull at the neck of his new white shirt or loosen the knot in his tie. This was a day of firsts for all kinds of things. A new suit, a new tie, and even new boots that shone with all the polish Haakan could apply. And it would be the first time he would have his photograph taken. Pastor Solberg had said that Uncle Hjelmer had arranged for a photographer to come from Grand Forks to take pictures of the graduating class, since this was the first for Blessing School.

Instead of running across the prairie as

was his wont, Thorliff rode in the wagon with his family.

His breath caught in his throat when he saw Anji waiting with the others by the front door of the church. A vision in a daisy-sprigged white dress trimmed with a yellow sash, she smiled nervously when he approached.

"You . . . you are . . . are . . ." He stopped to clear his throat. He who could cover a page with words so effortlessly — where had they all gone now when he needed them? She touched a hand to her throat where a cameo hung on a yellow silk ribbon.

He still hadn't found his vocal cords by the time they filed into the church to sit in the front row. His heart pounded so loud he was sure Pastor could hear it clear up by the altar.

CHAPTER SIX

The Sunday morning service proceeded as usual with the opening hymn, "Holy, Holy, Holy." All Thorliff could think about was the beautiful young woman beside him who kept giving him questioning glances when his voice continued cracking instead of rising strong on the familiar words.

Before the closing prayer, Pastor Solberg waited for the shuffling to cease. "And, Father God, we beseech thee to send rain in the right amounts this year. We confess to our fear of another drought and thank thee for thy great mercy in seeing us through the last one. Now to Him be all glory and honor as we praise His holy name. Amen." Pastor Solberg looked over his congregation. "As you all know, we will be having dinner together first, and then we will celebrate the graduation of four young people from our school. I invite all of you to attend and help these fine members of our congregation celebrate this large milestone in their lives." He smiled at the four in the front pew. "And now" — he paused and raised both hands — "the Lord bless and keep thee, the Lord make his face to shine upon thee . . ."

So often the words were just for closing the service, but today they smote deep into Thorliff's mind and soul. Every Sunday around the world those words were spoken and had been for centuries. And they would continue just as there always would be young people graduating from school and going on with their lives.

He glanced at Anji, who apparently feeling his attention, turned to smile at him. That, too, felt like a benediction, a blessing. He smiled back, wishing he dared take her hand. He could get lost in Anji's smile. His throat clogged, and the backs of his eyes burned. He looked forward again and commanded himself to take deep breaths. Together they stood for the closing hymn, each holding half of the hymnbook. His voice cracked on the first notes, so he swallowed and tried again, harmonizing as naturally as she did.

If life could get any better than right this moment, he was hard put to think what it might be.

■ ■ ■ ■

Sometime later Pastor called everyone back inside the church. "We are gathered again now to honor these young people of ours, the first graduates of Blessing School." Pastor Solberg beamed at the four in the front row. While some folks had left for home after the dinner, most had stayed for the ceremony.

After they sang a hymn, he led them in prayer, then beckoned to Anji.

"Miss Anji Baard will be our first speaker."

At the applause of the congregation, Anji took her place in front of the altar. Her smile quivered at the corners, but she only had to clear her throat once.

Thorliff felt his chest expand with pride. She was so beautiful, he felt his breath catch around his heart. *I love her, not only as a friend, but as a man loves a woman.* She shimmered in the golden light slanting through the window. He ducked his head to wipe the moisture from his eyes. *Anji, I love you. Do you know that?* Keeping his dancing body in the seat took a miracle of control.

"I want to thank all of you who have been my church family through these years. Pastor Solberg, you have taught all of us with such devotion. What would we have done without you? Mrs. Knutson, you gave me a love of reading. No one can make the Scriptures sing as you do when you read them aloud." She looked around the room, smiling at each person. "Ma and Pa, I am so blessed to be your daughter. Penny, you were my older sister, far closer than a cousin." She continued around the room, reminding everyone of things they had done to help her become the young woman standing before them. By the time she finished, folks were blowing noses and wiping eyes.

Thorliff felt as if he might burst apart with pride. She was theirs, but even more so, she was his. Surely she felt the same as he did.

When his turn came, the last, he swallowed hard and took his place. Like his beautiful Anji, he had no notes.

"God says in His Word that He has plans for each one of us, plans for good and not for evil. I believe our Father brought us to this country for good, for us to build new lives. I had a hard time believing that my far's dying in a blizzard was God's will, but looking back, I can see how He brought good out of that." He glanced at his mother and Haakan and felt a bittersweet smile flicker at the tears running down his mother's cheeks. "I think it is hard to know God's will every moment, and sometimes it is easier to see when looking back. Like Anji, I owe a tremendous debt of gratitude to so many of you. I hope to repay that debt by living the kind of life that will make all of you proud. But mostly the kind of life that will make our Father's heart glad. I want Him to rejoice over each of us. I want to run my life's race in a way that is pleasing to Him.

"He says to love one another." Thorliff tried hard not to look at Anji when he said those words. "That is the second of the great commandments. To love Him is the first. I have learned that it is not always easy to love those around us, especially when we disagree. But when we love, we make our world a better place, and I know we please our heavenly Father." He looked to each of the graduates. "So let us run our races with love and perseverance so that we might all hear 'Well done, thou good and faithful servant.' Thank you and amen."

Thorliff took his seat to a totally hushed congregation.

Pastor Solberg stood and had to clear his throat twice before he could continue. "We will now present these fine young people with their diplomas. Hjelmer Bjorklund, as president of our congregation, will assist me." He nodded, and Hjelmer rose and approached the front. He set four wrapped packages and four leather folders on the podium before turning to give Pastor a slight nod. The two men looked to the four young people, who rose as one to form a line in alphabetical order, as they had practiced, to the left side of the two men.

Thorliff could barely swallow past an Adam's apple that seemed to have swelled to boulder proportions. He heard Anji sniff in front of him. A wave of throat clearing, sniffing, and nose blowing broke over the congregation. Someone hushed a baby who let out a wail at all the unusual happenings. Judged by the volume of tears, one would have thought this were a funeral rather than a celebration.

"In the blessed name of our risen Lord, I present to you the graduates of Blessing School." Pastor Solberg turned from facing the congregation to smiling at Anji. "Miss Anji Baard."

Anji stepped forward to receive her diploma from Hjelmer with her left hand and to shake his hand with her right. As she faced him, Pastor Solberg handed her the wrapped parcel.

Pastor Solberg raised his hand to rest

lightly on her forehead. "The Lord bless and keep thee all thy days. Go in peace and serve our risen Lord."

Thorliff caught his breath. This part hadn't been rehearsed.

"Thorliff Bjorklund."

I'm graduating. This is the end of my schooling here. I cannot go back. Thoughts whipped through his mind like wheat chaff driven before a fierce wind. His hand shook and his eyes burned as he reached for the leather-bound diploma.

"I'm proud of you, nephew." Hjelmer shook his hand and whispered the words at the same time.

Thorliff nodded. He could do nothing else. He took another step and accepted the package from his pastor, mentor, and friend. His forehead burned at the touch of Solberg's hand, no matter that it rested lightly.

"The Lord bless thee and keep thee."

Please, God, do just that. Keep me from all wrong.

"Go in peace and serve the Lord. Amen."

Lord God, I will serve thee however you desire. If only I can decide what it is you want. Please make your will clear to me.

Thorliff sat next to Anji, his thoughts still racing. He glanced down at the two parcels in his lap. His hands had been sweating so that his fingerprints showed on the leather.

"Congratulations." Anji whispered without moving her head.

"Ja, and to you."

Manda took her seat on his left, soon followed by Jacob. He'd hardly sat when Pastor Solberg asked everyone to stand.

"The ladies of the church will be serving coffee, punch, and cake immediately following the ceremony, and then the photographer will be taking pictures. As we announced, families who would like their pictures taken may request that after our graduates are finished. Now let us pray." He waited for the shuffling to cease. "Heavenly Father, thou who knows all things, thou who loves us with unending love, we commit these young people into thy keeping. Do with them as you will that they might be useful in thy kingdom here on earth. As Jesus prayed for his disciples, I pray for you to keep these young people safe. May all that they do be for thy glory. In Jesus precious name, amen."

The hearty amen that echoed around the room showed everyone's agreement.

Pastor Solberg raised his hands and declared, "The Lord bless and keep all of us from this day forth. Go in peace and serve our risen Lord." He made the sign of the cross and nodded to the four. "You follow me, and we will greet everyone at the door."

As they greeted everyone, Thorliff's face felt as if it might crack from all the smiling, and his hand shook from shaking so many hands. When the line finally ended, he let out a sigh that made Anji giggle.

"If you will all get a drink first, then we will go right into the picture taking. Mr. Haganson is setting up his things out in front of the church."

Manda groaned loud enough to earn a raised eyebrow from their pastor, which set the others to giggling under their breath.

After wetting their dry throats with a quick drink, the four gathered outside the church, where a rumpled weed of a man ducked out from under a black-draped camera perched on a tripod.

"First we will do the group picture and then, ladies first, the individual ones." A New York accent spoken through his nose brought on raised eyebrows and stifled giggles. "I think we shall have the young men seated, please."

"That's because you are too tall for the picture." Manda elbowed Thorliff, who was already over six feet tall and still growing.

Thorliff felt his ears go red. "Shh."

"Now you must hold your pose until I

release you. I want a formal expression here."

"He means smile on pain of death," Thorliff muttered. Manda sputtered, Anji poked him to be quiet, and Jacob choked on his swallowed laughter.

By the time the photographer had finished with them, families were lining up. A photographer coming to town was indeed a rarity.

"Can we open our presents now?" Jacob looked to Pastor Solberg for permission.

"Of course, although I'm sure you've guessed what they are."

Together they carefully slit the wrapping paper and removed Bibles printed in English and signed by both Pastor Solberg and Hjelmer Bjorklund.

"The women of our congregation insisted that you each needed your own Bible now. Those came clear from Minneapolis."

Thorliff nodded as he read the flyleaf and inhaled the aroma of printer's ink, new pages, and the leather cover, on which his name was stamped in gold.

"Mange takk." He had to swallow before he could talk. "Such a wonderful present."

"I think that shall become a tradition here. You need to thank Mrs. Valders and Mrs.

Lars Knutson. They instigated the whole thing."

"Ja, I will." Thorliff looked to the line of people where his aunt Kaaren smiled back at him. So many of the books he owned had come as gifts from her.

As the graduates visited and ate their cake, several people slipped envelopes into Thorliff's pockets, always with the comment, "So you have money for college."

After he had walked Anji back home and had trotted across the field to help with the milking, he pondered the day, bringing each treasure to mind.

Ingeborg had set a lamp in the kitchen window. A verse floated through his mind. *"Let your light so shine . . ."*

Would he get to attend college like so many wished for him? Where would God have his light shine?

CHAPTER SEVEN:
NORTHFIELD,
MINNESOTA

"You look tired, my dear."

"I know, Papa, but exams will be over soon." Elizabeth toyed with the potatoes and gravy on her plate. The hand holding up her head, braced by her elbow on the table, said as much as her tone. Had her mother been at the table, Elizabeth would be sitting straight and proper. Anything to keep from seeing that pained look her mother put on at similar infractions.

Bosh on Mother. I'm too tired to care.

"You don't have to put yourself through this torture, you know." Phillip Rogers looked over his half glasses and shook his head. Smile lines crinkled around his gray eyes, gray that tinged the temples of umber hair kept short to control the curl. No matter how much good food Cook fed him, he could still be called by a childhood nickname — Bean Pole.

"I know. I could go to work at the newspaper full time like you want and still have time to be the social butterfly Mother wants."

"Many girls — er, women" — he changed his wording at the glare his daughter sent him — "sorry. Many *women* would be ecstatic to be in your position. You play the piano close to concert quality, you can carry on a conversation with anyone you come in contact with, you are lovely to look at . . ."

Elizabeth rolled her eyes. "Remember, beauty is in the eye of the beholder."

"Be that as it may, I've seen young men's heads turn when you walk by."

Elizabeth thought to the encounter with Hans and his wayward lips at the newspaper office.

"And, lest all that go to your head, you can set type faster than many a journeyman."

"But I hate dancing, and poor Mother is about at her wits end trying to teach me how to manage a household, and the only needlework I like is stitching up a wound."

"Which I've heard excellent reports on from the Hardesty clan. The father says you can barely see the scar on his son's arm, besides the fact that the hand still works."

Elizabeth thought back to the day they brought the young man into the doctor's surgery. While Dr. Gaskin had been out bringing another baby into the world, young Hardesty was losing blood fast on a tear from wrist to elbow. Elizabeth put a tourniquet above the elbow and stitched the wound closed with nearly a hundred stitches. All the while she checked the blood flow, and when they removed the tourniquet, nary a drop of red leaked out. She'd read about sewing nerves back together too, but near as she could see with all the blood in the wound, the major nerves and blood vessels were intact.

"I was lucky, and so was he."

Phillip shook his head. "No, child, that was all by the grace of God."

"Well, if God had been watching over that young man like his father said He was, the accident wouldn't have happened. And I . . ." She blinked at the remembered panic that had surged through her at the first sight of the wound. Then she'd taken a couple of deep breaths, considered waiting until the doctor returned, and went ahead on her own. The fact that gangrene had not set in pleased her more than the fine stitching.

"You did one good job." Her father reached for her hand and cupped it palm up in his own. "Not that long ago you were hanging on to my hand with these long fingers so adept now."

"Years ago, Papa."

"I know, but years pass by so swiftly, too swiftly." He slipped into the shadow-focused look that told his daughter he was thinking of an editorial.

Phillip Rogers would rather write than run a newspaper. The fact that the newspaper gave him a platform for his writing was all that kept him at the helm. That and the immutable fact that he couldn't afford to hire a manager. He'd dreamed of his daughter's assuming that role on a permanent basis after seeing the skill with which she helped out. During each summer break from school, she managed to bring his accounts receivable current and to increase his ad revenue by charming everyone who came into the office to take out more inches, allowing her father more time to write. The quality of his editorials improved too.

"Mother is a good manager."

"I know." He'd tried to get his wife to help, but she detested the whole environment, including the smell of ink and the noise of the press. Besides, she felt she was busy enough taking care of the house and the gardens and raising a daughter who was far too independent for her own good. And as a Doncaster, she had a certain role to fulfill in town and in the church. She drew the line at politics.

Until her husband chose to run for city council. Then she had campaigned quite energetically, helping him with teas and soirees as fund-raisers and convincing the women to persuade their husbands to vote for him. Phillip's solid reputation in the community helped also.

Elizabeth fought back a yawn. She couldn't sleep yet. She had reams of notes to go through first. "Excuse me, Papa, I must get back to my books."

"Of course, my dear." He rose when she did, and together they headed for the library, he to enjoy his cigar and newspaper, she to the books she had scattered all over the desk and table.

When her mother returned from the symphony she'd attended, she found them both writing furiously. He at one end of the walnut table, Elizabeth at the desk.

"Well, my dears, you look positively industrious." She crossed the room to drop a kiss on her husband's cheek first, then on her daughter's. His only response was a nod and the half-snort, half-grunt male greeting that said, "Hello. I'm glad you're safe at home again but please don't bother me."

"Did you enjoy the evening?" Elizabeth

asked, feeling as though she was being pulled out of a fog.

"Yes. I'm just sorry you couldn't attend with me." Annabelle leaned against the edge of the walnut desk and pulled her gloves off, finger by finger. Elegant with her dark hair smoothed in the usual chignon, she fulfilled the picture of classical beauty, but for the detested dimple in her chin. "Though I believe you play better than the pianist they had."

Elizabeth tightened against the words she knew were coming. In the secret place of her heart she wished she could be the daughter her mother dreamed of.

"If only you would give your piano playing the concentration you apply to your lessons. Why, with a . . ." Annabelle dropped her extended hands back to her sides and sighed.

Since they'd discussed this topic to death more times than she cared to count in the last couple of years, Elizabeth just nodded. Much as she loved the piano and music, she loved medicine and helping people get well far more.

Annabelle sighed again. "Would either of you like a cup of tea?"

Elizabeth made herself look up and smile. "Yes, please." When her mother left the room, she and her father exchanged a glance. Tea was not necessary, but quiet was. Fighting the guilt that stalked in on stiff cat legs, Elizabeth struggled to get back to her studies. Her mother could say more with a sigh than a ranting politician could say in an hour.

Three days later Elizabeth staggered home from her last exam and collapsed to sleep around the clock. She woke to someone tapping on her door; in her dream the tapping had been the sound of her pencil against the desk as she failed her biology test.

"Yes?" Blinking her eyes open, she pushed back the covers and stared out the window. Dusk? But she was in her nightdress. The last she remembered was promising herself a nap.

"I was getting worried about you." Her mother crossed the room to sit on the end of the four-poster bed. "You're not sick, are you?"

"No." Elizabeth stretched her arms above her head, then pushed herself up enough to sit against the pillows she punched behind her back. "I feel like my head is full of wool, but other than that . . . did you come put me to bed, or did I dream it?"

Her mother nodded. "I couldn't let you

sleep in your clothes."

"Thank you."

"I haven't put you to bed for many years. Brought back good memories, it did." Annabelle clasped her hands around one knee and leaned against the bedpost. "You talked with me, but I knew you had no idea what you said. You were sound asleep again before I even turned out the lamp."

Elizabeth rubbed her grumbling midsection. "Will supper be ready soon?"

"As soon as you get dressed and come down. Since it will be just the three of us, if you'd rather stay in your wrapper, you may do so."

Elizabeth knew what a concession her mother was making by the offer. She leaned forward and kissed her mother's cheek. "Thanks, but no thanks. Give me a few minutes to wash and dress, and I'll be down. Perhaps we could go for a walk later."

"I'd like that." Annabelle stopped at the door. "Down along the river would be nice."

Elizabeth nodded. "Then tonight I am going to take a long, long bath with bubbles and candlelight and a novel. How long it has been since I read something for pleasure."

"I just finished the latest Mark Twain, *A Connecticut Yankee in King Arthur's Court.*

You can read it next, as long as you don't drop it in the water."

The two of them chuckled at the memory of the night Elizabeth had fallen asleep reading in the bathtub and was awakened by the splash her book made.

Elizabeth stretched again and, pushing her arms into the sleeves of her wrapper, wandered down the hall to the bathroom. By the time she'd washed and dressed, she felt ravenous enough to eat a . . . well, whatever Cook had chosen for the meal.

"So what are your plans for the summer?" They'd finished supper, and now Elizabeth and her mother were strolling along the river path. While mud showed the line where the river had nearly run over its banks, green horsetail weeds and grass were already poking through the gray. Elizabeth wrinkled her nose at the dirty mud stench. Half-furled maple leaves fluffed out the stark branches of the trees, and dandelions beamed like tiny suns in the new grass. Azure-winged swallows dipped for mud to build their nests and scooped bugs just above the river's surface.

Elizabeth stopped to point out the brilliant pink, rimmed with burgundy, of the flowering crab apple tree that hung over a brick wall. "Dr. Gaskin asked if I would help out in his surgery two days a week because his assistant nurse would like to be home with her children more. And I think Mrs. Gaskin would like to be out in her garden instead of in the office all day. Since I worked there last summer, they are counting on me. The rest of the time I will be helping Father like I usually do. Why?" She breathed in a whiff of sweetness from another flowering shrub.

"I thought perhaps we might take a trip to New York or perhaps Chicago for the world's fair. I'd really love to go to Europe, but I know your father would scream the house down at the expense."

Elizabeth nodded. She knew he would too. While it took a lot to get her father riled, her mother dipping into the principal of her inheritance was a bone of contention for sure. Just as he refused to allow her to spend her money on the newspaper.

"Most likely he would. If we went to New York, I could visit one of the hospitals and look into their medical school. But I've read so much about the World's Columbian Exposition in Chicago." She gave the fair's title a lilt like a barker at the circus.

Annabelle glanced at her daughter. "Most medical schools still don't take women."

"I know. But they will someday."

"Hmm. We shall see." Annabelle paused. "I heard Mrs. Andresen and Miss Livia Wahlstein will be speaking at the Columbian Exposition. We could go hear them."

"Then Papa *would* scream the house down." Elizabeth smiled at her mother. One thing they absolutely agreed on was a woman's right to vote. "I would love to hear them. I mean, reading their speeches and articles is fine and dandy, but to hear them and see them in person . . . Do you really think we could?"

"Not only could we, but we will."

"When will they be there?"

"I think in July sometime. I saw an article about them in the *Minneapolis Tribune*."

"Interesting that Father didn't pick up on an article of such timely import." Elizabeth glanced sideways at her mother, and the two of them burst into laughter. While Phillip Rogers thoroughly believed in the fourth amendment and would be incensed if ever accused of censoring the news, somehow he managed not to include information with which he heartily disagreed. Or else he gave it a two-inch space on the next to the last page or tucked it in the middle of the obituaries or the ads.

"I'd really love to see the women's building, along with the others, of course." Elizabeth thought of all the advertisements she'd seen and the articles about the beauty of the lakes and the ornate classical architecture and all the works of art. "And the Ferris Wheel. I definitely want to ride on that."

Annabelle shuddered. "I'll watch you from the good solid ground."

"Now, Mother, surely you don't want to miss out on a ride on the Ferris Wheel. It's a once-in-a-lifetime opportunity." The daughter laughed at the look of horror on her mother's face. Besides, she knew her father would love to ride with her.

"We could go to the symphony there too and shop at Marshall Field's." Annabelle took her daughter's arm. "What a marvelous time we shall have."

Elizabeth didn't mention the one place she wanted most to visit — the hospital for women, run by women, with women doctors treating the patients. She'd been wanting to talk with Dr. Morganstein, the head of the hospital, and this would be her opportunity.

CHAPTER EIGHT: BLESSING, NORTH DAKOTA

"We'll be at the church for quilting, then," Ingeborg reminded her husband. "Dinner is on the stove."

Haakan nodded. "You have a good time."

"I could come home and serve if you want."

"No. Astrid can do that. Time she took more responsibility in the kitchen anyway." Haakan stopped on the way out to kiss his wife's cheek and give her a pat on her sit-down place.

"I know. I just . . ." Ingeborg looked around the spotless kitchen. The stew simmering on the back burner lent a fragrance that could make anyone's stomach rumble, even if they had recently eaten. The bread she'd just taken from the oven lay on the sideboard, golden crusty brown, joining its yeasty aroma with that of the stew. "It's just that this is most likely our last time to meet until after harvest."

"You go on and have a good time. I hear Kaaren with the wagon."

"Ja, I will. Now you be careful in the field." She reached up and patted his cheek. "Did you see that the peas are starting to blossom already?" The glint in his eye told her he understood her change of topic. It meant *I love you, and I can't say it right now, but later* . . .

"Ja, and the potatoes are up." He winked at her and headed out the door to the barn where the boys had the teams and spans all harnessed, yoked, and hitched to the plows, harrows, and the drill for seeding the wheat. With all of them, including Baptiste, working and the weather holding, they were getting spring work done ahead of schedule.

Ingeborg took her basket of quilting supplies, another basket with a wedge of cheese, a freshly baked spice cake, and a loaf of bread still warm to the touch. Whoever was the hostess for the day would have a kettle of soup steaming on the church stove, and everyone else brought whatever they had. Ingeborg's cheese was always a welcome addition.

"Bye, Mor," Astrid called from the garden where she was planting beans with the assistance of the twins and Trygve. When they finished one garden, they would go to the other house and do the same there.

"Uff da. I hate to be gone like this." Ingeborg set her baskets in the wagon bed and climbed up, using the wheel spokes for steps. "Good morning, Kaaren, Ilse. Did you get all your quilt squares sewn?"

"Ja, that machine makes short work of piecing the quilt top. Ilse and I each did one. Surely is different from piecing it all by hand." Kaaren waited for Ingeborg to settle herself on the board seat before clucking the horses forward. "I need to go by the store and leave off a list for Mr. Valders to fill while we quilt."

"Oh, I forgot to bring cheese for the store."

"You want we should go back?"

Ingeborg shook her head, wrapping her shawl more closely around her shoulders. "That breeze is chilly. You think it will bring rain?"

"I hope not. On one hand we need rain, but on the other it slows down the planting. Good thing we can leave such decisions to God himself."

"Did you tell Andrew that Penny is in the family way?"

"No." Kaaren glanced at the woman on the seat beside her. "Why?"

"He asked, nei, rather informed me that

she was." Ingeborg shook her head. "That boy. He is an observer all right."

"She will most likely mention it today. I know how she feels. After losing two, you get afraid to mention the new life growing inside you in case you frighten it away."

"She is past her fourth month, and this time she looks good and healthy." Ingeborg dropped her voice with a glance over her shoulder. After all, they shouldn't be talking so freely in front of one not yet married.

But Ilse, though sixteen years old, sat at the end of the wagon with her feet swinging over the edge just like the children. Snatches of her song could be heard above the clumping of the horses' hooves and the jingle of harnesses. The wheels sang their own song, one needing greasing, so the squeak could be irritating after a while.

"I'll take the list in and walk on over to the church," Ilse called as the wagon pulled to a stop in front of the general store, owned and run by Penny Bjorklund. Her husband, Hjelmer, owned and operated the blacksmith, livery, and machinery lot next door. Hjelmer was the last living Bjorklund son who emigrated from Norway. A raised board sidewalk connected the two buildings and on to the old granary that now housed Uncle Olaf's furniture and woodworking shop. The new grain elevator stood next to the train station, so new that it still needed a coat of paint. The Blessing Boarding House, owned by Bridget Bjorklund, now wife of Henry Aarsgard, stood taller than any building but the elevator, and with the new additions, it took up more ground. The new dining room was now open to the general public for three meals a day. Bridget's home cooking was well known among the railroad workers and traveling businessmen. She'd met Henry when he was still working for the railroad. Now he tried to keep her from working too hard, an arduous task in itself.

"Mange takk." Kaaren handed the paper over. "And if they have any needles, bring a packet along to the meeting. We can never have too many needles."

"Not like it used to be." Ingeborg waved her list too. "This one, please?"

"Ja, sure." Ilse paused. "Anything else?"

Both women shook their heads. "Just remind Penny to hurry if she hasn't left already."

The street had dried to ruts from the spring mud, so the wagon bounced on its way around the corner and back to the Lutheran church built next to the school. Pastor Solberg's soddy was occupied by

Sam and his family now, since Pastor and Mrs. Solberg lived out on Zebulun Mac-Callister's farm with Zeb's two adopted daughters, Manda and Deborah.

Kaaren stopped at the hitching rail, and Ingeborg climbed down to tie the horses. Removing their bridles, she tied the lead shank to their halters and then to the rail. The ten-foot-high cottonwood trees planted and hand watered by the schoolchildren were leafed out enough to offer a bit of shade as they rustled secrets in the breeze. Baskets over their arms, the two women followed the sound of laughter and happy chatter up the three broad steps and through the open church door.

With the benches pushed back to line the walls, tables now filled the center of the room. Three quilting frames took up one side, and someone had brought her sewing machine along. A chorus of greetings welcomed the last comers as women cut and ironed quilting pieces from scraps brought in or material donated. Since the sewing machines had speeded up their quilting, the women made quilts to donate to the needy too. The Indian reservation to the north received many of their warm quilts.

"We thought perhaps you had decided not to come today," said Mary Martha Solberg, her loose-fitting dress failing to disguise her advancing pregnancy. Her warm smile rivaled the sun streaming in the tall windows. While her dark curly hair was now worn properly in a crocheted snood, tendrils resisted her combing and curled around her heart-shaped face like petals cupping a blossom.

"Had to sidetrack to the store first." Kaaren glanced around the room. "Penny's not here yet either?" She dropped her voice. "She's all right, isn't she?"

"Far as I know." Mary Martha leaned in closer, her words for their ears alone. "I have good news. We had a letter from Zebulun." Back in '89 her brother had left for Montana to round up horses after his wife, Katy Bjorklund, died in childbirth. The baby didn't live either, adding to Bridget Bjorklund's deep grief at the death of her youngest daughter. They rarely heard from Zeb, only enough to know he was still alive. He'd taken up homesteading in Montana, writing that his farm in Blessing held too many sad memories.

"What did he have to say for himself?" Ingeborg knew her tone carried a bite to it, but watching his two adopted daughters grieve not only Katy but him too made her want to grab the young man and shake him.

"He loves the mountains and the valleys, his horses are doing well, and . . ." She paused, eyes twinkling. "He's coming back to visit."

"When?"

"This summer. He's bringin' a herd of horses to sell." When she got excited, Mary Martha's Missouri accent grew more pronounced. "I reckon he'll leave some here for Manda to train for him. That girl has such a gift with horses, I swain?"

At the arch of Kaaren's eyebrows, Mary Martha broke into laughter. "Forgive me. I nigh to forgot where I am. *I swain* is a bit like you sayin' *you know,* but you always put a question mark after."

Kaaren and Ingeborg exchanged questioning looks. "Do you think she is saying we talk funny?" Ingeborg asked.

"Lawsie, Miz Bjorklund, where all would she get such an idea?" Kaaren, in spite of her Norwegian accent, slipped into a perfect imitation of Mary Martha's drawling speech.

"You two!" Mary Martha laughed along with them, drawing other gazes their way.

"Sorry I'm late." Penny Bjorklund blew into the room like a human tornado. She set her baskets on the table and waved her greetings. "God dag. Did I miss anything?"

Ingeborg and Kaaren shrugged while Mary Martha shook her head. "Nothin' other than Zeb is comin' home with a herd of horses."

"Well, my land, about time. Did he say anything about, you know, someone coming with him?"

"Like as in a female, perhaps a wife?"

Penny smiled, all innocence. "That's exactly what I meant. Thank you, Ingeborg, for clarifying that." She smiled around the room. "Are we having our meeting first or quilting?"

"I thought we should set up, then have devotions, then quilt, and have our meeting while we eat." Mrs. Valders, her black felt hat pinned to cover her receding hairline, looked around for anyone who disagreed. With a nod that set her two chins to quivering, she finished. "That's settled then. Who would like to start at the frames and who wants to cut?"

As women volunteered for each job, their laughter and discussion set the church to ringing. Those with small children left them in the care of Ellie Wold, Goodie's ten-year-old daughter. One young mother nursed her baby, then laid her in a basket at the edge of the room. As the other children were herded out to play, peace floated into the

116

room like a welcome guest, and voices settled more into murmurs.

"I sure would love to have Kaaren read to us while we stitch," Mrs. Odell from over at the quilting frame said wistfully. "I do love to be read to."

"Me too," said another. "The only reading I hear is Thomas, and second graders don't read real smooth yet." She gulped. "Sorry. It's not that he's not reading good for a second grader, you know."

Chuckles rose like soap bubbles popping.

"I would be glad to read." Kaaren set her flatiron back on the stove and left her ironing board to retrieve her Bible from her basket. "Any favorite passages today?"

"I do love Psalm 91." Goodie pushed her needle through the three layers of material and wool batting with her thimble.

"Anyone else?"

"First John."

After a couple more suggestions, Kaaren, the sun glinting off her braided hair as if she wore a crown of gold or perhaps a halo, opened her Bible and paused. "Shall we pray first?" As the women bowed their heads and silence settled over the room, she began. "Our Father in heaven, we thank you for your house where we can come together. We thank you for the work before us and the blessings our quilts have been to those less fortunate than we. We thank you for sending your Son to live and die here on this earth that we might have eternal life. Oh, Lord, most holy, please fill us with your love and joy. In Jesus' precious name we pray, amen." The amen whispered around the room like the rustle of willow leaves in the breeze.

Needles darted in and out, flatirons pushed out wrinkles, and scissors snipped away as Kaaren read of sheltering in the shadow of the most high God and how God called them his beloved children.

Mrs. Magron, her nose twitching like the mouse she resembled, sighed. "I do love how He tells us to love one another. Sometimes . . ." She paused and sighed again. "Sometimes that ain't the easiest thing on this earth."

Ingeborg and Agnes glanced at each other with a slight nod that said they were thinking the same thing. Even in the most forgiving terms, Mr. Magron would not be described as loving. Not that he was cruel, or at least they hoped not, but he never had a good word to say about anyone or anything. At least he didn't carry on about it like some others they knew, but still . . .

"I'm a'goin' to make sure I call on her

this summer, maybe invite her and the mister over for supper." Agnes, her once round face now more bone than flesh, nodded as she whispered, "Get so tied up in my own things, I forget about her."

Ingeborg reached over and patted her friend's hand. Agnes and Joseph Baard had come to the area not long after the Bjorklund brothers, and the women had been friends ever since the first time they met, back when they were both a lot younger. "You always do so much more than most of us anyway."

"Look who's talking."

At a disapproving glance from Mrs. Valders, who liked things just so, they returned to their cutting, sharing a secret smile.

God, what is happening with my friend? Are you not listening to our prayers for her health? She looks like something is eating her alive from the inside out, and while I know she wanted another baby, the swelling I see isn't new life growing inside of her. Ingeborg kept her attention to the quilt pieces she was cutting out, for she knew if she looked at Agnes again, she would burst into tears. And *that* would be entirely unseemly.

"Ingeborg, are you all right?" Penny leaned close to whisper in her ear.

"Ja, I will be."

Kaaren's voice leant music to the words as she concluded her Bible reading with the Beatitudes from the Sermon on the Mount. " 'Blessed are they that mourn: for they shall be comforted. Blessed are the meek. . . .' "

When Kaaren closed her Bible, thank-you's skipped around the room, and those at the quilting frames switched places with those working at something else. The treadle of the sewing machine beat out the time as the needle blurred up and down.

"Can we have cookies now?" One of the children called from the doorway.

"Yes, I suppose it's time." One of the mothers rose and, taking a basket outside, let her son pass the cookies around. At the same time, Penny stood and took up the coffeepot, then motioned to Ingeborg to bring the tray of cups. Together they made the rounds so that everyone had coffee and cookies.

The fragrance of hot coffee mingled with that of the beef and noodle soup simmering on the back of the stove, all seasoned with a dollop of laughter and rising like a veil of incense before the altar. A child shrieked in play outside, and the chant of "Red rover, red rover, send Amy right over" made more than one woman smile.

"So when is the baby due?" Ingeborg set the tray down and turned to Penny.

"In September. I've been afraid to say anything, you know, afraid I might lose one again."

"I thought that might be what was keeping you silent. But you look wonderful this time, not like the others."

"Mange takk. Now . . ." She rolled her eyes so that Ingeborg nodded and smiled.

"Those first months can be pretty miserable for some."

Penny laid her hand over the beginning mound under her apron. "I believe we are finally going to have a baby to lay in the cradle Onkel Olaf made so long ago."

"It's been put to good use."

"I know. The Johnson baby outgrew it and then the Solbergs' little Johnny. One thing is sure, we all put things to good use around here."

"Well, Metiz told me some time ago that this time you would carry the baby to full term. I didn't even realize you were that way again." Ingeborg cupped one hand under her elbow as she sipped from the cup of coffee she'd poured herself.

"I wish she would come to these meetings."

"Me too, but even after all these years she doesn't feel really welcomed by everyone."

Penny nodded and lowered her voice, leaning closer to Ingeborg's ear. "I heard someone mention that it was a shame all our lovely work went to cover some lazy Indian who couldn't be bothered to take good care of anything."

Ingeborg squinted her eyes. "Still going on about that, eh? I think we better have Kaaren read about the sheep and the goats again. We seem to need regular reminders that there, but for the grace of God, go I." *And why do I have no doubt who's been saying such a thing? Oh, Lord, preserve us.*

At a sound they both turned toward the window. Was that someone screaming or was it one of the children playing? They listened again and just as they were about to dismiss it as one of the little ones, the scream came again.

"Ma-a-a!"

Ingeborg flew to the door to see the now quiet children staring out across the land. She took the steps running and rounded the corner of the church to look to the north. "Mary Martha," she called back, "it's Deborah!"

CHAPTER NINE

"It's Ma . . . Manda. . . ." Deborah collapsed into Ingeborg's arms, out of breath from running as fast as she could.

Mary Martha charged down the steps. "What is it? Deborah, what?"

"M-Manda."

"I'll get the team." Ingeborg handed the child to her mother and headed for the hitching rail. "Someone go find Pastor." With shaking fingers she slipped the knots, bridled the horses, and leaped into the wagon, all the while muttering, "God help us. God help us. Please, God, take care of Manda." She backed the horses and turned them, aiming to circle the church and head north.

"Kaaren, you come too." Mary Martha and Deborah climbed up the wheel.

"It's her arm. A horse threw her," Deborah said, having finally caught her breath.

"Is she bleeding?" Ingeborg asked the little girl.

"No, not in the arm, but here." Deborah pointed to a spot on her forehead. "But not bad."

"The bone isn't sticking out of her arm?" Ingeborg slapped the reins. "Giddup." When they only trotted slowly, she slapped the reins again.

"No. But she can't move it. And it hurts somethin' fierce. Manda never cries."

"But she did this time?" Mary Martha clutched the little girl close.

"She screamed, Ma, then cried and said some bad words." Deborah, shock written all over her slender face, stared up at the woman who was really her aunt but had taken over the care of the girls when their father, Zeb, left home.

Ingeborg kept her gaze on the team and the road. "Where is she now?"

"She was sittin' up against the corral fence. She sure be mad at that horse." Deborah leaned into Mary Martha's side. "I didn't take time to catch the horse or nothin'. I just ran hard as I could."

"Do you have bandages rolled?" Kaaren asked from her place right behind the wagon seat. "If it's broken, we'll have to set it."

"Yes, I always keep some of different widths. We haven't needed them much."

"Good. And some willow bark for tea will help with the pain."

"I have some that Metiz left when the baby was born. And we have some spirits too, if we need them. And laudanum."

"Where is Pastor today?"

"He had some folks to call on south of town. Dropped me and the babies off at the church and said he'd be back in time for dinner." Mary Martha slapped her forehead. "I ran off and left the babies. Thomas is going to be screaming hungry when he wakes up."

"Someone else will nurse him. He won't starve."

"Land sakes, what is Mrs. Valders going to have to say about all this?"

Ingeborg and Kaaren looked at each other, eyes wide, jaws tight, and lips rolled inward, fighting off the laughter that threatened to erupt in the otherwise stressful moment.

Mary Martha sent Ingeborg a sideways glance. "Not that I'm afraid of her or any such thing."

That did it. Ingeborg lost control first. She tried to turn her snort into a cough, but that snort was mighty stubborn and snort it stayed. Kaaren's chuckle perched in the back of her throat as if she were trying to swallow it. Tears brimmed her eyes at the effort. But they made the mistake of looking at each other, and they could disguise their mirth no longer.

"I don't for the life of me see what y'all are laughin' at. I reckon you might've lost your minds." But a giggle escaped her too, and Deborah, after looking at each of the women as if trying to figure out who was the looniest, giggled along with the others.

Ingeborg slowed enough to turn into the ranch without tipping or skidding the wagon but picked up the pace again on the straight-away. When she brought the team to a stop at the corral, dust blew in a cloud, and the horses were blowing.

"Manda?"

"Over here against the barn wall in the shade." Her voice carried an undercurrent of tears.

Mary Martha climbed over the wheel and headed for the gate. "Darlin', how bad hurt are you?"

The others followed her.

Manda sat in the dirt, tear tracks streaking her cheeks, her right arm cradling her left. "Fool horse." She glared at the animal, which stood as far away from her as possible. If he could have squeezed through the corral rails and run off, he probably would have. His flicking ears told them he was taking it all in.

Mary Martha knelt beside the girl. But when she reached out to touch the arm, Manda yipped and flinched away, gnawing her lip at the pain.

Ingeborg and Kaaren looked at each other, then back at the shaking girl.

"Mary Martha, come with me," said Kaaren. "Let's get the supplies we need. We can set it right here before we move her. We'll save some pain that way, and it'll be better for the arm."

"I ran fast as I could." Deborah's lower lip quivered as she stood by her sister.

"I know. Thank you." Manda, her britches-clad legs straight out in front of her, tried to smile at her little sister. "Could you get my hat, please?" She nodded to the battered lump of felt that looked only remotely like something to be worn on a head.

Ingeborg knelt next to Manda and put her hand on the girl's shoulder. "We'll take care of this." She called over her shoulder. "You better bring the laudanum too. I think we're going to need it." Her attention back on the suffering girl, she stroked the hair back off Manda's sweat-beaded forehead. "Now,

Manda, you know I have to look at that arm."

"I know. But I can't move it." Her shoulders curved forward to protect her arm.

"I promise I'll be careful, but let me probe it. You know I'll be as gentle as I can."

A deep sigh preceded the "All right."

"Show me where it hurts the most."

"All over, but mostly here." Manda pointed to midway between the wrist and elbow.

With prayers flying heavenward even as she leaned forward, Ingeborg gently pushed Manda's shirt sleeve up her arm, then touched the arm with her fingertips. Although already swollen, the flesh gave enough for her to feel the bump. Closing her eyes, she focused on what she was feeling, all the while murmuring soothing words.

Manda gasped, then groaned.

"Easy, hold still."

"I'm trying."

"I know." *We're going to have to pull hard to set this. Oh, Lord, have mercy. Give us strength, especially Manda.* Ingeborg tugged a handkerchief out of her apron pocket and handed it to her young friend.

"I . . . I'm not goin' to lose my arm or some such, am I?" The whisper told of the weight of her fear.

"No, no. It's just a simple break. People your age heal quickly."

"How long?" Manda flinched away from Ingeborg's questing fingers.

"Oh, a few weeks. We can be grateful it wasn't your neck. What happened?"

"The dog chased a barn cat through the corral, and that fool horse thought it was a cougar, I swear. He went higher'n that barn wall, and I wasn't hanging on tight enough. When he landed, I took a header."

"And landed on your arm." Ingeborg sat back on her heels and glanced up at the barn. "High wall."

"Seemed it at the time." Manda sounded more like herself. By the time this story got around, the horse would have jumped clear over the corral poles, if Ingeborg knew anything about Manda's storytelling abilities. Though she was quiet too much of the time, once she got going on her horses, she'd keep an audience enthralled till the end of the tale.

"Can I get you a dipper of water or something?" Deborah sat beside her sister, her arms clenched around her updrawn knees, her eyes taking up most of her face.

"Bring the whole bucket and pour it over me."

"Really?"

"Nah, a dipper would be good." Manda's eyes followed her sister, as with bare feet flying she headed for the rails, slid between two, and ran to the well. "Scared her right bad."

"She ran all the way to the church."

"Poor kid." But pride shone in Manda's hazel eyes. Since their ma died and their pa had left for supplies and never returned, the two had been inseparable. Zebulun Mac-Callister had saved them from dying of starvation on their homestead near the Missouri River and had brought them with him on his own flight that stopped with the folks in Blessing.

Kaaren and Mary Martha returned with the supplies in a basket, along with two pieces of kindling to be bound for the splint. Kaaren poured a couple of glugs from the flat brown bottle into a cup of water and handed it to Manda.

"Drink this. In a couple of minutes you won't feel any pain at all."

Manda made a face but drank it all down. She wiped her mouth with the back of her good hand. "Ugh."

"Now, Manda, Kaaren is going to take your hand, and I'll hold your elbow. On the count of three we'll give a hard, steady pull, and please God, that bone will snap right back into place. Then we'll splint it and wrap it and get you up to the house before you fall sound asleep on us."

"Don't got no choice now, do I?"

"Not really." Kaaren stroked the wisps of dark hair back off the girl's forehead. "You can scream if you need to. No one to hear but us, and we won't tell."

Manda looked to see where Deborah was. "Why don't you send her to the house for something? She don't like to see pain. Scares her some bad."

Mary Martha nodded. "I'll take care of that." She handed the stick she'd been wrapping in strips of an old sheet to Ingeborg. "We'll go get something going for dinner." She met Deborah at the corral. "Come, we need to get Manda something to eat."

"But I got the water." Deborah slipped around the partly open gate and headed for her sister, her gaze tight on the dipper so she wouldn't spill any water. Only after Manda drank the whole thing did the little girl turn and run back to Mary Martha. "Can we have some molasses cookies? That's Manda's favorite."

"I know." The two of them headed for the house hand in hand.

131

"You ready?" Ingeborg asked the injured girl.

Manda nodded. "I feel woozy."

"Good. That's the way we want you." Ingeborg took hold of Manda's elbow with both hands and Kaaren did the same with the wrist.

"One, two, three." They both pulled. The grating of the bone sounded worse than fingernails screeching on a blackboard. But with a slight snap, it settled back into place. Manda's eyes flickered open.

"Done?"

"Done. Hold steady now while we wrap this up." Ingeborg and Kaaren worked together as they had so many times before in tending to injuries of all kinds. Metiz had passed many of her healing skills on to Ingeborg through the years, and that combined with what her mother had taught her made Ingeborg the closest thing to a doctor in the area. Within minutes they had the arm wrapped and bound close to the girl's chest with a sling tied around her neck.

"I . . . I don't think I can walk." Manda, her eyes out of focus, shook her head.

"We'll help you." The two women bent over, Kaaren taking the good arm while Ingeborg put her arm around Manda's waist. "Again, on three. You get your feet under you, and we'll help lift."

By the time they had Manda standing, Ingeborg and Kaaren sighed at the same time. They half carried, half walked the girl through the gate and to the house, navigating the steps with some difficulty, as Manda barely heard their instructions to lift her feet.

"One thing sure," Kaaren said when they laid the girl on her bed. "She's not a little girl anymore."

"No, she's a young woman, whether she likes to admit it or not." Mary Martha leaned to pull off Manda's boots, but Ingeborg gently pushed her out of the way. "You've got us to do the heavy work right now, so take advantage of it."

"I'm just pregnant, not an invalid."

"I know. Let's go eat." They left Manda snoring on her bed, pillows propped against her side to keep her from turning over.

"What about Manda?" Deborah looked from her sister to the women and back.

"She'll eat when she wakes up." *And please, God, let that be a long time from now.* Ingeborg glanced back at the sleeping girl. They should have taken her dirty clothes off, but they could do that later.

Heavy footsteps pounded up the wooden steps, and Pastor Solberg burst into the

133

house. "What happened?"

"Manda was thrown by a horse and broke her arm. She's all set and resting, darlin', so you can calm down now." Mary Martha met her husband in the middle of the room. "We're just goin' to eat. Have you had dinner yet?"

"No. I came straight here. She's going to be all right?" He looked to Ingeborg for the answer. At her nod, his sigh could be heard clear to the schoolhouse. "Thank God."

"I should never have left them. . . ."

"Don't even think of that. Manda is seventeen years old, a grown woman. Why, many girls her age are married already and starting their families."

"Speakin' of families, I need to go back to the church for our babies."

"What?" Pastor Solberg looked like someone had struck him.

"Don't worry. They're being well taken care of," Ingeborg said.

"I know, but . . ." Mary Martha took in a deep breath and let it all out, then turned to the others. "Come, I have a dinner of sorts on the table. Or rather Deborah does."

As soon as they'd eaten, Pastor Solberg headed his wagon back to the church for his children, and Ingeborg and Kaaren followed. By the time they'd picked up their supplies and told the story for everyone to exclaim over, the afternoon was half over and it was time for everyone to head for their wagons and go home.

"We didn't do much quilting today." Kaaren set her basket in the rear of the wagon beside Ingeborg's.

"You never know what's going to happen, that's for sure. Uff da, that poor child."

"We better quit calling her a child, you know. I've seen the looks she and Baptiste exchange when they think no one is watching."

"Ja. Astrid said she saw them walking out by the river one day. Baptiste had his gun along but hadn't shot anything."

"Hard to see game if you're only looking at Manda." Kaaren raised one eyebrow.

"But then, perhaps she is the game he is after."

"Ach, those poor children. They would receive nothing but censure." Kaaren raised her hands when Ingeborg turned on the wagon seat. "I know. Not from us, but then everyone doesn't love Metiz and Baptiste the way we do."

"As if the color of one's skin or hair should make any difference." Ingeborg flipped the reins again so the horses would pick up their feet. "But I heard that comment today about where our quilts go. Made me want to go over and shake her. We, who all have so much compared to others, should be generous."

"Funny how many of them don't really think of Metiz as Indian any longer. She's helped about everyone in Blessing and others for miles around at one time or another."

"Ja, but there is always the bad apple that rots the barrel."

CHAPTER TEN

June arrived with no rain in sight.

Thorliff lifted the yoke off the oxen for the final time until haying would start. The sun burned, tanning him through the fabric of his shirt. *With no fieldwork to do after dinner, maybe I can go over and visit with Anji. We could walk down by the river.*

"I think we all need to go fishing," Haakan said to his sons as he hung the harnesses up on their pegs. "What do you say?"

"I say that's the best news I've had since graduation." Thorliff took off his wide-brimmed hat to wipe the sweat off his forehead. So much for seeing Anji today. Perhaps tomorrow night.

"Go ask your mor if she wants to go too. Maybe we'll have a picnic supper with the fish we catch."

"I will." Andrew took off for the house before anyone could answer.

Thorliff and Haakan shared the kind of

look grown-ups give at the antics of one younger. Pleasure sat on Thorliff's shoulders like a purring kitten.

"You've worked hard as any man, son. I want you to know I appreciate it. Both of you boys have." Haakan stretched his arms above his head, then lifted and resettled his hat. "Let's go eat." Throwing his arm around Thorliff's shoulders, he strode on up to the house with his son at his side. They paused and turned, as if by secret communication, and looked out over the newly seeded fields. In some, the growing wheat softened the black soil with a veil of green. The most recently seeded ground still lay smooth and black, absorbing the sun that would bring the seeds to life.

"Now if only the rains would come, gentle and lasting for a couple of days. Wouldn't that be the perfect picture?"

"Ja, it would." Thorliff dipped water, warmed by the sun, into the washbasins lined along the house wall. Towels hung on a rod above the bench, and soap rested in a dish so that none would be wasted. They washed, tossed the wash water over the roses by the front door, and followed their noses into a kitchen redolent with the smell of baking chicken, sage, onion, and bacon to flavor the greens. Biscuit perfume floated

138

over the other aromas like frosting on a cake.

Haakan inhaled a chest-swelling draught and touched his wife's arm as she hurried past. "I could smell this meal clear out in the fields. That's why we raced around the last turns. Did you see the horses at a dead run and me whipping them on?"

"Ach, the way you go on." Ingeborg gave him a poke with her elbow. "Call Astrid, will you please?"

"Where is she?"

"Gathering eggs. I thought to take a wagon with eggs, cheese, and butter into the store this afternoon."

"Ja, I'll call her, but doesn't fishing and a picnic sound better than a trip to the store?"

Ingeborg shook her head. "Fishing is what sounds a treat. What if you men go fishing and Astrid and I bring food to go with the fresh fish down in time for an early supper. Then we can all help with the milking. Surely the cows won't mind our being a bit late."

"Ah, leave it to you to figure the best way."

"I'll call Astrid," said Thorliff. The thought of an afternoon of fishing banished the tiredness he had carried to the house, so he jumped down the steps and trotted across the yard to the chicken coop.

"Dinner, Astrid." He looked inside to see

a few hens on the nests but no laughing girl, not even behind the door. He found her in the coolness of the springhouse, damp cloth in hand to clean the eggs she was setting into the wooden egg crates. A pan of water sat beside her for any eggs too dirty to buff off.

"Dinner's ready."

"So soon?"

"Ja, we finished the planting. Guess what we get to do this afternoon."

"Weed the garden?" Her laughing smile said she was teasing. Weeding the garden was one of Thorliff's least favorite chores. He'd been accused of daydreaming while leaning on a hoe handle more than once.

Astrid laid aside her washcloth and followed him out the door. "So are you done for real?"

"All but the haying, unless Onkel Lars needs us over on the north piece."

"I thought Mor and I were going to the store."

"You are, then you're coming down to the river."

"Ah." Astrid poked him in the side. "What if I invite Anji to come back with us? What would you pay me for that?"

"Pay you?" Thorliff poked her back. "She's your friend too."

"But I'm not the one who goes all dreamy eyes when —" She squealed as Thorliff gave a yank on her braid. The two of them mounted the back steps still laughing.

When they bowed their heads for grace, he dug her in the ribs with his elbow so that she spluttered on the first words of "I Jesu navn," earning them both a look of reprimand after the amen.

"You two." Ingeborg shook her head, but the twinkle in her eyes said she didn't blame them. The end of spring work was a good time to celebrate. Not that there wasn't still plenty to do.

Down at the slow flowing Red River they swatted mosquitoes and watched their corks bob on the quiet surface. When Thorliff's cork dipped under, he jerked on his willow pole, and a fish flew over his shoulder to land on the bank. Paws yipped and sniffed the flopping fish. When it curled and flipped, smacking him in the nose, he leaped backward, scrambling to get his feet back under him.

"Hey, Paws, you want to hold my pole?" Andrew rubbed the dog's ears while Thorliff removed the hook and jabbed a forked stick up through the gills of the fish. Haakan had yet to catch a fish big enough to keep, so every time one of the boys caught a keeper, their quiet giggles made their father sigh more loudly.

With a new worm on his hook, Thorliff tossed his line back into the eddy where he'd caught the last perch.

Andrew yelped as his cork took a deep dive. "Catfish, I bet."

"Hang on to him." Haakan rammed the end of his willow pole into the dirt and reached to help his son.

"I can do it." Andrew stood and, keeping the tip of the pole in the air, eased the dragging fish closer to the bank. "He's a big one."

Haakan rolled up his pants legs. "I'll grab him." Wading into the stream, the mud squishing up between his toes, he reached for the string.

"Pa, your pole." Thorliff leaped for it, but the pole headed out toward the middle of the river, whatever pulling it large enough to get it beyond reach in a breath.

Haakan grabbed the string taut from Andrew's line and hauled in a huge catfish, its feelers upright and side spines wriggling. The mouth looked big enough to swallow the dog.

"Three feet if it's an inch."

"But, Pa, your pole."

"I got more string and another hook. No one's caught one this big for years. Good job, Andrew." Careful to keep from getting stung by the spines, Haakan rammed a stick through the gills before standing up and clapping his son on the shoulder. "We got enough fish for supper already."

"We're not gonna quit, are we?" Andrew looked up from baiting his hook again.

"No, we'll keep fishing. We can have fried fish for breakfast too, or Kaaren and Lars can have some."

Haakan cut himself another willow pole, tied on some string, a hook, and a worm, then tossed the line out into the river. Hands locked behind his head, he leaned against a tree trunk, his pole dug into the black dirt by his side. Swatting a mosquito on the side of his neck, he clasped his hands again.

Thorliff yanked in another fish. Andrew followed. Their father's pole remained upright, no wiggle.

"Maybe he just came to watch us fish." Thorliff's stage whisper made Andrew giggle.

"Good thing he has us, or we'd all have no supper." Andrew baited his hook and threw it back out.

"You think he could get the fire going?"

"I hope so. We're too busy catching fish."

"Paws, get 'em!"

Paws thrashed his tail in the leaves and whined.

Thorliff lurched for his pole as it started to follow a fish. He jerked, and another fish flew through the air, missing Haakan by mere inches.

"Well, I never . . ." Ingeborg stood near a tree not ten feet away. "Is this the way our men go fishing?"

"We . . . we got lots of fish, Mor." Andrew pointed to the pegs in the riverbank. "Me and Thorliff did. Pa's been taking a rest." His burst of laughter made his mother chuckle too. Andrew's laugh had always been as contagious as a cold.

"Where's the fire for frying them?" Astrid set her basket down at her mother's feet.

"That's Pa's job." Thorliff untied his string from the pole and, sticking the point of the hook in the cork, wrapped the string around it and put the ball in his pocket. "Andrew and I'll get the wood."

That night after a supper seasoned with laughter, when the cows were milked and the chores finished, the family trooped back to the house.

"Oh, Thorliff, I forgot. I'm so sorry." Ingeborg fished in her apron pocket and pulled out a letter. "It's from St. Olaf."

Thorliff stared at the envelope for long seconds before reaching for it.

CHAPTER ELEVEN: NORTHFIELD, MINNESOTA

"Elizabeth, I have bad news." Annabelle knocked a second time.

Elizabeth fought through the fog of a dream that vanished like smoke in a breeze. "C-come in, Mother." Blinking in the brightness of morning, she shoved herself up on her pillows and yawned, arms reaching above her head to get a good stretch. "What did you say?"

Annabelle crossed the deep red Oriental rug to stand by the foot of the four-poster bed. "Mrs. Gaskin died in her sleep last night. Went to bed feeling fine but never woke up. The doctor would like you to come. . . ."

"Mrs. Gaskin? Oh, Mother, are you sure?"

"Old Tom brought the message. Dr. Gaskin wants you to come take care of the office today."

"He's not going to see patients, is he?"

"No, but if there is an emergency, he

146

wants you to help or send them over to the new doctor. Looks like his nurse assistant chose a bad time to be away."

Elizabeth threw back her light covers but paused in the act of standing. "Mrs. Gaskin gone . . . I can't believe it." The doctor's wife not only ran her house and the surgery, but she had always taken time to encourage Elizabeth, ever since she was a question-asking ten-year-old. While others suggested Elizabeth become a nurse, Mrs. Gaskin always said she would be a fine doctor one day.

"How ever will the doctor manage?" Annabelle sat on the end of the bed and leaned against the post. "His wife has been his right hand since the day they opened that office."

Elizabeth fought the moisture brimming her eyes and flooding her nose. "She . . . she was such a wonderful friend." She sniffed and nodded when her mother handed her a handkerchief. "Th-thank you." After wiping and blowing and wiping again, she looked up to see that her mother had tears streaming down her face too.

"I better get dressed. Where's Tom?"

"In the kitchen. Cook is coddling him with coffee and doughnuts. Breakfast will be ready for you as soon as you go down."

Elizabeth crossed to her armoire, drew out a serviceable blue cotton dress, and tossed it across the bed. "I know the neighbors will be taking food to Dr. Gaskin's house as soon as they hear, but I'll take a basket along. Oh, and let Father know so he can start on the obituary. I'm sure he'll want to do a front-page story on her life — she was such a boon to all of Northfield." She stopped and wiped her eyes and nose again. "I know death is part of life, but that doesn't mean I have to like it."

"No, dear. And it doesn't get any easier as you get older either. My mother always said, 'Life changes in an instant, and only God is in control.' " She paused at the doorway. "No matter how much we think we know."

Elizabeth knew that last was for her. She and her mother had often discussed her vendetta against death. *I know, but I am still going to keep it at bay for as many people as I can for as long as I am able.* By the time she made her way down the curved walnut stairs, she had herself in hand, and only the slightest reddening of her eyes spoke of her tears.

But then she saw the hound-dog misery in Old Tom's eyes and a fresh tear track down his corrugated face. "Oh, Tom, I'm so sorry." She knew that Mrs. Gaskin had cared for Tom like a brother for all the years he'd lived above their stable, tending the garden, the horse and buggy, and driving whenever Dr. Gaskin needed him. Although she had no idea how old Tom really was, he looked ancient in the cheery kitchen. She laid a hand on his slumped shoulder, feeling the bones beneath her fingertips, so bereft of muscle that he looked more like a walking skeleton than a man.

"She was so good to me. God don't have no finer saint in heaven than Mrs. Doc."

"I know." Elizabeth took her place at the table and smiled up when Isabel Ames, better known as Cook, set a plate with two fresh doughnuts and a bowl of rhubarb sauce in front of her.

"Now, you eat up, missy. This going to be a long, hard day." She returned with the coffeepot and filled Elizabeth's and her mother's china cups to the brim. "I got me another batch of doughnuts started. I'll send what's done with you. Folks going to be needing coffee and doughnuts when they come to call." Like a perpetual top, Cook spun from stove to counter to larder and back, keeping three things going at once yet pausing to pat first Elizabeth's shoulder and then Tom's. Elizabeth shared a secret smile with her mother. They were both very capable in the kitchen, but Cook got such pleasure out of doing for them, they rarely let on.

"That woman was most as good a doctor as the doctor himself," continued Cook. "Why, that concoction she made for my lumbago made me feel better in a snap."

Elizabeth secretly wondered if the honey and whiskey base hadn't done as much as the medication, but she never mentioned such a thing. If Cook knew what was in some of Mrs. Doc's concoctions, she would throw her apron over her head. But they did work. Or at least many claimed so.

"No one makes doughnuts like these." Tom reached for another. "You could start a shop. You'd near need to beat people off with a stick, they'd come buy so much."

"Oh, pshaw." Cook rolled her eyes. "The way you carry on."

Elizabeth rose, at the same time wiping her mouth with a napkin. "Come, Tom. If you're finished flirting with Cook, we can be on our way."

"Ah, missy, I ain't flirting no ways." But the glint in his eye said differently. "Thankee for the repast," he shot to Cook over his shoulder as he followed Elizabeth out the door to where he had left the horse and buggy. "Doc wanted you to come quick, not waste time walking."

"I appreciate that." She had planned a long walk this morning, down along the river and back up the hill. Since school let out she'd gotten lazy. "Where is Dr. Gaskin?"

"Busy with laying out the missus. He wanted her to look nice, knowing that was important to her. She always looked nice, din't she?"

Elizabeth nodded. Mrs. Gaskin had always worn her graying hair crimped on the sides and rolled around a rat in the back. A white apron covered whatever dress she wore, but her face always caught attention, not for true beauty but because of the love and laughter that shone from it. Comfort oozed from every pore, and her hazel eyes bestowed a benediction on those she met. Unless of course they crossed the doctor's orders. Even the Catholic priest trembled when she got after him.

Biting her lip and sniffing to keep the tears at bay, Elizabeth wound her handkerchief around her finger. The house would feel so empty. How would Dr. Gaskin endure it? How would Henry, the little black-and-white dog that followed his mistress everywhere, get along?

When they turned into the driveway that

led to the cutstone house surrounded by roses about to bloom, Elizabeth sucked in a breath. Already black wreaths hung on the gateposts and the front door, announcing that someone had passed on to their reward.

Old Tom glanced at her. "I hung those for him. Couldn't bear to have him nail them up. Nothing but bad memories that." Years earlier the wreaths had been used to announce the death of Dr. Gaskin's only son, who had died of consumption.

"You're a good man, Tom. I know how much the doctor appreciates you." Elizabeth picked up her basket.

"Here, I'll take that. You go on in the front door and see that all is well."

"Thank you for coming," Dr. Gaskin said as Elizabeth entered the house. He stood at the foot of the black-draped dining room table.

"You're welcome, and of course I would come." When he took her hand, she could feel his trembling. She fought her tears so she could smile for him. Often he had commented that her smile could charm the most brokenhearted. Today, he fit that part. His eyes looked as lifeless as a flower stalk in a winter garden. Deep commas bracketed his mouth, and he looked to have lost ten pounds or more, so shrunken in on himself was he. The gray of his face now matched his hair.

"How can I help you?" She fought the quivering of her lips.

"Just see to the folks for me. I cannot bear to hear how much they all loved her and how they'll miss her so." He rubbed a dry hand across his eyes and furrowed forehead. "I-I always thought I'd go first, and I knew she was strong enough to-to go on without me." He clung to both her hands. "But now I have to go on alone, and . . . and I'm not strong like she was." He leaned forward to peer into Elizabeth's very soul. "She was, wasn't she? I mean we haven't believed wrong all these years?"

"I know with everything I am that Mrs. Gaskin is sitting right now at the very feet of Jesus and the angels are singing glory hallelujahs because she's come home." The doctor's gulping sobs tore chunks out of her heart. She held her dear mentor and friend in her arms while he sobbed like a small child.

When the storm passed, he drew himself upright and, taking a handkerchief from his pocket, mopped his face. "Thank you, my dear. You are an immense comfort. I thought putting Helen here in the parlor was better for those who ask to see her."

"You could have waited for some of us to help you."

"I know, but . . . it was just something I had to do. The funeral will be tomorrow."

"All right."

"I will be either upstairs or out in the garden with Tom. His gentleness is such a comfort, and I think he loved her as much as I. Call me if you need me."

Elizabeth wiped her eyes and took in a cleansing breath. "I will." But inside she knew only someone bleeding to death on his porch would merit that call.

She spent the morning comforting callers and sending a few who needed to see a doctor across town to the new man, Dr. Johanson. Her father was the only one she sent out to the garden to visit with Dr. Gaskin.

Gifts of food covered the counters in the kitchen and filled the icebox. One of the church women volunteered to stay and manage the kitchen, to keep the coffeepot simmering and plates filled with cookies, cake, and sweet breads.

Everyone who came brought something — a jar of jam or pickles, fresh-baked bread, hot dishes, and salads — enough to feed a platoon of hungry soldiers.

As the flow of grievers trickled off in the afternoon, the women sent some of the food to the neighbors' iceboxes to wait for after the funeral. What they could serve, they did.

Elizabeth made her way out to the backyard as the late afternoon sun sent long shadows across the lawn and flower beds. Two men sat in the gazebo set near a small pond.

"Have you two eaten?" she asked as she drew near.

"No, but maybe we could take a little somethin' now." Tom looked to the doctor for confirmation. At his nod, Elizabeth smiled.

"Good." Inside she rejoiced at how much better he looked. Color had returned to his face, his eyes weren't as red as before, and his appearance was not so ghostly. "I'll bring you each a plate."

"H-how's it going in there?" Dr. Gaskin nodded toward the house.

"We have enough food to feed half of Northfield, but we're taking care of it. Mrs. Warren chose to stay and help. There are flowers all around the parlor. Pastor Mueller sent a message to say he wants to come by later."

"Good. Helen had the service all planned. I found it in the box she always told me to look in if she died."

"That sounds like her, always making

things easy for others." Elizabeth turned and blinked several times, forcing the tears back where they lurked, ready to spring forth at the least provocation.

"She even wrote me a letter." The doctor shook his head. "Wrote it a couple of years ago." He looked up to Elizabeth. "You think she had an idea this might happen?" He jerked his head. "If she was sick, she should've told me. After all, I am a doctor. I could've helped her." Frustration coated with anger made him clench his teeth. He pounded one fist into the other palm. "She should've said something."

"I don't think she knew. I think she just wanted to be prepared." Elizabeth tried to think of something comforting to say, but no wise words made their way to her tongue. She shook her head. "No, I don't think she had any idea."

He acts like he is angry, Elizabeth thought on the way back to the kitchen. Surely he isn't. All his dear wife had done was to make things easier for him, just as she had done all her life.

Choosing from the wide variety of food in the kitchen, Elizabeth fixed two plates and, setting them on a tray along with coffee, rolls, and a plate of desserts, headed back out the door. Like the men, she'd rather be out here in the peace of the garden than in the parlor where more tears were being shed.

When she finally went home later that evening, she could hardly make herself climb the stairs to her room. Moonlight streaming through the sheers at her window painted squares of light on the floor. Thoughts of the doctor pacing around that big house all by himself made her eyes smart again. While she'd suggested he drink a glass of wine to help him sleep, she doubted he would.

Lord, take care of Dr. Gaskin tonight. Let him know you are with him and that Mrs. Gaskin is in heaven with you. Please help us all get through tomorrow. While Elizabeth had been to funerals, none were for someone as close to her as this. She'd thought of staying at the doctor's house during the funeral tomorrow to help prepare for the repast to be served after the burial, but when he'd asked her to sit with him in the front pew, what could she say?

Lord, that's the last thing I want to do. She sighed and turned on her side. *I know they both looked on me as a daughter, but, God, right now I'd rather be in Africa.*

She turned again and reached for the glass of water that always waited for her on her nightstand. One thing for sure, crying so much made her very thirsty.

The morning dawned bright with sun, but the house as well as her heart felt like rain. She donned the black dress her mother had hung on the armoire door. Freshly brushed and pressed, nevertheless, the black silk looked like what it was, a dress of mourning. Rows of pin tucks fitted the bodice to the waist, and mutton sleeves puffed at the shoulder and fitted from elbow to wrist. The skirt fell straight to the tops of her shoes in front and gathered in the back to a small bustle. The black hat with a small feather and full veil sat on a form on the side of her dressing table.

"I hate wearing black," she told the pale face in the mirror. "I look bad enough this morning without unrelenting black."

"What's that, dear?" Annabelle stuck her head in the doorway. "I was just on my way to wake you."

"Nothing." Elizabeth knew that complaining would do no good. One wore black for mourning, and that was that. No sense in starting a scandal. If she wore anything but black her mother would be mortified, and while her father's eyes might dance in delight, he'd never admit that he liked it.

The organ was playing as they entered the church — sad, dark music that managed to even take the color out of the sun streaming through stained-glass windows. Long faces, handkerchiefs held to sniffing noses, dark clothing — all the accoutrements of sorrow.

Boughs of cherry blossoms filled large vases and pots, bringing not only a burst of pink and white to the darkness but also a cool fragrance as Elizabeth made her way down the aisle and slid into the first pew next to the doctor.

He took her hand and shook his head at her whispered question asking how he was.

The service passed. That was about all she could say for it. Her throat clogged so badly on the hymns that she could not sing. From the sounds of the standing-room-only congregation, others were doing no better than she. Only by keeping her gaze on the empty cross above the altar could she keep from breaking down.

After the benediction Elizabeth and the doctor followed the pastor out the side door and into the cemetery. A mound of dirt was piled by the oblong grave. Men from the congregation, including Phillip Rogers, carried the coffin to its final resting place under the spreading boughs of an ancient maple. A sob broke from Dr. Gaskin's throat, but he never said a word, even when they lowered the casket into the hole in front of them. Her fingers felt about to shatter from his grip on her hand as the pine box disappeared. Elizabeth let her own tears flow unheeded.

Back at the house she stood beside the doctor, greeting the mourners as they arrived. Ladies of the church directed visitors, served the food, and made sure there was plenty of coffee.

"You don't have to stay here with me," Dr. Gaskin murmured to her when there was a pause in the line of mourners.

"I know. But I want to." She bit her lip against the lie. No, she didn't want to, but she felt she should.

When the last person left, she wandered out to the garden, where Tom and her father were in deep discussion by the roses. She angled away from them and took a seat in the gazebo. She and Mrs. Gaskin had sat there so often, talking about everything from the doctor's cases to Elizabeth's latest beau. Or imagined beau. She'd scared most of them away with her talk of medicine. True, that wasn't the most ladylike topic of discussion, but it was what interested her.

She smiled to herself. One time she'd asked a young man how his gall bladder was. She'd never heard from him again, but then, that was the purpose of the question. He'd been so full of himself she'd wanted to stick him with a pin to burst his bubble. The question worked equally as well.

Ah, Mrs. Gaskin, why'd you have to go and die like this? No wonder your husband is upset. We fight for life, and you just left it.

It had to have been her heart, she reasoned. *Perhaps it surprised her as much as it shocked us.* After all, think of going to sleep thinking of all you had to do on the morrow and instead waking up in heaven.

Father God, that's the only good thing about all this, knowing that our life continues in you. If I didn't feel so sure I'd see Mrs. Gaskin again, I'd . . .

I'd what? She didn't know. The thought of no heaven was too excruciating.

Swallows dipped and swooped over the pond, snatching their evening feast of bugs. Two frogs croaked from the cattails, a tenor and bass duet. Somewhere in the near distance, a child laughed and shrieked, "Higher, Daddy, higher." A dog barked, announcing an unwelcome visitor.

Elizabeth leaned back against the cushioned bench. Slight movement on the railing caught her attention. Two ants carried bits of something, maybe crumbs dropped by a grieving guest.

Life went on in spite of sorrow.

Would tomorrow be just another day? she wondered.

CHAPTER TWELVE: BLESSING, NORTH DAKOTA

Thorliff took the letter from his mother's hand. He glanced at the return address and felt his heart ricochet off his ribs. "From St. Olaf."

"Ja, aren't you going to open it?"

He nodded and dug in his pocket for his knife. He held the letter with his teeth, using both hands to open the blade, then slit the envelope along the top edge. His hands shook enough that it took both of them to shut the knife. Letting it slide back to nest next to an arrowhead he'd found in the field, he took out the paper and leaned closer to the lamp to read it. When he looked up, he held the letter out to his mother. "I've been accepted." At the same time he shook his head. "But where I'll find the money, I sure enough don't know."

"Don't you worry about that." Ingeborg folded the letter and tapped the edge on her finger. "The money will be there when you need it."

"But if we have a drought again . . ." Thorliff inhaled enough to stretch his chest. "I know Far is worried." Thorliff used *Far* and *Mor* and *Pa* and *Ma* interchangeably, being totally comfortable in either Norwegian, his native tongue, and English. While he still spoke with an accent, he no longer felt concern that people might not understand him.

"Instead of worrying, we must trust that God will take care of us. He always has. Why would he stop now?"

"But what if Far says no to my going? He's not been agreeable so far."

"When the time comes, he will do what is right and best."

Thorliff cocked his head. "So how does one know what is right and best?"

Ingeborg tapped him on his chest. "You listen to your heart. That's where God speaks to us. Haakan knows how much you want to go to school, how much you need to go away to school. He will come around. You just be patient and keep praying."

"But what if God says no?" Thorliff clenched his fists in his pockets. *Please, God, you've got to say yes.*

"If God says no, sometimes He means not yet. Waiting is hard but good for building character."

Thorliff groaned. *Surely I have enough character.* "I know." His shoulders slumped, and he stared at the floor. When he looked up again, his voice broke in the middle of the question. "So what do I write back to them?"

"That you are looking forward to attending St. Olaf and thank you for the acceptance."

"Really?"

"Ja. Really. If something happens, we can always cancel."

"Thank you, Mor." Thorliff picked his letter up from the table. "I'll answer this tomorrow." On the way up the stairs he thought back to the afternoon fishing at the river. If he went clear to Northfield, Minnesota, for school, there would be no more fishing, hunting, riding, or working with the men. And there would be no Anji. That thought made him clunk the toe of his boot on the riser and stumble. While he often tried to convince himself they were just good friends, none of his other friends made his heart race or his tongue get tangled in his teeth. When he walked with her, he knew he could wrestle a buffalo to the ground if need be. Not that he'd ever seen a live buffalo in the area, but he had picked up a wagonload of bones.

He hung his shirt and pants on the pegs lining the wall and crawled into bed beside his sleeping brother. Hands locked behind his head, he lay listening to the night noises. A nighthawk screeched. An owl hooted up the river. The curtains rustled in the breeze, puffing out like white clouds, then falling straight again. The house creaked. Andrew snuffled as he breathed. Crickets sawed their summer medley. Home sounds, comfortable like the down-filled pillow he rested his head on. Would he miss all these things too, or only his family and friends in Blessing? Surely there were crickets and curtains and peeper frogs in Minnesota too.

But no Anji or Andrew or Astrid. No Mor and Far and Tante Kaaren. Sadness bit his tongue like vinegar.

Breakfast the next morning was nearly over with, the cows already milked, and the rooster still crowing when Haakan gave his sons their chores for the day. "Thorliff, you go on over and help Lars today. Andrew, you can help the girls in the garden."

Andrew groaned. "I could help Onkel Lars."

"I know, but you're better on the hoe."

166

Haakan leaned over and tousled Andrew's hair.

Andrew rolled his eyes and propped one hand under his chin. "How come the weeds grow without rain and the corn and beans don't?"

Haakan looked to Ingeborg and shook his head. "I don't know. Ask your mor."

Ingeborg shrugged. "That's a good question for Pastor Solberg. But I do know that weeds even grew during Bible times."

"Tante Kaaren said a weed is just a flower in the wrong place." Astrid looked up from spooning oatmeal into her mouth.

"Tell that to the pigweed and thistles."

"I heard down in Richland County the thistles are so bad they have to wrap canvas around the horses' legs and bellies to keep them from being cut up." Haakan drained his coffee cup. "Sure am grateful that's not the case here."

"How come there were no thistles when we came here?"

"The prairie sod was so thick nothing new could grow. And before you ask, the thistle seed came mixed in with the seed wheat. Weeds don't need much invitation to take over." Haakan thumped his young son on the shoulder. "That's why we hoe the garden. If we don't get rain soon, we will have to haul water from the river again for the garden. Can't take a chance on our well going dry." He pushed his chair back. "Takk for maten," he said to his wife.

The boys echoed him as they followed his broad back out the door.

"Velbekomme," Ingeborg called after them.

That evening when the chores were finished, Thorliff wrote his letter to St. Olaf and slid it into the envelope. He'd washed before climbing the stairs to his room. With Andrew downstairs playing checkers with Astrid, he'd finally had a few minutes to himself. The letter was simple, but his dream wore shadows. How could he possibly take money from his family in a drought year to go to school? He could always wait another year. Postponing didn't kill dreams.

As Mor said, sometimes God answered with wait, not yet. He eyed the story he'd started about a young man who came to this country and made mistakes with the language. Something he knew a great deal about.

But instead of writing, he changed clothes, slicked his hair back, and letter in hand, descended the stairs.

"I'm taking this over to be mailed."

At his announcement, Astrid looked up from the checkerboard.

"You sure are dressed up to walk to the store." Her merry grin told him more was coming. "Thorliff's going courting, Thorliff's going courting."

"Hush with teasing your brother." But the smile on Ingeborg's face made Thorliff's go from warm to hot. "I have some quilt pieces to send to Agnes if you would please take them."

Now his ears felt on fire. "Ja, I will do that gladly." He shifted from one foot to the other as he waited for her to find the cloth bits and roll them together to tie with a scrap of cloth.

Giving him the packet, she patted his arm. "Don't stay out too late."

"I won't."

Freedom was running across the prairie with the moon rising behind him and throwing long shadows from every post and weed stalk. It was feeling his hair flopping in the breeze and shouting, "Anji! Anji!" with no one to hear. He slowed his pace to catch the breath cramping his chest, then shot off again, leaping a ditch, feeling pride at his long strides, wishing to dart and dip like the bats skimming the air for their evening bug feast.

He dropped his letter into the mail slot at Penny's store and headed back to the Baard farm. The dog barked at his arrival, then wagged himself nearly in half, as if apologizing for not recognizing the guest.

"Hey, Thorliff, you come too late to play horseshoes." Swen Baard, the eldest of the boys, leaned against the post of the front porch. Behind him rocked Agnes and Joseph, his mother and father.

"He don't want to play horseshoes, you horse breath, you," quipped his younger brother.

"Knute." The tone of his mother's voice even stilled the chortle at his brother's expense.

"Mor sent this for you." Thorliff managed to bump Knute with his knee as he passed on his way to deliver the fabric. "And I'll beat you at horseshoes any time you want."

"Well said. Have a seat." Joseph Baard indicated the steps with the bowl of his pipe.

"I . . . ah . . ." Confounded ears. Why did they go hot all the time?

"All of you, stop it." Anji backed out, pushing the door open with her hip, her hands full with a tray of glasses. "I already gave the little ones theirs." She set the tray

170

down on the stool Joseph removed his feet from and smiled at Thorliff. "I thought you might be thirsty after your run across the field and such."

He could feel his ears, nay, his entire face warm up. "Dark was comin' on fast."

"Help yourself, young man." Joseph nodded toward the tray as he took one glass and half drained it in one gulp. "Ah, must be the last of the raspberry juice. Was this just for us, or did you know we would be having company?" Thorliff prayed the moonlight wasn't bright enough to show his red cheeks and ears.

Anji ignored her father's teasing words and sat down beside Thorliff on the porch step, her own glass held between both hands, her elbows on her knees. "Mighty pretty evening."

Thorliff stared at her moon-kissed profile. The tip of her nose turned up in the nicest way, and while in the moon glow he couldn't see her freckles, he knew they were there, spattered across her nose and cheeks like dots of gold dust. When she turned to smile at him, his heart flip-flopped, and his Adam's apple nigh to choked him.

"You want to go for a walk?" He kept his query to a whisper in hopes the boys wouldn't hear.

"Sure." She stood and set her glass back on the tray. "Come on, I'll walk you partway home." Snickers followed them as they left the yard.

"I mailed my thanks to St. Olaf."

"Good for you. I'm glad. You've been wanting to go to college ever since I can remember."

"Far hasn't said yes yet, but Mor says not to worry." He locked his hands behind his back, the urge to take hers drying his mouth.

"Looks like drought again. I hope not as bad as before."

Who cares about the drought. What about us? "You thought any more about teaching?"

"Umm. Sure, I think about it, but not for this year. I don't dare leave Mor the way she's been feeling."

Thorliff lifted his face to the evening breeze. He sniffed the dryness, the dust-coated weeds, the wheat only half as tall and thick as it should be. "I don't know how I can leave if the harvest is poor. With the sawmill no longer running in the winter, Far needs every dime he can earn from threshing, and if they have to pay one more man to help . . ." His sigh sucked up dust through his boot soles.

"But if your Mor said . . ."

172

"I know, but she said I would know for sure in my heart." He turned to her and took her hands. "Anji, my heart says I don't want to leave you either."

"Our hearts speak alike." She withdrew her hands. "Good night, Thorliff. I need to be getting home and so do you."

Her lips were so close. What would it feel like to kiss her? Thorliff nodded. "God natt."

CHAPTER THIRTEEN

No rain nor even rain clouds.

Every day the men studied the western sky. Would this be a repeat of the drought years? Although harvest had been good in 1890, many had still not recovered from two years of harvest so poor it hardly fed the animals. No wheat to ship meant no money for the year — nor any to pay on mortgages.

The community-owned First Bank of Blessing had not foreclosed on anyone, but there was no money available for new loans. At the meetings, Hjelmer Bjorklund, who ran the bank, predicted dire consequences if no one added money to their accounts or repaid their loans.

"So the bank does not make a large profit this year." Ingeborg, whose cheese house was the only thriving business in the area, remained standing after her comment. "Our return of interest will not be as much, but there will be no talk of closing the doors."

"Amen to that." Penny, store owner and Singer sewing machine representative, stood beside her sister-in-law. "We operate on a cash basis. We did so before, and we can do it again."

Just before the benediction in church the next Sunday, Pastor Solberg stood in front of the congregation, a smile widening as he waited for them to settle again. "I have the great pleasure this morning of making an announcement that still has me thunderstruck." He looked around at the members, then nodded. "Good. Would Thorliff, Manda, Anji, and Jacob please come forward?"

Thorliff looked at Ingeborg, who shrugged her confusion also. Swapping questioning looks, the four young people made their way to the front.

"I know, I know. You have no idea what this is about, but I promise you will be as overjoyed as I am." He waved a letter, then carefully unfolded it. "This came to me two days ago from New York." He held it still to read.

"Dear Pastor Solberg,
   I'm sure your first group of young people have graduated from Blessing

175

School by now and that you have given them a good start. I would like to have the honor of contributing to their further education, so I have enclosed a draft for one hundred dollars to be given to each one of them. I hope they will use this money to further their education, but college is not the only place of learning, so they may use the money as they wish. For your school you will find another draft that I hope you will use for books for your library. It has come to my attention that you have opened the school library so that the good folks of Blessing may come to borrow books. I thank our God for people like you who help educate the future leaders of our great country.

Sincerely,
David Jonathan Gould."

Thorliff could scarce catch his breath as he heard the swift intake of those around him. A hundred dollars! He turned to look at Anji and saw her eyes shining with tears.

"Who is this Mr. Gould?" Jacob whispered behind his hand.

"A friend of my mor's. He helped her in New York when we first arrived from Norway." Thorliff flinched at a look from Pastor

176

Solberg.

"How did he know there were four of us?"

Thorliff shrugged. "My Mor, I guess. They exchange letters."

"So with that, I hereby present each one of you with a draft." Pastor Solberg handed out the envelopes with one hand and shook their hands with the other. Manda was still shaking her head.

"Now I expect you will each write the gentleman a thank-you note immediately," he said with a voice that could reach no farther than the four. At their nods, he turned to the congregation. "Let us pray." When the rustling ceased, he said, "Father in heaven, thou hast brought unexpected riches to these fine young people from a man who listens to thee. Help them to use the money in the way that thou wouldst have them go so that they may grow in grace and knowledge of thee and of thy will. In thy precious name we pray, amen." He dismissed them and motioned for everyone to rise. "And now, may the Lord bless thee and keep thee, may the Lord lift up His countenance upon thee and give thee His peace. In the name of the Father and the Son and the Holy Ghost, amen."

Thorliff could hardly keep his feet still. The paper burned in his hands. A hundred dollars. Surely that would pay for a good portion of his school year. Had God heard his prayers and thus answered by using a man far across the land? He barely remembered Mr. Gould but knew of him through Mor's stories and the letters she read from him.

When everyone around him rose, he stood and accepted the congratulations of friends and family. Folks bubbled with curiosity and joy over the tremendous gift given to them all. When some asked who this man was, Ingeborg told them briefly how he'd helped her in New York City when she was lost and that they'd exchanged letters ever since. When she finished, she glanced up at Haakan to see a cloud had settled on his brow.

"Can I see it?" Astrid asked, pulling on Thorliff's sleeve.

"Sure." He handed her the envelope and watched her open it carefully and remove the oblong piece of paper.

"This is really money?" She looked up to him with rounded eyes and mouth.

"No. This is a draft that can be taken to a bank and exchanged for real money." Thorliff turned his head enough to see Anji smiling at him. He nodded toward the door, and she tipped her head slightly to indicate she got his message.

Astrid handed the filled envelope back. "I'm glad for you, Thorliff. I don't want you to be gone so far, but I know how you love school."

Thorliff stared down at the little sister who so delighted in teasing him. Her lower lip quivered, and her blue eyes shone with unshed tears. "Ah, Astrid." He picked her up and hugged her close. She wrapped her arms around his neck and laid her cheek against his.

"I love you," she whispered.

"And I you." Thorliff could barely get the words past the lump swelling in his throat. He hugged her again and set her back down, catching his mother's damp eyes in the process. *God, can I really leave them all and go to school? Is this money to show me that's what I am to do?* But he'd caught the cloud on his father's face as his mother had.

Haakan was not happy. Thorliff wasn't sure about what, but he had a feeling the straight brows and mouth had to do with the gift.

As someone spoke to Ingeborg and Haakan, Thorliff slipped out the side and headed for the door. Anji would be waiting. He passed Manda and grabbed her hand. "Come on." At the same time he looked around for Jacob. The four of them needed to talk.

Anji stood by the cottonwood tree, the breeze teasing the blue ribbon she'd tied around her hair.

"I'm goin' to give that money back," Manda said as soon as they'd gathered.

"Why?" Anji asked.

"I ain't goin' to no more school. Only went the last two years 'cause Father said I had to."

"But the letter said there were other ways to get an education. What do you think he meant by that?" Jacob looked to Thorliff as if he knew more than the rest.

"Maybe Pastor knows. I sure don't. But I don't think you should send it back. Mr. Gould gave the gifts to us and said to use the money as we wanted."

"Still, it don't seem right. That Mr. Gould, he don't know me." Manda clamped her splinted arm to her chest.

"What are you going to do with yours?" Jacob asked Anji.

"I want to go to the college in Grand Forks and become a teacher." Anji wore a dreamy look, so unlike her.

"Is it enough?"

"I don't know, but I think perhaps I will inquire. Never hurts to ask anyway."

Thorliff knew teaching was her dream, but she'd never told anyone else.

"Anji, you want to ride home with us?" Agnes called from the seat of the Baard wagon.

Thorliff shook his head and said *Walk with me* with his eyes.

"No, Mor, but I'll be home shortly."

As all the wagons headed for their respective homes, Thorliff and Anji ambled slowly toward the Baard farm, laughing and waving as the wagons passed them by, cheerfully ignoring the teasing. When the dust drifted off to settle on the roadside grass and sun-burnished daisies, the two picked up their conversation again.

"Do you really think you could go?" Thorliff's hand brushed Anji's, sending a zinger up his arm. *Do I dare?* To answer his own question, he breached the chasm and took her fingers in his until their hands met, palm to palm. When he looked down at her, he read the answer in her eyes. She'd wanted that as much as he. *One of these days I'm going to kiss you too.* She must have read his mind, for she instantly turned red as the cardinal who sang on the breeze.

"I . . . I . . ." She sighed. "Like I've said before, I dream of it, but Mor needs me."

"Mrs. Sam could come help."

181

"I know, but . . ." Anji chewed on her bottom lip. "I'll just have to keep praying about it."

"Have you ever asked your mor what she thinks?" Her hand felt fine as a summer Sunday morning in his. He swung his hand a bit just to feel hers move with his.

Slowly shaking her head, Anji looked down at the ground. "No."

"But . . ."

She stopped. "Thorliff, if I ask her, she will say I must go. That's the way she is, always thinking of the rest of us and not of how sick she is. She absolutely refuses to talk about . . . about . . ." Tears shimmered, and one rolled over her lashes and down her cheek.

Thorliff wiped the tear away with one finger. Her skin felt like the finest cream. "Your Pa could take her to the doctor in Grand Forks."

"He tried. She won't go. She said that if the good Lord didn't heal her, then this is His will, and she must bear it."

"She's talked with Metiz and Mor?"

"Of course. Many times. Nothing seems to help." A sob caught her. "So you see, I cannot leave her. No matter what I want."

Thorliff turned to face her and took her other hand too. He knew the unspoken

182

words. If Agnes died, then Anji would be expected to care for the Baard home and the younger children. That's what the eldest daughter did.

"I . . . I wish it could be different."

"Ja." She nodded and wiped the tears away with her fingertips. Then slipping her hand back in his, she set their path toward the farm ahead. "I need to help get dinner on the table."

When Thorliff left her at the gate, he trudged home. No matter that the sun blazed in the sky, he felt under a cloud, a heavy black rain cloud. The blackness seeped inside his heart, heavy with the knowledge there was nothing he could do to help Anji.

"God, it's not fair," he said to the sky. But as Mor had often said, life wasn't fair, but God was always good. Thorliff shook his head. How could God be good in a situation like this?

Chapter Fourteen:
Northfield,
Minnesota

"Housekeepers are hard to come by. Good ones, that is," Elizabeth said with a sigh. Still shaking her head after interviewing the last candidate for Dr. Gaskin, she poured cups of tea for her mother and herself. "Did you have this kind of trouble looking for Cook?"

"Yes. You look and look and then the right person walks through the door and you know it immediately. Are you sure Dr. Gaskin shouldn't be looking for household help himself?"

"Perhaps. But he can hardly manage to treat his patients right now. He looks to have aged about ten years. . . ."

"And he wasn't a spring chicken anyhow." Annabelle sipped from a china cup sprinkled with forget-me-nots. She closed her eyes and savored both the fragrance and the flavor.

"Has he ever said anything to you about

his plans that I should take over his practice?"

Annabelle's eyes snapped open. "No, never. Why?"

Elizabeth's eyebrows shrugged along with her shoulders. "Just a comment he made —"

"About?"

"About . . ." Eyes slit, Elizabeth tried to recall his exact words. "About how he was keeping it together for me." She pursed her lips, then rolled them together. "I'm not sure if he meant keeping on going now for me, or if he was referring to the practice." She leaned forward and her voice deepened in intensity. "Mother, I don't want to take over the practice here in Northfield. Not that it's not a good thing, but I . . . I . . ." *I what? I don't know what I want. I just know what I* don't *want.*

"You don't have to make a decision now." Annabelle covered her daughter's hand with her own. "For all you know, your interests will change, and —"

"No, Mother, don't keep hoping that way. You raised me to think for myself and to care for others. I *will* become a doctor. It's just how and when that is not yet clear."

Annabelle sank back in her chair. "What if they won't let you into medical school?"

"Then I'll find another way. But I *will* find a way." *And, Mother, there is a way, just perhaps not the easiest.*

Her mother's sigh spoke only of disappointment, but not of giving up. Elizabeth felt like sighing herself. While her mother was not vociferous with her disapproval, Elizabeth felt it keenly. Glances, sniffs, and sighs could communicate a wealth of opinion. Changing the subject was always a good line of defense.

"Have you gotten the tickets yet for the Chicago fair?"

"Yes, they came yesterday. I have both our train and hotel reservations also. We leave on July first. Your father will come to join us for the fourth. I've heard rumors that the Fourth of July celebration will be a stupendous spectacle. I cannot wait to see the French Pavilion. Parlez-vous Français?"

"Of course, and it might be a good chance to practice my French."

"And German and Italian." Hands in the air, Annabelle sketched an all-encompassing gesture.

"Not that I'm that fluent in the latter two."

"Your father speaks excellent German, as you well know. Ask him to help you."

"Actually he wants me to help him down at the paper. With all the time I've put in

186

helping Dr. Gaskin, I'm behind in the accounts again." Elizabeth laid her napkin on the table and pushed her chair back. "I better get on down there and see what I can do." She kissed her mother's cheek. "Don't hold supper for me. I'll be home late."

"Remember that the Audisons are coming for supper tomorrow night. They are bringing a cousin along."

"Male or female?"

Her mother's slight flinch answered.

"Never mind. I shall be here, but I am not looking for a marriage partner."

"I know, dear." But had Elizabeth been looking in a mirror, she would have recognized that the stubborn tilt of her mother's chin nearly matched her own.

The stroll down to the newspaper office took her past yards with honeysuckle-sweetened air, two pinafored girls laughing and playing fetch with a dog, and a gnome of a man calling hello from a rocking chair on his front porch. Having lived in Northfield all her life and having walked this route almost daily, she knew and greeted them all.

The bell tinkled over the door when she pushed it open and stepped into her world of newsprint. A thudding printing press released the bite of ink into the air, and her

187

father was uttering some rather uncomplimentary words to the aging equipment. He needed one of the new printing presses she'd seen advertised in a catalogue, but since she did his accounts, she knew he could not afford one. She took her place at the front desk, opened the account book, and began filling out invoices.

She didn't realize the presses had stopped until her father laid a hand on her shoulder.

"I'm going home for supper. You want to walk with me?"

"No, thanks." She smiled up at him. "You better wash first."

"Ink on my face?"

"Umm." Her glance perused his shirt. "Didn't you wear your apron?"

"Of course." He looked down at the inkblot on his linen shirt. "I need one that covers me head to foot." His sigh told her they both knew what he would hear when he walked in the door at home. "So are you ashamed to be seen walking your old man home?"

Elizabeth rolled her eyes. "Of course not. I need the time to get your accounts in order so you can buy that new press you need so badly." She motioned to the books in front of her. "If you kept these in the same good shape that you do that monster

188

back there . . ."

"That monster is what keeps us in business. Most people get around to paying me sooner or later."

"Usually when they want to place another ad." She sent a look ripe with rebuke. "Some haven't paid since the last time I billed them. Like Flanagan's Market."

"Ol' Mike's going through a hard spell since his wife died. He'll get around to paying me when he can."

"What about the creamery?"

Her father shrugged.

"And Asplund's Smithy?"

"Are they behind too?" He peered over her shoulder, shaking his head. "I didn't mind carrying old Oscar, but that young whippersnapper . . . Send 'em a bill and add on a hefty charge for being late again." Her father stomped across the room to the hat rack by the front door. "I'll remind Mother to keep your supper warm." He huffed once more before the bell announced his departure.

It was quiet but for the cleaning noises coming from the pressroom, and Elizabeth settled back into her job. The stack of invoices grew with the passing minutes, accompanied by sighs as she found some accounts seriously in arrears. After she finally

189

closed the book, she took a stack of envelopes and began addressing them, folding the papers to insert in the envelopes before sealing. With each one she thought to the recipient, alternately praying for them or uttering imprecations upon their heads. How could so many take advantage of her father's good heart?

"Are you leaving, then?" She looked up to see Hans leaning his elbows on the counter and staring at her, hound-dog eyes sorrowful as ever.

"No. I'm waiting for you."

"Why would you do that? I told you —"

He raised his hands as if to fend off blows. "I know, but your father told me to wait and walk you home. He don't want nothing happening to you."

As if you would be any help in an attack of any kind. She snorted and jerked her head briefly in disdain.

"Now don't go gettin' all het up. I do what your Pa says, or I lose my job."

"Like when you —"

"You said you would forget all about that," Hans broke in.

"I know." Elizabeth felt her high horse stumble. He was right. She wasn't being fair. Her father was the one she should be after, not poor Hans. Muttering more to herself than to him, she shut the books and straightened the desk. All the while she could feel his gaze following her every motion. She fumbled and dropped the big ledger, sending papers flying every which direction. "Now look what you did!"

"Now, Miss Elizabeth, I didn't even go near to you . . ."

She clamped her lower lip between her teeth and counted to ten. "I know that." *Why am I being so hard on him? What's the matter with me?* She picked up the book, shoved it in place between three others and slammed a hunk of granite as a paperweight on the stack of haphazard papers. She'd straighten it all tomorrow when she didn't have an audience.

"Here." She thrust the stack of envelopes into his hand and crossed to turn off the gaslight. Glancing around the room in the glow from the streetlight, she pushed a chair back in place and let him hold the door for her.

"Ain't you going to lock it?"

Elizabeth gave him a questioning look. "Since when?"

"Since that money was gone the other day."

"What money was gone?"

"Five dollars from the cashbox." The look

191

in his bony face clearly stated his wish that he'd never brought this up.

"And who does my father think might have taken it?"

"Don't know. He just said to lock the door from here on out."

Why in heaven's name didn't he tell us? Or tell me at least? But she knew the answer. Her father couldn't bear to face the censure from her mother, who frequently admonished him to stop being so trusting. Like some of the accounts that she'd read were paid in full. She knew of one debt for sure that he'd forgiven because of a tragedy of some kind. He'd so often said, just like the doc, that a bill hanging over someone's head was like the French guillotine about to fall at any second. A man could hardly hold his head up under the weight of it. If the debt was forgiven, her father believed that the man could build his business better, and the next time he would pay promptly or not run an ad.

They'd reached the post office by this time, and she waited while Hans leaped the steps three at a time and shoved open the heavy brass-trimmed door to slide the letters into the mail slot. She sniffed the breeze, catching remnants of a fried chicken dinner, the night-blooming nicotiana, and freshly turned rich garden dirt. Her ears hurt from half listening to Hans's rambling tale by the time they reached her gate.

"Thank you for walking me home." She pushed the gate open and slipped inside. "I will tell Father that you did your duty nobly."

"Good night, miss." Hans touched the brim of his porkpie hat and, shoving his hands into his pockets, headed off, whistling a tune just enough off-key to set her teeth on edge.

Elizabeth greeted her parents, then headed straight for the piano. For the next hour the notes spread like a balm over her spirit, soothing the ache in her heart that she didn't understand.

The young man who accompanied his relatives to the Rogerses' house the next night made her teeth itch again. Sitting across from him, Elizabeth felt like kicking him under the table, if her foot could only reach that far. If he smiled once more at her in that condescending way, she'd slump down in her chair far enough to ensure that her foot connected with his shin, no matter what her mother would have to say later.

"Surely you've been to see the art exhibit at the World's Columbian Exposition."

That did it. Elizabeth dropped her napkin onto the table and pushed back her chair. "Excuse me, please, I have a headache." *And an ache in my back. Just let me out of here.*

"Oh, I am so sorry to hear that."

My right foot, you are. You don't know what sorry even means. Refusing to look at her mother, Elizabeth turned and sailed out of the dining room and up the stairs to her bedroom. When she thought about it, she really did have a headache — one compounded by the look on her mother's face when she introduced her only daughter to the insufferable, pompous donkey down there. If that was what wealth brought, she wanted none of it.

Once in bed, guilt stole in on the breeze and hung in the air, taunting her. *You could have been polite a few more hours. You know your mother considers him a fine catch.*

A rumbling purr told her Jehoshaphat had nudged open her door. He leaped up on her bed to knead his head under her hand.

Elizabeth flipped over on her side, the better to pet her cat. She grabbed a picture of the bones of the hand from the table by her bed and, starting at the fingertips, began naming them. Distal phalanges, middle phalanges, proximal phalanges, and metacarpals. Soon the rhythm of Jehoshaphat's

194

purring lulled her to sleep.

A pounding on the front door below her window woke her some time later.

CHAPTER FIFTEEN

"Help me, please help me!" The pounding on the front door sounded as urgent as the cries for help.

Elizabeth leaned out her window into the moonlit night. "What do you need?"

"My baby, he . . . he ain't . . . he ain't . . ."

"You need to get the doctor."

"He must be out on a call. He don't answer the door."

And Dr. Johanson is clear across town. Elizabeth considered the options. "Where do you live?"

"Out beyond the college. Can you come? You helped deliver my boy."

"What is it?" Elizabeth's father asked from right behind her.

"The man's son . . ." She leaned back out the window and made out the man's face in the moonlight. "I remember where your place is. You go on and see if Dr. Johanson can come. You know where he lives?"

"Yes. But you'll come right now?"

"I'll take you out there." Phillip Rogers spoke over his shoulder as he headed for the door.

Elizabeth called out the window again. "You go on. We'll be at your place as soon as we can get there." She pulled her head back in and dashed for her armoire, pulling her nightdress over her head as she went. Dressed in seconds, she bundled her hair into a snood when she reached the bottom of the stairs. Her black bag, a gift from Dr. Gaskin, sat by the door. Taking her instructions from the doc, she kept the bag packed with emergency bandages, salves, sutures, and supplies necessary for birthing. As she climbed into her father's buggy, she remembered she hadn't learned what happened to the little boy.

Dear God, please let him be alive. She had heard the terror in the father's voice. *"My boy ain't . . ." Breathing* was the word she inserted in the blank. But surely he would have brought the child with him if that were the case.

Her father needed no encouragement to set his pacer at full speed. The thud of hooves on the hard-packed road ticked away the seconds, seconds that could mean life or death.

Lord, please, no tracheotomy. Elizabeth had assisted the doctor in one, but the thought of cutting into a child's throat sent terror clamping her own. Where was Dr. Gaskin? If he was home, why had he not answered the door? So many questions and no answers.

"Turn here." She pointed to the right. Thank God for moonlight. She'd never have known where to turn if it were pouring rain. But then, a pouring rain would be welcome relief from the drought. Living in town, she hadn't felt the full brunt like the farmers had, but no one talked of much else.

"I think it is the third farm on this road."

"All right." Her father's gentle voice helped calm her racing heart. "That house with all the lamps in the windows must be the place."

He slowed the horse, whose breath whistled through extended nostrils from its fast pace. When they turned into the lane, a dog leaped from the ditch, barking at the buggy wheels. The pacer ignored the dog and picked up speed again, the rougher road rocking the buggy.

Elizabeth hung on to the seat with both hands. Getting her or the bag tossed out of the buggy wouldn't help anyone.

"Thanks." She leaped to the ground the

instant the buggy shuddered to a stop. The door flew open, and the weeping mother grabbed her arm. "In here. Where's the doctor?"

"I don't know. I sent your husband for the new doctor, but I'll help if I can."

"Baby's got the croup. Even quit breathing for a time. God help us." Her sobs shattered the words into quivering fragments.

Elizabeth heard the wheezing before she entered the room. While the sound sent chills to her very shoe soles, at least he was still alive.

"Get a kettle of water steaming." She set her bag on the bed and turned to the baby.

The baby coughed and choked, his little back arching clear off the bed.

"How can I help?" Phillip Rogers stood in the doorway.

"We need to tent a sheet or towel or something over the kettle. I'll hold his face in the steam to see if that helps him breathe."

She picked up the child and set him against her shoulder, gently rubbing his back, trying to calm him. She paced to the kitchen, crooning comfort all the while.

As soon as the steam began to rise, she showed her father and the baby's mother how to make the tent and then ducked under it to hold the baby in the hot, moist air. Within minutes she could feel the baby relax as the air penetrated his swollen airways. By the time the doctor and father arrived, the child lay sleeping on his mother's shoulder as they sat in a rocking chair under the steam tent.

Dr. Johanson nodded to Elizabeth, his smile of congratulations warming her heart. "You did exactly what needed doing." He listened to the baby's lungs and nodded again, then turned to the parents. "Now you know what to do if this happens again. The sooner you get him into the steam, the better he will be."

"He'd been coughing throughout the day and had finally gone to sleep, so I thought he was better." The mother patted her baby's back. Not quite a year old, the little boy now slept soundly, a faint whistling reminding them of the emergency.

"Miss Rogers, we can't thank you enough." The boy's father reached for Elizabeth's hand. "If it weren't for you . . ." His voice choked.

"I'm just grateful that he responded so quickly." She didn't mention a tracheotomy, but the look she exchanged with the young doctor communicated the words she didn't say. A slight shudder let her know he didn't want to do one any more than she did.

She listened as he gave the parents instructions on caring for their baby, then followed him out the door. Once in the buggy heading back to town, she leaned against the seat back, feeling as if someone had pulled a plug and all her energy had drained out. Knowing how close the little boy had come to dying made her hands shake. Surely there must be something that could help children like that. Eyes closed, she reviewed her book of herbs and plants used for medicinal purposes. Nothing came to mind. But at that moment getting anything to stay in her mind was beyond her ability.

Her father shook her awake when he stopped the horse at the front door. The sky had faded from deep azure to gray.

She fell into bed and missed the sunrise. Only when her mother brought in a tea tray at midmorning did she stir.

"You should have wakened me." Elizabeth threw back the sheet.

"You needed the sleep." Annabelle Rogers set the tray on the end of the bed. "Dr. Gaskin said that when you wake he would appreciate your help in his office. Your father said that if you have extra time, he needs help in his office too."

Elizabeth pushed back her hair and cocked

an eyebrow. "And you'd like some help in your office?"

Annabelle laughed and shook her head. "I can handle my office just fine." She poured a cup of tea and laid cinnamon toast points on the saucer. "Here."

"Thank you." Elizabeth inhaled the aroma. "Sure better than the last steam." She sipped her tea, ate her toast, and told her mother what had happened.

"So many things we have learned in the medical field, so many wonderful advances, yet a baby can die of croup."

"It sounds to me that you did what had to be done. According to your father, you're a heroine."

Elizabeth humphed and shook her head, her hair falling in a veil as she stared into her teacup. "Someday, Mother, I want to find ways to save babies and mothers having babies."

"You think to learn those things in medical school?"

Elizabeth tucked her hair behind an ear and gazed at her mother. "I hope so. I certainly hope so."

A robin singing in the tree outside her window was the only sound as the quiet second stretched into minutes. Elizabeth let her mind explore the images of babies and mothers that peopled her head. Laughing, crying, living, dying — some she'd known and others existed only in her dreams. Who were they, and how could she help?

She heaved a sigh and leaned forward to set her cup and saucer on the tray. The pink rosebud in the crystal bud vase caught her attention. She reached a gentle finger and caressed the furled petals.

"Thank you, Mother. You bring such beauty into my life." She looked up to catch a gleam of tears in her mother's eyes. *I don't say thank-you enough. None of us do.*

"You're most welcome." Annabelle set down her cup and reached to hug her daughter. "Moments like these I will treasure all my life."

A song sparrow added his aria to the robin's. Honeysuckle wafted in on the breeze that teased the sheer curtains at the window.

Elizabeth stretched and set her feet on the floor. "I better go see what Dr. Gaskin needs. Fortunately I found a housekeeper to start tomorrow for him. Her name is Hope Haugen."

Her mother arched an eyebrow.

"He needs a nurse too."

"I know. He thinks he has that in me."

"But we will be leaving for Chicago next week. Then what will he do?"

"That's another one of my jobs — to find a nurse to fill in while I am gone. I've already arranged for some to come in for interviews today. Here's hoping whoever we hire will like being there so much she will stay on."

On her way out of the house, Elizabeth thought longingly to the gazebo in the backyard. Set to catch any errant breeze and perfumed by the wisteria and roses that grew over and around it, the gazebo beckoned. She loved curling up in the hammock to read and dream away a hot summer afternoon, that is, when these two offices weren't calling for her.

Wearing a lightweight yellow daisy-sprigged cotton dress as a concession to the temperature, she slipped into the side door of the doctor's house so she wouldn't have to go through the waiting room.

"Elizabeth, is that you?" The doctor's voice came from one of the examining rooms.

"Yes." She debated checking those patients waiting or answering the querulous tone that told her Dr. Gaskin was already fed up to the eyebrows with seeing patients when the day was not yet half over.

"I never realized all that his wife did for him," she muttered under her breath. He'd always seemed such an even-tempered man before.

But he'd never lost his wife before, remember? The voice in her head made perfect sense. She took in a deep breath and headed for the nearest closed door of the two examining rooms. She tapped and entered on command.

"Hold this arm for me, will you?" the doctor instructed.

The tears on the boy's face told of his pain.

"What happened, Johnny?" Elizabeth took in the situation at a glance. The boy's mother held a handkerchief to her eyes instead of comforting her son. Usually she was the one in that family who came running to the doctor with every headache or feared disease.

"I . . . I fell out of the apple tree."

"I told him not to climb trees, that he was going to fall and break something, and now, see, he has done just that. Oh, this is giving me such a headache." The woman sank down in the chair, her face pale and beaded with perspiration.

"It is awfully warm in here," Elizabeth said. "What if I open the window and see if we can find a breeze?"

"Hold his shoulder there first." Doc

indicated with a nod. "It's just a simple break. I want to make sure the bones are in alignment."

"Easy, son, this will be over in a minute."

With Elizabeth's hands on the shoulder, the doctor pulled gently on the hand and wrist. A soft snap, a muffled shriek from the patient, and a sigh of satisfaction from the doctor. "There now. I'll splint it, and you can wear it in a sling for a few weeks. But don't you go climbing any more trees."

"Hear that? You have to do what the doctor says." A large sniff accompanied the pronouncement.

Elizabeth and the doctor exchanged glances, then turned their attention back to the boy on the examining table.

"Someday I'm going to be a doctor." Johnny's gaze followed every movement Dr. Gaskin made.

"Really? Me too."

Johnny looked at her, disgust evident in his hazel eyes. "You can't be a doctor. You're a lady."

That's what you think. But Elizabeth only raised one eyebrow.

"You better hope she gets to be a doctor." Dr. Gaskin continued to wrap gauze around the splinted arm. "She's going to take over for me."

"Why?"

"I'm getting too old. That's why." He knotted the tails of the bandage. "Now you be real careful with this. You don't want to end up with a crooked arm. You'll never make a doctor if you have a crooked arm."

Elizabeth took a square of white cloth from a drawer and folded it into a triangle. Slipping it under his arm, she tied the tails in a knot behind his neck and then pinned the other corner around his elbow.

"Now promise me you will keep this sling on all the time."

"Even when I'm sleeping?"

"No, you can take it off then. Come back in three weeks and let the doctor see it again."

"But . . . but I can't play baseball like this."

"That's the point."

"And I can't go swimming."

"I know."

"This is going to be a terrible, awful summer."

"At least you won't be climbing any more trees." The mother rose and headed for the door. "Come, Johnny. Thank you, Doctor. You may send the bill to my husband's office."

Even Elizabeth could tell that wasn't a question. And since she was the one doing the accounts, she knew the woman's husband didn't pay his bills regularly. This time she would include a more forceful reminder whether the doctor wanted her to or not. This family was different from many. They had the money to pay their bills, or at least it seemed that way.

She waved Johnny off with a reminder to keep the sling on, then straightened up the room. More patients awaited attention.

Later, when a lull finally occurred, she pointed the doctor to an easy chair in his office. "I'll get you a glass of lemonade."

"There isn't any. I drank it all."

Elizabeth thought of the large pitcher she'd made the day before. Did he take a bath in it? "I'll make more," she said and headed for the kitchen. Thank goodness the new housekeeper would be there in the morning. When she returned some time later, Dr. Gaskin lay back in his leather chair sound asleep. Dark shadows circled his eyes, and new lines channeled from nose to chin. His cheeks appeared sunken, as if he'd not eaten for weeks.

A soft snore fluttered lips that used to smile more than frown. Somewhere along the way, they'd forgotten how.

She set the glass down on the blotter of

his desk and gently closed the door behind her.

He must have been out on a call most of the night.

But he wasn't. When he told her later that he hadn't heard the man pounding on his door, she started to say something and stopped. How could he not have heard?

"Were you sick?"

He shook his head, not meeting her gaze. Suddenly she understood the smell of peppermint. He'd chewed mint leaves to cover the odor of whiskey.

She closed her eyes. How had she missed the signs? How would the new housekeeper tolerate this?

"I need to go interview the nurses. I'll have them go into the parlor."

"I'd rather you stayed on."

"I know, but I start school again soon, and then what?"

"You can apprentice under me and not go on to school."

Only as a last resort, Elizabeth promised herself. "We've been over this before." She patted his arm. "Call me if you have an emergency."

She interviewed three women before she knew she had the right one.

"Is that Miss or Mrs.?" Elizabeth glanced

from the paper in front of her to the bright-eyed woman who reminded her of the gray squirrel that sometimes visited outside her bedroom window.

"Miss." The smile that accompanied everything she said made Elizabeth automatically smile back. "Miss Matilda Browne."

"And you can start immediately?"

"Yes. I found a place to live yesterday. Something just drew me to this town. Must be the hand of God at work."

"Well, you are needed here. Dr. Gaskin's wife died two weeks ago, and while I can help off and on, I will be leaving next week for a trip with my mother. She would be so disappointed if we had to cancel."

"Now, dearie, you go right ahead with your plans. I've been a nurse for fifteen years and would still be in Wisconsin if my doctor hadn't sold his practice and gone west." She shook her head. "Sometimes men get the wanderlust, and there is nothing to do about it." Clasping her hands in her lap, she leaned forward. "I worked at the hospital for two years too, so I can help in most instances."

Elizabeth named the salary the doctor had instructed her to offer and waited while the woman in front of her pondered.

"Done. I can be here at eight-thirty in the

morning, or do you want me earlier?"

"No, that will be fine." Elizabeth felt like some giant had just removed a huge pack from her back. "I'll take you on a tour through the office now. Most of the patients should be gone. And you can meet Dr. Gaskin." *And please like him. He is such a dear man.*

By the time she walked toward home, the doctor's office was set to rights, and his supper was on the table. All she wanted to do was sit and stare at a wall. Even reading a book would take too much energy.

How had Mrs. Gaskin handled it all? And kept her cheerful attitude?

"Your father is wondering when you will get to the newspaper office. He sent Hans over to get you a few minutes ago, for the third time."

Elizabeth groaned. Dreams of a soaking bath and early bed went flying out the window like a bird heading south.

"You don't have to go."

"Yes, I do. I promised."

"Then have a bite to eat first and perhaps you'll feel better."

Elizabeth let her mother lead her toward a dining chair, and she sank down on it. She rested her elbows on the table and her head on her hands.

If answering an emergency in the middle of the night made her this tired, how was she going to handle hospital work?

Chapter Sixteen: Blessing, North Dakota

"Please come, Miz Bjorklund. Mira's wailing something awful," a voice called urgently, waking both Haakan and Ingeborg.

"I'll get the door while you get dressed." Haakan pulled on his pants and headed for the door.

Ingeborg shed her nightdress and put on her dark skirt in nearly the same motion. Not bothering with camisole and slip, she buttoned her waist and slipped her arms through the straps of her voluminous apron with pockets for her supplies, quickly tying the bow in the back. Since this was a second baby for the Mendohlsons and all had seemed all right during the last months, she knew the baby could come quickly. She also knew Mira didn't handle pain well. Birthing basket in hand, Ingeborg strode into the kitchen.

"Is there anyone with her?" She skipped a greeting, knowing that young Mr. Mendohlson was too upset to think things through anyhow.

"Only Ossie and he's asleep."

"When did the pains begin?"

"Just before I left. She woke up screaming, you know."

Haakan held the door for her. "You want to take the horse and wagon?"

"No, I'll ride with Abe here." She looked to the man with his hat in hands and feet shuffling from one to the other. "Or did you come on horseback?"

"No, I got the wagon in case Metiz wanted to come too."

Ingeborg hesitated for only a second. She and Metiz always worked together if there was a problem with the birthing. Should they go get her?

"I'll send you back for her if it looks like we will need her." She turned to look up at Haakan. "Tell Astrid to make pancakes for breakfast, and I planned on the last ham for dinner. It is soaking in the well house. She knows to go ahead and finish the bread." The night before Ingeborg had set the sourdough to rising, so eggs and flour were all that needed to be added, and then the dough would be ready for kneading. "If she has any questions, you know where I am."

Haakan smiled at her, the slow smile that

warmed both his eyes and her belly. "God bless."

"He does and will." She let the young man assist her up the wheel and to the board seat of the wagon. She settled her basket at her feet and pulled her shawl around her shoulders against the predawn chill.

When Abe set the horses to a gallop that nearly threw her off the seat, she hollered above the racket, "Take it easy. That baby won't be coming for some time."

He reined them in to a fast trot, which only rattled her teeth.

They heard Mira scream as he pulled the horses to a halt at the front porch. He wrapped the reins around the brake handle and leaped to the ground, racing into the house without bothering to assist Ingeborg down.

She chuckled to herself. How good it was to see a man so concerned for his wife. Young love. Perhaps they all needed a dose of it once in a while.

She made her way into the house, heat from the roaring stove smacking her in the face. A washing boiler heated on the front burner. He'd taken her request for hot water to heart, that was for sure.

Mira moaned.

A child's cry floated down the stairs from

the half story above. Mira's carrying on had wakened her year-old son.

Ingeborg kept on course to the bedroom just off the kitchen and found Abe comforting his wife.

"I'll see to her, and you go take care of the baby."

Abe nodded and whispered something in his wife's ear before heading out the door to climb the stairs. His son's cries now echoed down the stairway.

"All right now, Mira, let's see how you are doing."

"The pains. They are so bad." The young mother wiped the sweat from her face and neck with the sheet.

Ingeborg spoke gently. Calming a frantic mother was no different from comforting a hurting child. And the face that grimaced back at her was no more than sixteen anyway, still a girl but already a mother.

"You must be strong. We have a long way to go." But after checking, Ingeborg smiled at the resting patient. "Perhaps not so long after all. You are made for having babies easily."

"If this is easy, I . . . I can't think about hard."

Ingeborg took the girl's hands as another contraction began. "Go easy now. Breathe

216

through the pain. Don't fight it. If you breathe and ride with the pain, the babe will have less trouble, and you will too."

Whimpering rather than screaming this time, Mira did as she was told. When it passed, she smiled up at Ingeborg. "That was better, but then it is always better when you get here."

"Good." Ingeborg pulled back the sheet. "Now we will walk. Remember last time how we walked and you felt better?"

Mira started to protest, then changed her mind. Using Ingeborg's strong hand to help pull herself to a sitting position, she grunted and swung her feet to the floor. "I feel like a walrus from the north of Norway. My far told me about them." She panted as she struggled to her feet. When she stood, water poured down her leg to puddle on the floor. "Uff da, such a mess."

"No mind. I will mop it up. This means we could go fast now."

Abe entered the room, his son in his arms.

"Can you take him to a neighbor's?" Ingeborg, her arm around the young mother's heavy waist, asked.

"I-I guess so. Or for now I could take him to the barn with me. I leave him in the grain bin at times."

"Perhaps he will go back to sleep if you

give him something to suck on." While she spoke, the two women paced the floor.

"Ja, I will do that."

He'd just left, child on his arm, when Mira doubled over. "I can't walk no more."

"Ja, you can."

"No." The word trailed in a screech. "The baby's coming."

Ingeborg half carried the girl back to the bed and then checked on the baby's progress. After one mighty contraction, Ingeborg held a squalling baby girl, who waved her fists and howled as if she were being beaten.

"Uff da, I never seen a baby come so fast." Ingeborg laid the baby on her mother's chest, where mother and babe studied each other, lost in a world of recognition.

Mira murmured sweet words to her baby and stroked the perfectly shaped head with a shaking finger. "I told her you was coming, little girl baby, and so you did."

"Mighty big hurry she was too." Within minutes all was finished and cleaned up, the cord cut, and the babe swaddled in a baby-sized sheet and laid in the crook of her mother's arm. Both of them promptly fell asleep, leaving Ingeborg to add wood to the fire and set the coffeepot to heating. Remembering the kitchen from a year earlier, she found all she needed to make pancakes and eggs for breakfast and had it all ready when Mr. Mendohlson brought in a foaming pail of milk to set on the counter.

"Go see. They are doing fine."

"The baby is here already?"

"Ja, and a fine little daughter you have there." Ingeborg slipped into Norwegian, as she knew he understood that more easily.

"So soon." He left the room shaking his head.

Ingeborg poured circles of batter to bubble on the griddle and broke two eggs into the frying pan.

"They are sound asleep." Abe returned, still shaking his head.

"I know." Ingeborg pointed at the table. "Take a seat."

"Ja, after I go back out and check on Ossie. He fell back asleep too. Then I wash."

Ingeborg set the filled plate in the warming oven and poured two cups of coffee. As soon as he returned, she asked, "You want me to butcher a chicken and start it cooking? Chicken soup always tastes good after birthing a baby."

"No, no. That is too much bother. I will take you home right after we eat." He smiled his pleasure at the food swiftly disappearing. "You are one fine cook, Mrs. Bjorklund. Tusen takk for all you do for us."

"Mira did the work, short that it was. She nearly dropped that baby on the floor." Ingeborg cut off her chuckle with a gentle cough at the scandalized look on his young face. Sometimes men just didn't see the humor in things like that.

A while later she stepped down from the wagon and retrieved her basket. "I'll send Ilse over to help out for a bit. Just let that chicken stew till the meat is falling off the bones. It will go real well with dumplings. You have anything in the garden ready yet?"

He shook his head. "Nei, we got a late start what with . . ." He made a motion of a big belly.

"Ja, that is so. We will send some greens along." Ingeborg thought to the few remaining green beans she'd dried in their pods, which they called leather britches. "I'll send some other things too. You remind Mira she has to drink lots of milk and water so she has plenty of milk for the baby. She nursed like a greedy little pig already."

At the red flaming up his neck and face, she waved and turned toward the house. Men. They didn't mind making babies, but they sure didn't want to hear about the birthing or the baby's care. Her chuckle preceded her into the house, where Astrid was forming the dough into loaves.

"My, but it smells good in here," Ingeborg said.

"You are back soon."

Ingeborg nodded. "Easy time she had. How would you like to run over to Tante Kaaren's and ask Ilse if she is free to go help the new mother for a day or two?"

"I could go help, Mor." Astrid slid the final loaf into the pan and dusted off her hands.

"I know you could. You are so capable in the kitchen already." Ingeborg put an arm around her daughter's slim shoulders. "But it is good practice for Ilse. She might soon be having a house of her own."

"Not without someone courting her, she won't." Astrid washed the bread dough and flour off her hands in the basin kept on the back of the stove.

Ingeborg cocked her head. "You are wise beyond your years, Astrid. Sometimes you amaze me."

Hauling water from the river to the garden took up a good part of the day for Andrew and Astrid, even with the twins and Trygve assisting. Andrew backed the sledge pulled by the oxen right down to the water, so all of them kept cool from the water splashed as they passed the filled buckets from hand to hand and Andrew dumped them in the barrels. With the barrels full, the oxen pulled the sledge back to the gardens, and the children, barefoot and soaked, raced back to start the reverse. They poured water carefully at the base of each plant, making their way down the rows of growing beans, corn, carrots, and potatoes.

"There must be an easier way." Andrew wiped the sweat from his forehead with the back of his hand. He handed a small full bucket to Trygve. "Now you be more careful. Water is too precious to waste."

"Why not pour it in the rows like a river?" Trygve demonstrated what he meant. The black soil sucked up the water, never letting it flow to the next plant.

"Takes too much water. The earth is too dry."

"But it runs off the plants when we pour."

"Maybe we should build dams around them." Andrew fetched a hoe and heaped dirt so the water couldn't run off. "There now. That will help."

Astrid, her sunbonnet hanging by its strings down her back, came back to see what the boys were doing. "That's good."

Andrew handed Grace, the deaf twin, the

hoe and signed his instructions. All the children and many of the adults had learned sign language at school. He showed her how to mound the dirt, and she flashed him a grin that said she understood. The three barrels never went far enough, but they kept the plants growing, even though not at the speed a good rainstorm would have provided.

Day after day, week after week, the sun had been shining, with hardly a cloud to dim the heat. When thunderheads did build up in the west, they all prayed for rain, but the clouds passed over, the heat lightning flickering in the distance like a broken promise.

"If only there were some way to water the fields like you children are doing the gardens." Haakan and Lars watched as the twins emptied the last of their buckets.

Andrew emptied the last of the barrel water into a bucket for Astrid. "We could try."

"If we could save the pasture, that would help. When you've finished giving the gardens a soaking, go out in the pasture and throw out buckets of water."

"You think once would help?" Lars rubbed his chin with thumb and forefinger.

"I wonder if we could build a sluice, you

know, like those they built in Montana to bring the logs down from the mountains?"

"But how . . ." Lars shook his head. "We don't have a hill to run the water down."

"Don't need much of a drop."

"I know, but the river is already so low you'd have to go up the banks and then over to the fields. Hard to believe it's not even July yet."

Haakan sighed. "Guess you're right, but there should be a way. Seems to me I heard about some newfangled machine that pumps water."

"Better'n our windmills?"

"Ja. If only we dared pump more from the well . . ."

"If the wells go dry, we'll be hauling water for the stock too." Shaking his head, Lars turned his head and spat. "Bad times."

"But we are so much better off than others." Haakan stared out at the crops that should have been knee high already. "We made it through the other years. We can survive this one too."

"Ja." Lars hawked and spit again. "We best start the haying tomorrow."

"Let's sharpen the scythe bars then. I'll get Thorliff too."

"I can help." Andrew spoke from beside his father.

Haakan tousled his son's hair, knocking his hat to the ground. "You keep the water flowing, son. At least until we get the fields turned and raked. Then we'll all haul hay."

The short hay dried nearly as fast as the mowers laid it over. What should have taken weeks was finished in a matter of days. While the barns were full, there were only two outside stacks.

"We're going to have to sell some of the cows," Haakan announced one night at supper. "We won't have enough to feed so many through the winter."

Ingeborg sighed. "I know, but the cheese house is what kept us going before. It can do so again."

"Ja, so true." Smoke from his pipe circled his head.

Thorliff sat at the kitchen table writing another story. The look he gave his mother made her force a smile to lips that wanted to quiver. "God will sustain us. He always has and He always will. Before we do anything, we will pray and seek His will." She waited until each of her men looked her in the face and nodded. *Father God, I speak so surely, and yet my heart is screaming out fear. I don't want to sell any cows.*

Haakan stood and stretched his arms

above his head. "Bedtime."

"I want to finish this." Thorliff motioned to his paper.

"Blow the lamp out when you're done." Haakan tamped his pipe out into the open stove, took out his knife, and scraped out the bowl. He yawned as he settled his pipe on the rack he'd carved. "Morning comes soon."

"I'll be done in a bit."

Ingeborg set the dried beans to soaking. She would bake them in the morning. When Haakan and Andrew had left the room, she crossed to stand behind Thorliff, laying a hand on his shoulder. "No matter what happens with the drought, you are not to consider staying home from college. Do you hear me? I can see it in your face when you hear discussions like this."

"But, Mor . . ."

She gripped his shoulder harder. "No. You *will* go to school. I believe with everything in me that God is calling you to St. Olaf, and you must not doubt." She stepped to his side and turned his chin up so he had to look at her. "Promise me."

Thorliff struggled against the clasp on his chin, then wilted like a plant gone without water. "I . . . I cannot promise. It all depends."

"Ah, Thorliff. God asks for faith the size of a mustard seed. It all depends, all right. Your school, my cheese house, our farm, our family — we all depend on Him. Isn't that what we believe?"

"Ja." He stopped the "but" before he said it, but it rang like a church bell in the silence of the kitchen.

CHAPTER SEVENTEEN:
JULY 1893

"Guess who came home."

Thorliff shrugged. "How should I know?" He studied the look on Manda's face. Manda rarely showed much emotion unless someone had made her mad, which happened more often than not. "Baptiste?"

"He wasn't gone anywhere." Disgust was another of her visible emotions, and right now it dug under his skin.

"Why can't you just tell me?" He felt like someone had clapped him upside his head. "Your pa?"

"Well, Zeb." He was her pa, but by adoption. Her real father had disappeared back in South Dakota on a trip to the store for supplies years earlier. Some said he had run off, but Manda pounded whoever said that right into the dirt. No matter what had happened, no one had ever seen a trace of him. Zebulun had found Manda and her sister starving in a dugout near the swollen Missouri River and convinced them he would help them if they came with him. Eventually they had all ended up in Blessing.

"When did he get here?"

"Last night."

Thorliff waited for her to continue. When she didn't, he sucked in a deep breath. Getting information from her was about as hard as dragging it out of Baptiste. Neither one ever wore out their tongues from talking.

"So how many horses did he bring?" He knew that was the subject she'd most likely be excited about. Manda was already gaining a reputation as a good horse trainer.

"Ten." Her eyes sparkled. "Says he has more in Montana."

"You going to train them for pulling or for riding?"

"Some of each. He's got a real purty filly. She's smart too."

"How do you know that already?"

"Worked with her since sunup. Already got her bridled and saddled. She stands good as can be."

Thorliff could tell she'd like to keep the filly, but knowing Manda, she wouldn't ask for such a gift. Just getting to train the horse would give her hours of pleasure.

"He's going back, then."

"Yep. And he don't know it yet, but I'm

goin' with him."

"But what about Ba—" He stopped himself before finishing.

"That's what I come to ask you about." She scuffed her boot toe in the dust before looking back at him, the skin tight around her eyes. She cleared her throat. "You think Baptiste will come along?"

Thorliff knew what it cost her to ask. He squinted his eyes to think better. The silence stretched as he considered all the possible answers.

"I don't know. Guess all you can do is ask him." The look she gave him said what she thought of his answer.

"Sorry." Thorliff had known for a long time that Manda and Baptiste were sweet on each other, no matter how hard they had tried to keep it a secret.

While it made no nevermind to him, he knew others in the community would have six kinds of conniption fits. It didn't matter that Baptiste and his grandmother had helped out nearly everyone in and around Blessing. Some still thought of them as Indian and didn't hold much truck with Indians. Especially not Indians and whites sweet on each other.

Thorliff hated the thought of anyone hurting his friends. It didn't make sense. When

230

he and Anji were together, people smiled at them, benevolence evident in everything said or not said. Some teased them, sure, like Astrid. He thought sometimes of stuffing a rag in her mouth. If only he wouldn't blush so fast. Burning ears stood out like flaming torches. But even so, no one meant any harm.

Not so for Manda and Baptiste.

"I wish it were different."

Manda sighed. "Me too." Her lower jaw tightened. "But it ain't, and wishin' don't make it so." She turned and slid her foot into the stirrup, swinging aboard smoothly as any man. She'd given up skirts the day Zeb left for wherever he was headed, taking Ingeborg's stories of the early homesteading days for her model. That was back when Ingeborg had scandalized some settlers by wearing britches while out working in the fields or hunting. Her shooting ability embarrassed some of the men because she was so good.

Manda touched the brim of her felt hat with one finger. "Don't go frettin', Thorliff. This'll all come right in the end."

Or you'll make it so, Thorliff thought but didn't bother saying aloud. "God willing."

"Yeah, there's that too." She nudged her horse with her heels and loped back down the lane.

Thorliff watched her go, listening to the argument going on in his head that he should have had something wiser to say to her. *How come I can come up with a million questions but never any answers?* He climbed up on the metal seat of the cultivator and *hupped* the team back to the corn rows. Slow as the crop was growing, this was still the last pass through with the horses. If only they would get a day or two of slow drenching rain.

Since the team would follow the rows almost without him, Thorliff let his mind wander from story to story and back to Manda, then from Manda to his own concerns about leaving home for school. Often enough he'd heard Pastor Solberg say that worrying was a sin, that it showed lack of trust in their heavenly Father and caused all manner of problems. How come it was so easy to believe something and so hard to put it to work?

When Thorliff told his mother about Manda that night after supper, Ingeborg laid down her knitting. "She cares for Baptiste, doesn't she?"

"Ja, but how did you know?"

Ingeborg smiled her mother smile. "Thorliff, I'm not blind, and I have been around enough springs to see budding affections."

"They been friends for a long time."

"I know. Like you and Anji."

Anji, the flower of my heart. Thorliff could feel the burn start in his neck and ears. And his mother wasn't even teasing him. All he could see was love in her eyes, and he knew that love applied to Manda and Baptiste too. He nodded. "I don't know what to do for them."

"Not much you can do."

He debated telling her what Manda had said about going to Montana but decided to keep the confidence. Instead, he stood and crossed to stare out the window. The moon shone bright enough he could have taken his book outside to read. Questions bubbled and snorted within him like an awakening volcano. Guilt rose like steam. *How can I dare think of going away to school when we've had no rain? Yet how can I not go? Lord God, what is the best?*

"Son, what is it you are stewing about?" His mother's voice floated softly through the dimness and called him back to young boy days when he had sat at her feet and told her his stories.

Thorliff shook his head. *I'm supposed to be a man now, and yet I want to hide my face*

in my mor's apron and let her tell me every-
thing will be all right. "Nothing, just —"

"If you are still worried about going away, put those thoughts from your mind. You have the bank draft from Mr. Gould, and I have money put aside. You'll find work there to help pay also. Remember the story Jesus told about the talents? The only man he scolded was the one who buried his talent in the ground."

"I know. But I would only be postponing, not burying. I can write here too."

"How many stories have you written since school was out?"

"Only one, but winter is when I write the most. There's more time then." He leaned against the window frame and looked at his mother. While her face was in shadow, the moonlight caught the clicking knitting needles and the whiteness of her fingers passing the yarn around the dancing ivory. He could feel her gaze upon him, a gaze of love and imbuing strength. Ingeborg Bjork-lund did what needed to be done, no matter the cost. While she wasn't his birth mother, she was the only mother he'd ever known. After his father, Roald, died in the blizzard, she'd kept the family and the land together by sheer will. He remembered her working the farm and the fields, breaking the sod and planting, doing the work of a man, of several men, really. And they had survived.

Could he do less?

"Is it wrong to want something else than the farm? Far is so set on —"

"Andrew will till the soil, and you will till men's minds. Both are needed. Deep down, Haakan understands this."

He noted she'd referred to him as Haakan. Strange how he had lost both mother and father and yet gained new ones who meant the world to him, perhaps more so because he was not of their blood.

"But, Mor, you nearly gave your life for this land."

"Ja, and I would do it again, but not at the cost of your life. You are meant for another purpose, and God will use you in ways we do not yet begin to know. You keep your eyes on our Savior and let him guide you. That is all I ask."

Thorliff took a deep breath. "That I will."

"And no looking back. No saying 'Should I or shouldn't I?' Look only forward, like the apostle Paul says about keeping our eyes on the prize and running with patience the race set before us."

"It is not that I don't love this land."

"I know that. This black soil is part of our

very souls. You will go with our blessing, and you will return with rejoicing."

Thorliff turned and looked out the window again. If he closed his eyes, he could see his doubts and fears rising on the moonbeams as an offering to the keeper of his heart and soul.

"Mange takk."

"You are indeed most welcome."

But putting and keeping the worry out of his mind was far easier said than done.

CHAPTER EIGHTEEN

"Ah, Zeb, it is so good to see you."

"Thank you, Miz Bjorklund. Good to see all my family again." Zebulun MacCallister indicated all the folks gathered around and visiting after church. "I feel like the prodigal son."

"As right you should." Mary Martha Solberg snaked an arm around her lanky brother's waist. She leaned her head against his arm. "Strange how the mail lost all your letters to us."

Zeb had the grace to both blush and flinch. "I did write one."

"I know. Manda and I wore that little piece of paper out with our rereadin'." She gazed up at him. "I wish you were goin' to stay." She patted her rounding middle. "Little Emily here would like to get to know her uncle."

"Emily? Are you prescient or somethin'?"

"No, but this one feels like a girl. Besides,

Metiz told me it was a girl, and she is always right."

"Ma-a." Little Johnny Solberg tugged on a fold of her shirt.

Mary Martha leaned over and cupped her son's round face in her hands. "What do you need?"

"Thomas won't let me have the train engine."

"Is he playin' with it now?"

"Yesss." Hands on hips. "But I want it now."

"You must wait your turn."

Zeb leaned down and scooped up the child, setting Johnny up on his shoulder. He squealed and clamped an arm around the man's head, a tiny hand sealing off his left eye. "Hey, Thomas, see! Onkel Zeb givin' me a ride."

Zeb grinned at his sister, winking with his available eye. He removed the clamping hand so he could see.

Mary Martha shook her head. "Children." But love colored both her voice and her eyes. She watched as Zeb galloped off with his cargo shrieking in delight. Other children followed after him as if he were handing out cookies.

"He loves children, doesn't he?" Ingeborg watched the activities with a smile.

"Always has. I know that's why he couldn't leave Manda and Deborah in that dugout." Mary Martha sighed. "If only he would stay here. Perhaps someday he'd find another wife, and . . ."

"Does he talk about Katy?" Thinking back to the deaths of Zeb's wife Katy and her newborn baby brought the sting of tears to Ingeborg's eyes. She and Metiz had fought so hard to save them both, but they lost the battle. She sniffed and looked to see the tears trickling down her friend's cheeks. They took out handkerchiefs at the same time.

"I miss her every day. And if *I* do, how much more does Zeb?"

"I know. Even after all these years, something will trigger my memory, and all the sorrow after Roald died comes crashing back, in spite of the fact that I have a good husband and my life is all I ever dreamed." Ingeborg dabbed at her eyes again. "But Zeb is all alone."

"He needn't be." A slight tightening about her mouth showed Mary Martha's true feelings.

"He reminds me of a wounded animal going off by itself to lick its wounds."

"Sometimes those solitary animals never heal. They die."

"Ja, that is true." Ingeborg shook her head. "But men so often act this way."

"I know." Mary Martha flinched and rubbed the side of her belly. "This baby is a busy one, runnin' to keep up with the others and not even out of the womb yet."

Ingeborg waved when someone called good-bye from over at the long line of wagons. "We'd sure like it if you all would come for dinner."

"Let me ask John, but I see no reason why not." Mary Martha paused, a frown wrinkling her brow. She lowered her voice and moved closer to Ingeborg. "Have you heard anything about Baptiste and . . . and Manda?"

"I know they are good friends. Have been for years."

"Um." Mary Martha rubbed her belly again. "I reckon I just have me a feelin'."

Ingeborg waited, watching the emotions play over her friend's face like clouds chasing tag around the sun.

"Mor, can Ellie come home with us for dinner?" Andrew skidded to a stop in front of his mother.

"If Goodie says it's okay, she may."

"Good. She said the same." Andrew threw a "mange takk" over his shoulder and ran off to play a game of Run Sheep Run with the other children.

"Uff da, such energy." Ingeborg turned to see Mary Martha smiling at her.

"Do you ever say *no* or *wait* to someone coming for a meal?"

Ingeborg shrugged. "Why would I? We can always stretch what we have a little bit more." She tipped her head a trifle to the side. "God has been good to us. I am just grateful that we have much to share."

"True, and most of us would come just for the cheese if the rest of your larder was bare." Mary Martha sighed. "Back to the question."

"What is it you are afraid of?"

"I reckon I don't rightly know. But it seems Manda is more secretive than ever, if that's possible. Maybe secretive isn't the right word. She's always kept her own counsel. She doesn't ask for anything unless absolutely necessary and always does more than I could ask, as if she were beholden and wanted to work off the debt."

"All that responsibility made her old before her time."

"I know. She really looks up to you. You think perhaps you could talk with her?"

"I can try, but . . ."

"Perhaps after dinner?"

Ingeborg nodded and answered Haakan's

241

beckon from the wagon. "I'll be right there."

"We need to go by home first, so it'll be a little while before we come. I have a chocolate cake baked, and I'll bring that." Mary Martha put an arm around young Johnny, who'd returned to his mother as the other children departed. "Come, let's get in the wagon so we will be ready to leave when your pa is ready."

"Pa went back in the church." Johnny pointed to the open doors.

Ingeborg and Mary Martha headed toward the two remaining wagons.

By the time everyone gathered for dinner, the group had swelled to party size, with the women inside putting the meal together and the men setting up the sawhorses to make tables. Thorliff and Baptiste hauled benches out of the granary while Andrew and Astrid drew the other children into a circle around Metiz, who sat cross-legged in the shade of the cottonwood.

"Tell us about Wolf," Andrew asked as he took his place beside Ellie. "Do you think he will ever come back?"

Metiz smiled, showing her few remaining teeth. The wrinkles in her face folded into each other, a map of the years. "Long time since he come back. Brought pups to show us." She nodded, her eyes gazing into the past.

"One winter before any of your people came to our valley, I find a young wolf caught in a trap by front paw. He near to death. Men say kill him, but I spring trap and carry him back to tepee where Baptiste live with me . . ." Her voice trailed off, and she nodded. "I clean and bandage foot. Wolf lay by fire. We feed him small bits of dried meat. Give him water to drink. Baptiste think Wolf die, but he live. When time of new grass come, he can walk again, limps . . ." She dipped her shoulder as if she were favoring one foot. "Slow, slow he go. We come back here for hunting and fishing. Wolf come too."

"Did he ever bite you?" Ellie asked.

"No. Wolf know we his friends. He soon hunt again, stay near us but not in tepee. When Bjorklunds come, he see we friends. We all his pack. One winter he chase off other wolves so sheep not die."

"When I was little, I got lost in the tall grass, and Wolf found me. He licked my face and stayed with me all night, then in the morning he led me back to my mor." Andrew shared a smile with Metiz. "I miss him."

"One winter he not come back until time

243

of new grass again, and he bring mate and two pups to show us. When they left, I think he not be back. He lead own life." Metiz stroked the rabbit skin she'd been pulling back and forth over a stick in her lap to soften it. She passed the tanned skin around for the children to feel. "Great Spirit give us all we need to live."

"So soft." Ellie held the fur side up to her cheek. "What will you make with these?"

"More mittens. Soon have enough for vest. Moccasins for baby feet."

"Here come the Solbergs." Andrew stood. "I need to go take care of their horses."

"My vest is too little." Trygve moved over into Andrew's spot so he could smile at Metiz.

"Ah, you want another?" Metiz took his broad hint.

"Ja. I gave mine to Lydia."

"When Metiz makes a vest, it never wears out." Ellie propped her elbows on her knees since she and all the children sat in the same cross-legged pose as their storyteller. "Tell us about when you were little. Please?"

Metiz chuckled. "You know stories by heart."

"But you tell them better."

When Ingeborg rang the bell for dinner, Ellie and Andrew stood beside Metiz in case she needed help getting up. Sometimes she did and sometimes she didn't. Today she allowed them to help her. After the other children ran to be with their parents, she turned to her young helpers. "You two fine friends. Thank you." She gazed up at Andrew, who'd passed his mother's five foot seven inches a month earlier. "You fine man one day. Take good care of land." She reached for Ellie's hand and put it into Andrew's. "And Ellie."

"Ja, I will." He crooked his arm for Metiz to hold on to as they made a slow way over to the tables.

Ingeborg watched them come, the two children making Metiz look even smaller between them. *She's growing more frail and smaller each year. Lord, help me be ready to let her go when her time comes.* She let out a breath in a puff, glancing over to where Joseph was helping Agnes to the table. Metiz and Agnes, her two best friends. And both of them weakening before her very eyes. "Lord God, how can I help them?"

"What did you say?" Penny stopped beside her.

"Oh, nothing." Ingeborg put her thoughts away and motioned to the tables. "Would you please ask Pastor Solberg to say the blessing?"

"Of course." Penny patted Ingeborg's arm as she left. "All will be well."

Ja, all will be well. I must remember that. I must remember that God is indeed in control, that He is the Good Shepherd. A soft chuckle came from another part of her mind. *And not you, Ingeborg.*

She glanced down the tables to see that Anji stood beside Thorliff, and Manda, arm still wrapped but no longer in a sling or splint, was across the table from Baptiste. Somehow she had to arrange time with Manda, but how? Ingeborg chuckled at herself. Of course, she needed to check on that arm.

Quiet settled as Pastor Solberg asked everyone to bow their heads. "Most gracious heavenly Father, we thank thee for this family gathered together and that some of us are grafted into this family like we are all grafted into thee. Bless this food prepared with loving hands and, Lord, if it be thy will, please bring rain for our cattle and crops. In the name of Christ Jesus our Lord, amen." Everyone spoke a heartfelt amen along with him and took their places, laughter rising like steam from a washtub.

Bowls of mashed potatoes, gravy, and greens, followed by platters of sliced pork, venison, and beef made their way along the diners. Since everyone had brought whatever they'd had baking in the oven for dinner, the tables soon groaned under full plates. Kaaren poured coffee from the gray granite coffeepot, and Ilse carried a jug of milk in one hand and buttermilk in the other. Ingeborg refilled bowls and platters as fast as they emptied, until the pots and pans ended up in a tub of hot soapy water.

No one left the table hungry, but there weren't even crumbs left of the cakes and pies.

Goodie Wold headed up the cleanup crew, since her family had joined the others for dinner as well. She insisted that those with a bun in the oven should put up their feet and Ingeborg and Kaaren should join them. She and the younger ones could wash and dry the dishes.

On one of her treks to the kitchen, Ingeborg stopped Manda, still favoring her arm. "Manda, how about I check your arm while all this is going on?"

"All right." Manda used her shirttail to wipe sweat from her brow. "Sure is hot today."

"I know." Ingeborg pointed to the bedroom. "Let's go in there."

She sat Manda on a stool and took the chair for herself.

"Mor?" Andrew's voice made her roll her eyes.

"Can't get away anywhere, can we?" She went to the door. "In here. What do you need?"

"Can we go swimming?"

"Perhaps later. You just ate."

"So we can go in a little while?"

"You must ask the other folks too. And you must have Thorliff along."

"Baptiste said he would like to go. I'll ask everyone else."

"What are the men doing?"

"Playing horseshoes."

She returned to her patient.

"I would like to go swimming too." Manda slumped against the back of the chair.

"Let me see your arm first."

"You mean I could go?" Straightening, she held out her arm. "Looks awful dirty, I know, but that sling and the splints" — she shook her head — "just got in the way somethin' awful."

"Have you been training horses anyway?"

Manda looked at her, one eyebrow raised. " 'Course. But one handed weren't too easy."

While they talked, Ingeborg cut the knots off and unwound the bandage, resting Manda's arm between her hip and elbow. "Can

248

you move your fingers without pain?"

Manda never flinched as she moved her fingers.

"Did that hurt at all?"

"Not enough to bother." The girl started to clench her fist but seemed to think the better of it.

"I see." With gentle fingers, Ingeborg probed the area of the break, studying Manda's eyes for any sign of pain she'd try to hide. "Now clench your fist slowly and stop if it hurts."

Manda did as she was told and bounced on the stool when she could close her hand tight. "Look, it don't hurt." She rubbed her arm with her other hand. "But my arm shrunk." Manda held the two arms straight out. The left one was not only white and wrinkled but was indeed smaller than the browned right.

"That happens when you can't use it. You will have to rebuild the strength in it, and that takes time."

Manda sighed. "Everything takes time."

"True. Wrap it up when you're doing hard work. You could rebreak it so easily. Otherwise use it like always. Just don't expect it to work as well as the other."

Ingeborg wished she could have had different news because the cloud settled back on Manda's brow. How to get her talking?

"Have you been having a good visit with Zeb?"

Manda nodded, keeping her gaze on one thumb rubbing the other.

"Sure wish he was going to stay around here." Ingeborg picked up Manda's now healed arm and began to massage it.

"He has more horses at his ranch in Montana."

"Is he planning to take the heavy stallion back with him?"

Manda shrugged. Years earlier Zeb had taken the train back to Ohio and brought a Belgian stallion to service all the area's mares so they would have sturdier horses for the fieldwork.

Ingeborg waited, hoping Manda would get uncomfortable with the silence and volunteer something. But nothing came forth. "You must want to see his ranch real bad."

Manda glanced up, eyes slightly squinted, then down again. "He said he'd bring more horses for training next year."

"Thorliff said you are really a good trainer."

Manda nodded.

"Is Baptiste going back with Zeb?"

Manda shrugged again, letting Ingeborg see only the part in her hair.

Ingeborg patted her arm. "Does that feel better?"

"Yes, it's fine. Thank you." Manda bolted from the room.

Mary Martha is right. Something is definitely going on. Ingeborg turned at the sound of stamping feet.

"It's not fair." Astrid and Sophie, arms clamped across their chests and chins jutting a mile, stopped in the doorway.

"What's not fair?" Ingeborg asked over her shoulder, putting her supplics away.

"The boys get to go swimming and we don't."

"Ah." Ingeborg knew without further questions. She thought a moment, finger to her chin. "I have an idea."

"What?"

"There's enough ice left in the icehouse — we'll make ice cream."

"And they won't get any?"

"We'll share, but we'll get first helpings." As the girls turned, Ingeborg grabbed Astrid's arm. "Now don't you go telling, you hear?"

"We won't." But the dancing lights in her daughter's eyes told Ingeborg differently.

"As soon as they leave, you fetch the eggs and cream from the springhouse. We'll get Haakan to bring over a gunnysack of ice."

"We can get it."

"After the boys go, I'll go with you." The thought of the shady coolness of the icehouse was inviting. Why hadn't she thought of this earlier? If only they had lemons too. Surely there were a few strawberries left.

Later, as she and the girls crossed the field to the icehouse, she thought again to Manda. Where had she gone?

Suddenly a scream echoed from the river.

CHAPTER NINETEEN

"Help! I'm stuck!"

Thorliff turned in the direction of the voice. The sun- and shade-streaked river made locating the problem difficult.

"Help!"

"It's Hamre." Baptiste threw himself back into the water and swam out to the floundering boy.

"Andrew, go get Far." Thorliff ran into the sluggish water and dove out as far as he could. *God, please don't let him drown. Please let him live.* He gagged on a mouthful of water as he stroked with all his strength.

Hamre struggled in the water, arms flailing. "I'm caught. My foot is caught in something."

"Take it easy. I'll go down and see." Baptiste jackknifed, driving himself straight down. When he came up, he shook the hair out of his eyes. "I can't see anything. The water is too muddy."

"Hamre, can you swim upstream?" Thorliff treaded water using the breaststroke to stay in one place. While the river appeared to be hardly moving, it kept pulling him downstream and dragging Hamre under.

Hamre went under again and came up spluttering. "I am trying."

Thorliff studied the riverbank. Was there anything there they could use? A willow tree grew near the edge. If they climbed that to bend a branch down, would it reach to Hamre?

"I'm going down again." Baptiste dove under the water. When he came up, he gulped air. "Feels like a root or tree branch. If I could stay down longer . . ."

Thorliff turned toward the shore. "Trygve, get my knife out of my pants."

"I have one too," Trygve responded. Hamre gulped water and choked.

Thorliff swam back to shore. With the river so low, at least he didn't have far to swim. He took one knife and thought a moment. Handing it back, he pointed to the clothes on a tree branch. "Get my shirt and your knife."

Trygve splashed up the bank and, grabbing the shirt and knife, dragged them back. "Here."

Thorliff tied the sleeves in knots and put a knife in each, then buttoning the shirt around his neck, he swam back out to Hamre and Baptiste.

"I . . . I can't . . ."

"Yes, you can. Turn and face upriver."

"I can't. My foot . . ."

"All right. Baptiste and I will take turns cutting the branch."

"Don't cut my leg."

"We won't." Thorliff turned back to Baptiste. "How big is the branch or root or whatever it is?"

"We need a saw."

"Can one of us stand on the thing and hold Hamre up?"

"No. It goes straight down."

"Then we'll have to try to chop on it."

"I'll go first." Knife in hand, Baptiste sucked in a huge breath and dove again.

Thorliff counted the seconds. One minute passed.

"Did he drown?" Hamre's eyes looked big as plates.

Baptiste's head broke the water. After he got a breath, he held his finger about three inches apart. "That far below his foot, I cut on that side of the root. Feel it with your fingers. You can't see nothing. I cut downward like slivering kindling."

Thorliff nodded. He took two deep breaths and dove, his ears popping as he followed Hamre's leg down. Thanks to Baptiste's instructions, he found the cut, and digging the knife blade in, he tried to slice the strips off. The waterlogged root seemed hard as granite. His lungs screamed for air. He made another slash, pushed against the root, and headed for the surface. His head broke the surface just as he thought he'd suck water.

Gasping and floundering, he felt the blessed air fill his starving lungs. "We'll never get through that with these knives. I'm going for that willow tree. Hang on, Hamre."

Thorliff swam to the bank, beckoned Trygve and another boy, and pointed to the willow. "I'll go climb up the tree first. You come if we need more weight." He climbed the trunk hand over hand up the branches until the tree began to bend. "Come on, we need more."

"Thorliff, what are you doing?" Haakan ran down the shallow bank with Lars following right behind him.

"Got to bend the tree over for Hamre to hold on to while someone saws off the root that's holding his foot."

"Andrew, go get a saw." Haakan started

for the tree. "Get two."

Thorliff climbed higher. The tree bent, but not enough.

Baptiste reached for the nearest branch and missed. Hamre went under again. Baptiste yelled to Trygve. "Get a reed, up there." He pointed upriver. "A dry one that's hollow."

Trygve slipped and slid on the black mud bank, but he reached the cattails and picked a dry stalk from the last winter.

Thorliff inched further out, Haakan behind him.

"Be careful. This thing lets go, and it could throw you clear to Grafton." Haakan's head was now even with Thorliff's feet.

"You too."

"Nei, I'm too big. I'd only go as far as the barn."

Thorliff glanced back to see Ingeborg standing on the upper bank. Good. Now they had someone who could be praying too, although his mind screamed for supernatural help between breaths.

Lars stood in the river up to his chest. He ripped off his shirt and moved upstream. "Here, Baptiste, hang on to this and then Hamre. Maybe we can keep him stationary that way."

The shirt floated to Baptiste, and he

grabbed hold. He reached for Hamre, who'd gone under again. When he struggled back up, the two joined fingertips.

"Closer."

Lars took another step and down he went. He came up sputtering. "Hole there. Maybe I can do this from the other side."

"Here." Trygve waded out to his waist, handing the reed to Lars.

Baptiste took it to Hamre. "Breathe through this." He put it in his mouth to show how. "Breathe through your mouth."

Hamre did as shown and leaned back in the water. When his face went under, the reed stood up. He floundered up again. "It works. I can breathe." Lying back, his face inches under the surface, he breathed through the reed.

"Thank God. Good thinking, Baptiste." Haakan tapped his son on the knee. "Thorliff, you come down even with me, and we'll go down together." When they were both standing on the ground again, Haakan threw his arm over his son's shoulders. "No wonder my mor used to go white when she saw us up in the pine trees. Bending them for fun is one thing when you're young and foolish, but knowing what could happen to your son is quite another."

Andrew ran down the bank, the saws

clanking against his side. "I brought the crosscut too." He doubled over, trying to catch his breath. "Where's Hamre?"

"Breathing through that stalk under the water."

"Really?"

"Really." Ingeborg clenched her young son's shoulder.

Haakan took a saw and swam out to where Baptiste paddled. "Now where did you start the cutting?"

Baptiste explained, and on three the two of them dove under.

"We will go next." Lars looked to Thorliff.

Alternating so that one hand was always on the saw, holding it in place, the four finally sawed through the root and dragged Hamre with his foot still bound but floating free to the bank. "M-mange t-takk." Hamre stuttered through trembling lips. "You saved my life — all of you. Baptiste, how did you think of the reed?"

"Grand-mère told me of braves who did that long ago. I just remembered."

"But all of you risked your lives for me." Hamre shook like he had the palsy.

"You would have done the same." In spite of the heat Thorliff grabbed his shirt and pants. "If I'm freezing, what about you?"

Hamre shivered and nodded.

While pulling on his pants Thorliff mentally shook his head. In all the years they'd lived on the same farm, he'd never heard Hamre say so many words at once. Thorliff's second cousin, Hamre Bjorklund, had come to America with Thorliff's grandmother, Bridget, in 1886, after his mother died of consumption. Though strongminded, Hamre was not one for much talk.

"Ach, look how swollen." Ingeborg probed the ankle with careful fingers. "We must pray the swelling is only from the root. Your poor foot has been mauled."

"Let's cut the rest of the roots off, and we'll carry him to the house."

"No, to the icehouse. We'll pack the foot in ice for a time after we've scrubbed it clean."

Sawing the last section of root took care, but they managed without cutting the skin. With his arms over their shoulders and their arms around his waist, the two men and Hamre made their way to the icehouse, where Ingeborg filled her apron with ice chips to pack around the injured ankle.

Teeth chattering, Hamre shook all over.

"Get some blankets," Ingeborg said. Andrew ran for the house. Trygve, carrying all the pants and shirts from the tree branch, held them out so they could get dressed again.

"At least you didn't swim in your birthday suits," Haakan muttered, pulling his pants over his soaking underwear.

"Ja, I thought that's why you didn't let the girls go along." Ingeborg checked the boy's skin under the ice pack.

"Just didn't seem right, that's all."

"Perhaps you listened to God's good advice."

Hamre coughed, then threw up. When he finished heaving, he lay back with his wrist over his eyes. "And I still dream of going fishing. On the ocean. At least the water will be clean."

Thorliff snickered, Baptiste chuckled, and Haakan laughed. Ingeborg shook her head as all the males around her laughed until they hiccupped.

Thank God they could laugh instead of cry. So different the ending could have been, so terribly different.

When Andrew carried in two quilts, he looked a question at his mother. She shrugged and took the quilts to wrap around the shivering Hamre.

Later when they all returned to the house, Astrid, Ilse, and Kaaren had the ice cream all churned and packed in ice chips.

261

"It's nearly ready to eat. Sounds to me like we have something wonderful to celebrate."

"That was too close a call." Haakan took off his hat and smoothed his hair back before setting his hat back again. "We all smell like river water, that's for sure."

"Right now, that's a right good smell." Lars hugged Trygve between his knees. "Took all of us working together to keep that boy alive." He stroked his son's head. "Didn't matter how little, huh, Trygve?"

The boy leaned back against his father's chest. "I never been so scared." His lower lip quivered.

Astrid handed Hamre the first bowl of ice cream. "Here, this should make you cold on the inside too." She glanced at his apron-bound foot, his toes red with cold. "That still hurt?"

Hamre nodded. "Some." He nodded again, this time at Baptiste. "He thought of breathing through a cattail reed."

Astrid's eyes grew wide. "And it worked?"

"Ja, right good."

They finished the ice cream just in time for everyone to leave for home to start the chores. With good-byes and God blesses ringing like church bells, the wagons raised a cloud of dust driving down the lane.

"How did your talk go with Manda?" Kaaren asked as she set the bowls into a pan of soapy water.

Ingeborg shook her head. "She's about as closemouthed as can be. If she and Baptiste do marry, there won't be much conversation in that house."

"You think that will happen?"

"I wouldn't be the least bit surprised."

"Harvest is going to come early." Haakan, Lars, Andrew, and Thorliff stood on the edge of the wheat field, which was already turning yellow, but not the rich gold of regular harvest and only half as high. Dark earth could be seen in patches and between the sparse rows.

"Is it this bad everywhere?" Thorliff stuck his hands in his pockets.

"Some worse out toward the west." Haakan tipped his hat back. "I heard all the water holes are dried up, and those cattle ranchers are in worse trouble than we are. At least we've been able to keep our livestock watered, and while the pasture is grazed down, we have enough land to move them around. We'll graze the sheep on this field as soon as harvest is finished."

"Thanks to the young'uns, we have gardens too." Lars kicked at a clod of dirt.

"Thank God we got the loans paid off. If we have to, we can grind some of the wheat for feed."

"What makes no sense to me is why the thistles grew better than the wheat." Andrew pointed toward a clump of thistle. "They had the same rain."

"God only knows," Lars answered. "I thought to go chop it out, but we'd kill some of the precious wheat in the meantime."

Haakan leaned down and, thumb and forefinger around a stalk of wheat, pulled the length of the stalk so that the kernels slid into his cupped hand. He rubbed the wheat between his hands and blew off the chaff. He extended his hand to each of the others. "Help yourself."

They chewed one kernel at a time, testing for moisture content and ripeness.

"Still tastes some green." Andrew chewed another kernel.

"Right. It's not ready yet, but it will be in less than a week if this heat continues."

"We'll be lucky to get enough seed for next year."

"I read about a new wheat strain in the *Grange News*." Andrew pulled a wheat stalk and chewed on the end, the twitching wheat spears shimmering gold in the sunlight. "It's not supposed to get the blight."

"Got to have rain to get blight." Haakan turned with a sigh. "Let's go work on that steam engine. Get it in top shape so we are ready to roll as soon as the wheat turns." He clapped a hand on the shoulder of each of his sons. "Thorliff, how about you take a list in to Hjelmer so he can order us some belts. We put one more patch on that long one, and it'll be more patch than belt."

"Take my wagon. He can reset the rims on that." Lars shaded his eyes, looking toward the houses.

Thorliff chewed another kernel of wheat that seemed more shell than heart. They always kept the finest wheat for seed. This poor stuff might shrivel during the winter and not even sprout come spring. Let alone feed all the cattle. Then what would they do?

CHAPTER TWENTY:
NORTHFIELD,
MINNESOTA
JULY 1893

"How soon will you be ready?" Annabelle Rogers stood in the doorway of her step-daughter's bedroom. Dawn had yet to lighten the sky.

"Ten minutes?" Elizabeth turned from the small trunk she had set up on the bench at the foot of her bed. She most likely should have chosen a larger trunk, but taking too many clothes seemed such a waste of both time and money.

"Why didn't you pack a larger trunk?"

Elizabeth rolled her eyes. Leave it to her mother to ask the question she'd just been asking herself. "I hate to take so much along. After all, we're not touring Europe or anything."

"But we will be dining in places that require evening dress, and hot as it's been, you might want to change more often."

Elizabeth threw her hands in the air, her shoulders sagging in defeat at the same time. *Why didn't I just let you pack for me in the beginning?* "Now I need more than ten minutes."

"I'll help you." Annabelle Rogers pulled the cord in the corner, another thing Elizabeth tried never to do. She had two feet and a strong constitution made more so by running up and down the stairs. With the larger trunk ordered, Elizabeth returned to her armoire, pulling out frocks to hang on the doors for her mother's approval. Sometimes giving in was the better part of valor.

"I can't help how much room hats take," her mother said with a sniff when Elizabeth complained about the amount of luggage they were loading onto the back of the hackney. "After all, we *are* going to be gone for ten entire days."

Please don't remind me. How father and the doctor are going to get along without help is beyond me. While Dr. Gaskin now had two full-time employees, he was still running behind in seeing his patients, something that had never happened when his wife was alive. Even with Elizabeth taking care of the accounts, the office was still in a muddle. Caring for accounts had not much helped her learn medicine. However, ordering supplies and restocking his cabinets did send her thumbing through his pharmacopoeia books. The thumbing turned to studying as she memorized which potion treated which malady.

Once they were safely ensconced on the train, Elizabeth took a slender volume from her reticule and, leaning into the corner of the wall and seat, read about the latest findings in delivering infants and caring for postpartum mothers.

"What are you reading?" Annabelle fanned herself with the black silk fan she always carried in the summer. "My, but it is warm." She patted her upper lip with a handkerchief.

Elizabeth showed her the cover, keeping her place open.

"My word, child, couldn't you find something more . . . more . . ."

"I could have brought any number of books, Mother, but this is what I want to learn."

"But . . . but such a topic is not proper for a young woman of your sensibilities. And to be reading it in public like this." Annabelle looked around as if every eye might be locked on the title of her daughter's reading material.

Elizabeth glanced around the car. Three businessmen were playing cards at one table. A mother with two small children was reading them a story. Two ladies were conversing in the seats across the aisle from her. One elderly lady looked up from her knitting to smile when she caught Elizabeth's gaze.

As if they could read the title anyway. She was careful, however, not to let her mother see the diagrams and drawings. Now that would set her off for the entire trip. Perhaps bringing this specific book was not such a good idea after all. With a sigh she closed the offending volume and tucked it back into her reticule for later study.

"Are you happy now, Mother?" Keeping the sarcasm from her voice took a strong act of will or acting skill, she was never sure which.

"Yes, dear." Annabelle turned back from gazing out the window. "The country surely is dry, is it not?"

Droughts do that. But Elizabeth kept her thoughts to herself. Her mother had not been out treating farm families, had not been for a ride in the country for some time, as she felt her house and garden took too much time for much gadding about. Due to a good well and the services of the gardener they shared with the neighbors, the gardens were nearly as lovely as ever. Except for the dust on the leaves of shrubs and trees. Only a good rain would wash them clean.

Elizabeth stared out the window, her fingers itching to return to her book. Rather than offending her mother again, she took out a bound journal and pencil, writing down in outline form all she could remember having read. She included her experiences in assisting the doctor in birthings, fitting them into the information from the book. She'd helped in a breech, a stillbirth, and a dozen or so normal deliveries. In one case the mother had died due to excessive bleeding. Of all of them the stillborn was the most difficult, the second, losing the mother.

When her mother opened the basket Cook had prepared, Elizabeth ate without paying much attention, other than giving a vague smile and the requisite thank-you. She dug another book from her reticule, this one on childhood diseases, and only glanced up when her mother pointed out something for her to see.

"Next station: Chicago, Illinois." The conductor repeated his call as he made his swaying way down the aisle.

Elizabeth closed her book to watch as they rode between three- and four-story brick buildings with washing hanging from lines on pulleys attached to the walls. Broken windows, trash in the handkerchief-sized yards, fences with missing slats, children playing on an empty lot. A woman, heavy bellied like those she'd been reading about, sat on an iron fire escape, her hair hanging in clumps, fanning herself with a folded newspaper.

Elizabeth shivered in spite of the heat. While she knew from reading that many people lived in squalor like she'd just seen, she'd not noticed it on the train to Chicago before. Was it only that because of the heat people were outside, or had she just not looked with eyes that wanted to see? She glanced at her mother. Serene, stylish, and with total absorption, she plied her needle in and out, the burgundy yarn adding to the flower petals on a needlepoint canvas. She'd made needlepoint seats for eight of the twelve chairs in the dining room. Most likely she'd finish another on this trip.

I wonder . . . Surely there are medical facilities for these people. Will that woman have someone help her when her time comes? Midwives had been around for centuries, in fact only recently had doctors had anything to do with childbirth, believing it a natural occurrence beneath the dignity of a man trained for better things. And besides, seeing a woman in such a state was not really proper.

Elizabeth sighed. The latest information she'd read about hospital births didn't bode well. More women died of fever there than at home. She'd noted a chapter in her book on home delivery versus hospital, but she hadn't had time to read it yet.

By the time they arrived at their hotel, Elizabeth had caught a bad case of Columbian World's Fair fever. No matter that her mother had drilled into her that eavesdropping was improper and unladylike, Elizabeth's ears burned from the strain of listening in on others' conversations.

One couple rhapsodized over the Ferris Wheel, he bragging, she simpering. "If only there hadn't been all those people in the bucket. That fat man nearly crushed me into the corner."

"But think of all you could see, all of Chicago laid out around us. I'd go again in a minute."

Two men talked about Little Cairo but dropped their voices when they got to the part about the dancing girls.

Elizabeth was sure her mother would not allow a trek through such sin. Showing female skin was next to murder in her list of proprieties.

A dairy farmer from Wisconsin kept shaking his head as he told his friend about the seven-hundred-pound block of cheese in the Agriculture Building.

Elizabeth gaped at the huge posters along the streets until her mother poked her with an impatient elbow. Wishing she were a little girl again who could get away with such things, Elizabeth bit back a retort that surprised her with its audacity. One did not say to her mother, "Whyever not? There's so much to see. I don't care if the whole thing is gaudy or not." At the same time her fingers ached to find a piano and try out the new music she heard coming from a hotel. Different from any of the classics she played, the music the "hootchy-kootchy" was danced to sure set her toes to tapping.

When her mother insisted they take baths and lie down for a nap before supper, Elizabeth did so, hiding her mutinous spirit with difficulty. The last thing she wanted was to waste her precious freedom on a nap.

Once her mother was breathing the even rhythm of sleep, Elizabeth rose, careful not to let the bed squeak, and tiptoed into the parlor, where she dressed with nary a rustle of her bustle. The mauve upper drape on her skirt of darker burgundy settled with a whisper, the cream fringe swirling into decorous place. With the fitted bodice buttoned, she pinned a wisp of a hat forward so the froth of a veil covered her eyebrows. With a matching parasol to shade her face, she left the room, pausing in the entry. She couldn't leave without writing a note. Causing her mother undue worry would not bode well for a harmonious vacation.

"Gone for a walk. Will not be far. Back in time for supper."

The heavy oak door closed behind her with barely a click. The thrill of adventure made her wet her lips and smile a secret smile, almost giving in to skipping down the hall. She was alone in a bustling city with myriad sights to explore, and that without even venturing near to the fair. She stopped at the concierge's desk and smiled at the white-haired man in the gold-trimmed burgundy suit.

"Could you tell me please how to find the Morganstein Women's Hospital?"

"Are you ill, miss?" Ambrose McKnight's forehead wrinkled in concern.

"No, not at all." Her tone and gentle laughter smoothed the deeper wrinkles away and brought an answering smile in return.

"Oh, for that I am grateful." His blue eyes twinkled, and by the fine lines radiating from the edges, she guessed a smile to be his habitual demeanor.

She leaned slightly forward. "Me too. But I am interested in medicine as a career, and this woman is doing so much to help women and the downtrodden. I read about her in a magazine, and since I am here in Chicago, I would love to call on her." Elizabeth could hardly believe she'd told this man so much. How unlike her. But his smile and nodding head invited confidences. "You must be a wonderful grandfather." She could already hear her mother scolding her for such audacity, but then her mother would never know of this conversation if there were anything she could do about it. At his deep chuckle, she couldn't resist joining him.

"Ah, miss, you do not know the half of it. I love my grand babies, and they love me. Nothing in this world is finer than little ones. God's gift, for sure." He drew himself back to the matter at hand with a slight straightening of his shoulders. "And now as to the Morganstein woman. I hate to be the bearer of bad tidings, but that place of hers is not in a very good part of the city. I would not advise a young woman of your, your . . . ah, sensibilities to go there without an escort." He shook his head, his eyes darkening like a cloud covering the sun. "No, miss,

I cannot in all good conscience do that."

Elizabeth sighed. Out of the frying pan and into the fire, as Cook always said. "Do you have any suggestions for me?" *I know I can find the information other ways, but . . .* Determined thoughts took a standoff against more compliant ones that suggested returning to her room until her mother awoke and they went to supper. However, her mother would want tea brought up, and then she'd take a leisurely bath before she dressed.

Elizabeth swallowed an unladylike snort. By then the day would be gone, and she would be deciding whether to have supper at the hotel or go out to a restaurant.

"Well . . ."

Elizabeth stopped her foot in midtap and smiled her most winsome smile instead. And waited.

"We could send someone from the hotel to accompany you. I get the feeling that if I didn't help you, you'd find a way on your own."

"You are most perceptive, sir." Her wren-sized trill of laughter made his smile broaden along with hers.

"Ah, then, that is what we shall do. Wait here." He indicated a leather winged chair near the desk.

Elizabeth was tempted to take her fan from her reticule but chose instead to use the time to watch people. A silver-haired woman, wearing navy moiré that looked more fit for winter, settled her pince-nez on her rather pointed nose and studied a program laid out on a carved walnut table on which was centered a stunning arrangement of white gladioli and pink cabbage roses. Feeling herself stared at, the woman glanced up, but Elizabeth managed not to be caught gawking, as her mother would say. It was just that the woman had walked to the table as if something were wrong with her leg or hip. It was not exactly a limp, for someone like the grande dame would never limp, but rather a slight favoring. Her eyes wore the taut look of chronic pain, and deep commas bracketed her thin lips.

Now, what else would Dr. Gaskin tell me to look for? Elizabeth closed her eyes, the better to focus on her mentor's instructions. *"The whole person, Elizabeth, always the whole person."* With the woman back to her program, Elizabeth noted the shaking hands, a sheen of perspiration on the broad forehead, and the age-rippled upper lip. Of course, warm as it was, everyone's face shone to a degree, but did pain bring on more?

The woman beckoned to one of the staff, and a young man with the round pillbox hat of a bellhop strode to the woman's side.

"Ah, I have found just the right escort for you." The concierge broke Elizabeth's line of vision and brought her back to the matter at hand. She shook her head the slightest to dislodge the idea that the woman should go with her, that she needed to see a doctor. *But surely she has a physician of her own,* one side of her mind argued against the invasive thought.

"Oh, thank you."

When the woman turned, the slightest flinch marked her face.

"Mr. Jones will be right with us. Ah, is there something the matter, miss?" He turned to follow her line of vision. "Ah, Mrs. Josephson." He pronounced the *e* long. "A longtime resident of our hotel and quite a benefactress to Chicago."

Elizabeth knew better than to ask such a question, but it escaped before she could trap it. "Has she been injured recently?"

The concierge gave her a startled look. "How did you know?"

Elizabeth felt the heat creeping up her neck. "I . . . I observed her favoring her right side."

The concierge nodded, his mouth pursed,

his eyes studying her. "And you want to go call on Dr. Morganstein? I see."

Elizabeth felt like a bug stared at by three small boys about to poke it with a stick. "My mother is always after me for staring."

"Methinks you have a gift, young lady, a God-given one that should be nurtured." He thought a moment. "Would you like to meet her?"

No, I want to go to the women's hospital. Yes, I want to meet her. "If it wouldn't be any bother."

"None at all on my part. Let me go speak with her."

Elizabeth watched the exchange and nodded when Mrs. Josephson glanced her way.

Ambrose returned. "She will meet with you in the dining room in a few minutes." The right side of Ambrose's mouth twitched in a smile. "Methinks this meeting was destined. I really do."

"Do you go around doing things like this all the time?" Elizabeth crossed her hands over the reticule in her lap.

"And what is it that you are referring to as *this,* miss?"

"You know, fix things."

"Well, miss, I *am* the concierge. That is my job, making things happen for our guests. As to your other errand . . ." He nod-

279

ded again, the light from the chandeliers glinting in his hair, giving him the appearance of wearing a slightly skewed halo.

Mrs. Josephson crossed to the desk, spoke briefly with a man there, then made her way down the hall, which Elizabeth had already discovered led to the necessaries.

She sat back in her chair and gazed around the busy lobby again. Two small children, so closely resembling each other they might have been twins but for the two-or-so-inch difference in height, followed a young woman who most likely was their nanny. The boy dropped behind, lowered the hoop he had been carrying on his shoulder and, with a flick of the wrist, set it rolling across the polished floor. Before the young woman could stop him, he tapped it with his stick and trotted beside it.

"Tony! Anthony Martin, you stop that this instant." The young woman grabbed for him, missed, and tripped on the front of her skirt.

The little girl, clad in a sailor dress matching her brother's suit, giggled into hands splayed across her face, a cloth doll clutched in her arm.

The young woman valiantly tried to right herself but to no avail and ended up in a heap on the floor.

Ambrose snatched up boy and hoop and set both down with a stern look. "Now, Master Anthony, see what you've done."

"I didn't trip her." Hoop back on shoulder and hands on hips, the boy glanced from the red-faced woman who, with the offered hand of a young man fighting to keep a solicitous look on his handsome face, was helped to her feet. Hat half over her ear, she shook her skirt into submission, grabbed the little girl, and headed for the boy like a galleon in full sail.

Elizabeth watched the boy, knowing exactly how he felt. Too many times she'd been in the same predicament.

"I just wanted to see if it would roll as well on a shiny floor as on the grass." He shook his head and allowed her to take his hand, purposely hanging back just enough to cause her to pull him.

Elizabeth glanced up to see Ambrose fighting the smile that twinkled in his eyes. Was that a wink he sent the boy?

Ambrose turned to her. "If you will come with me, miss, I believe Mrs. Josephson is ready for you."

What am I getting myself into now? But Elizabeth swallowed her question and stood to walk with her escort. Her knees had begun to shake.

CHAPTER
TWENTY-ONE:
CHICAGO, ILLINOIS

"Mrs. Josephson, may I present Miss Rogers?"

"You most certainly may, you old reprobate." The sparkling clip in her upswept and rolled hair caught the light and drew Elizabeth's attention. Not a hair out of place, not a wrinkle in her clothing, everything perfect as perfect could be but for the sadness in eyes dimming from age. Was it sadness or pain? Elizabeth took the hand offered and felt the tremor.

"I am glad to meet you, ma'am. Mr. . . ." She stumbled to a stop. She didn't know the man's name. Turning to him, she caught the look that passed between the two, the kind of look that said in spite of the difference in their stations, they were friends of long standing. Friends who would do each other favors and depend on the judgment of the other in social situations.

"I think, Ambrose, you should tell her

your name. I have a feeling . . ." She let her sentence trail off, but her eyes never left Elizabeth's.

Scalpels could probe no deeper than that steady gaze, and scalpels could not penetrate a soul.

Elizabeth felt as though she'd met the sword of the spirit, that sharp, two-edged sword dividing asunder even soul and spirit. She swallowed, or tried to, an impossible task with no saliva left in her mouth.

"I am Ambrose McKnight, head concierge here at the hotel since as far back as I care to admit."

"Th-thank you, Mr. McKnight." Tearing her gaze away would be most rude, and impossible anyway.

"Sit down, please." Whether an order or an invitation, Elizabeth did exactly that before her knees gave way. Meeting the queen of England could be no more harrowing.

"And you will order the tea?"

"Yes, ma'am, of course. Anything particular that would please you?"

"Hmm."

While they carried on a discussion of cream puffs and canapés, Elizabeth took the moments to regain her composure. She could remember no time in her life when meeting someone had affected her this way. What was it about Mrs. Josephson? The direct gaze? The regal manner? Or a combination of everything?

Their discussion finished, the man left with a slight bow, and Mrs. Josephson turned her attention again to Elizabeth.

"Well, my dear, what do you have to say for yourself?" The eyes that peered over her half glasses now twinkled as if a child had come out to play.

Elizabeth could feel herself relax, the tension draining away like water from an unstoppered sink. "I believe I shall tell you two things —"

"Only two things?" Mrs. Josephson quirked an eyebrow. "We will have many hours to share secrets."

Elizabeth swallowed and snatched the glass of water on the table in front of her to drown her dry throat. Instead of pussyfooting around, she made a decision. *I will be as direct as she unless that offends her. Then I shall be more circumspect.* Having comforted herself with the thought, she returned the twinkling smile.

"I asked Mr. McKnight if you had had an injury lately."

"And the second?"

"I am studying to be a doctor, and therefore I watch people, trying to learn more about them through visual diagnoses."

"And your diagnosis in my case brought you to the conclusion that I have had an injury. What made you think injury instead of chronic problem?"

Elizabeth stopped to think and review the picture she had seen. What made her think injury?

"You were refusing to limp."

A chuckle greeted her statement.

"And I think if it were chronic, you would have no longer paid any attention to it." Elizabeth waited for anything more, then added, "In spite of pain."

Mrs. Josephson straightened her shoulders, if that were at all possible. "One must not give in to pain, or it will take over one's life, especially as one ages. I refuse to let something so mundane take over my life."

Elizabeth blinked and blinked again. If only more people had her strength of character. "So is this affliction recent or long term?"

"You were right about a recent injury, but it is only the aggravation of a chronic situation. And there, I refuse to spend more time discussing it. Either way, you would have been correct." She stared over her glasses again. "Now tell me about your dream of becoming a doctor."

"It is not a dream. I *will* become a physician. At the moment I attend St. Olaf College in Northfield, Minnesota, and take my science classes at Carleton in the same town. I live at home, and my father owns and publishes the *Northfield News*." She wasn't sure why she included that, but for some reason it seemed important.

"What year are you?"

"I will be a junior in the fall." Another sip of water. "Oh, and I work for the local doctor."

"And what do you do for him?"

Elizabeth rolled her eyes. *Other than hiring his help and keeping his accounts, you mean?* "I assist in his surgery and accompany him on birthings. You see, I want to take care of women and newborns. There is no need for so many to die." The last was said with a rush of passion.

"Ah. Has there been something in your life that causes such devotion?"

"Yes. My mother died in childbirth. I remember the day clearly even though I was only three."

"So tragic for such a little one." Mrs. Josephson paused with a minute shake of her head. "And you have really assisted at birthings?"

"Yes. Dr. Gaskin wants me to learn quickly and take over his practice."

"Is that what you want?"

Elizabeth shook her head. "No, I want to work in a women's hospital. That is why I was trying to find out the way to Dr. Morganstein's hospital. Mr. McKnight was doing all he could to dissuade me."

"Your tea, ladies." The announcement came from the concierge, and the tray was carried by a white-clad waiter wearing a tall hat.

"Will this be acceptable, madam?"

Mrs. Josephson glanced over the tray and nodded. "You have outdone yourself, Monsieur Claude."

"Mais bien sûr." He pointed to each delicacy, his French fast and fluid.

Elizabeth listened hard and fast, catching some and totally missing others.

"Merci beaucoup." Her smile held a note of propriety now, not the openness with which she'd greeted Elizabeth. And yet, they obviously knew each other, just on a more formal basis.

The chef, as Elizabeth now realized he was, withdrew, and Mr. McKnight fussed over setting things just right until Mrs. Josephson whispered, "Enough, Ambrose, let us enjoy ourselves undisturbed."

"Yes, madam, of course." With that same slight but still appropriate bow, he left, leaving Elizabeth the secret of his wink.

"Do you take milk with your tea?"

"Yes, please, and one cube of sugar." She accepted the fine bone-china cup and fluted saucer, setting it to the right of her place setting as her mother had drilled into her for years. At least she did know proper etiquette, although she'd never dreamed she would be needing it in a situation like this.

"So are you here in Chicago alone?"

"Oh no. My stepmother is upstairs resting from our journey. She will order tea in our rooms, have a leisurely bath, and finally dress for a late supper, most likely to be served in our rooms also." She tried to trap a sigh, but the perceptive woman across from her caught it.

"And you did not want to waste a perfectly wonderful evening in Chicago in rooms with curtains drawn and the need to not disturb a sleeping relative." Mrs. Josephson dropped a cube of sugar into her teacup with the silver tongs. After stirring it, she took a sip and closed her eyes briefly. "Ah, there is nothing like a pot of fine Indian tea shared by an interesting person."

Elizabeth nodded at the compliment. "Merci."

"You do speak French. I wondered."

"Not well enough to keep up with the gentleman, but I can carry on a conversation." Elizabeth took two of the tiny sandwiches off the crystal salver held out to her. "These look lovely."

"Claude is an artist, but with food instead of paints." Mrs. Josephson bit into a sliver of smoked oyster on a tiny cracker. "Delicious. The older one gets, the more one must appreciate every little delight in life. Gratitude is a dying grace, I'm afraid." After touching her mouth with her napkin, she leaned slightly forward. "I have decided to take you to visit Dr. Morganstein. Althea and I grew up together."

Elizabeth could not have been more shocked had the woman confessed to . . . she couldn't think of anything to fit. "Th-thank you. B-but why?"

"My dear, I do not believe in coincidences. Our meeting is God-ordained, like everything else that happens. How else would I be standing at a table where I never pause while you were trying to cajole Ambrose into taking you to see my friend?"

"I just wanted directions."

"Which you would not have been able to follow unless you had lived in Chicago a good long time, and even then you may not

289

have arrived at your destination."

"Even in the daylight?" Elizabeth barely rebuked a shudder.

"Lovely young women alone have been known to disappear without a trace." This last was said simply and without any attempt to frighten, thus making it all the more frightening.

"How can I thank you?"

Mrs. Josephson leaned forward. "By becoming the very best doctor you can be and accomplishing your dream. No amount of money can buy a good enough doctor when needed."

"And what happened to you to come to this place?" Elizabeth knew she was walking a thin line, but confidence begot confidence.

"My only daughter died in childbirth, the babe with her, due to her doctor's inexperience, or at least that's what they called it. I call it criminal negligence, but" — Mrs. Josephson sat back again in her chair — "it shouldn't have happened."

Wishing she dared lay her hand over that of her hostess, Elizabeth threw propriety to the chandeliers and did exactly what she felt was right. The woman clenched her fingers with a fierceness born of a soul-stripping need.

"I dream — I pray — she might have been

just like you."

As if nothing had transpired, Mrs. Josephson released Elizabeth's hand and picked up her teacup, using both hands to control the shaking.

"We will go tomorrow if that is acceptable to your stepmother. And now I suggest that you go ascertain that she is well and enjoy your time together. Chicago and the fair will wait. I will send you a note in the morning."

Knowing that she was dismissed, Elizabeth touched her napkin to her lips, rose, and inclined her head. "Merci beau-coup, madame. Is it possible I could — ?"

"No. I shall be fine."

Elizabeth sketched a curtsy and left the room, positive that her feet never touched the carpet. *What did Mrs. Josephson mean about many hours together? Does she not realize I live in Minnesota?*

CHAPTER TWENTY-TWO

"But I thought we were going to spend this time together." Annabelle Rogers frowned at her daughter, then smoothed out her brow as she looked around the hotel dining room.

"I know, Mother, we are. I'm taking one morning to go meet Dr. Morganstein, that's all. Perhaps you would like to come with us." Elizabeth knew the invitation was only polite. Her mother did not like to view suffering up close.

Annabelle sighed. "I should have known this would happen. You agreed to the trip too readily." Annabelle shook her head, sadness dripping from every pore.

Elizabeth tried warding off the arrows of guilt, but a few penetrated her shield. "After that, I am all yours, Mother. I'll even go shopping with you if that is what you would like." Going shopping meant spending hours looking at and trying on and dithering over choices of shoes and hats and gloves. Her own style was to walk in, point to a fabric, buy it, and get back to more important things. Then call their dressmaker and have her take care of it all. She knew Elizabeth's likes well enough. She could manage with only one fitting and that to check the hem. Therefore, a real shopping trip with her mother was a major concession.

Annabelle sipped from her after-supper tea and pondered her daughter over the rim of the fine bone-china cup. "And you won't grumble?"

"I won't grumble, and I won't sigh."

Annabelle's musical laugh drew attention from the tables immediately around them. Elizabeth joined in, knowing she'd confessed to something she'd sworn for years that she didn't do — sigh, that is. At least not on purpose. Well, sort of.

"Are you ready for dessert?"

"I cannot eat another bite." She didn't mention the delicacies she'd enjoyed with Mrs. Josephson only a couple of hours earlier. Some things were just better left unsaid.

"Fine, then let me show you what I have discovered. Mrs. Andresen and Miss Wahlstein are speaking at a rally in front of the

Women's Building at ten o'clock in the morning on the fourth. I know your father will be ecstatic to hear that, but he can go listen to the mayor or some such at the same time in front of the Agricultural Building. Then we can have a picnic dinner at the park and spend the rest of the day and evening seeing the sights of the fair."

"Don't forget the Ferris Wheel. Father will really enjoy that."

Annabelle rolled her eyes. "Just so the two of you understand, I will not be joining you."

"You'll be missing out. Everyone is riding it and talking about it. Cook will castigate you severely for declining such an adventure."

"Lord save us." Annabelle flashed her engaging smile at the waiter who set the chit by her place. After signing, she waited for him to pull out her chair as she stood. "Thank you. Come, dear, it's not too late to see some of the city from an open carriage. Such a pleasant way to end the day." Elizabeth followed her mother to the concierge's desk, where she made arrangements for a carriage tour. Eagerly the two of them set out.

"Oh, Mother." Elizabeth gazed at a white domed building outlined in incandescent light bulbs that created a magical view of the world's fair.

"Prettiest sight I ever seen." Their driver spoke over his shoulder as he held the horses still so the woman could enjoy the view.

"What is this world coming to that entire buildings can be lit up like that?" Annabelle took her daughter's gloved hand in hers. "I read about Mr. Edison's invention, but to see it displayed like this. One has to see it to believe it."

"You want to go on further?" the driver asked.

"No, thank you, not tonight. Is there always such a crush of people?"

"Thousands go through every day. Prettier lakes and parks you never did see, let alone the buildings and the statues and fountains and such. People are saying a week here is like attending a university, you can learn so much. Chicago done outdid herself."

Later as they drove back to the hotel, Elizabeth closed her eyes to keep the fairyland imprinted on her mind.

Elizabeth didn't receive a note from Mrs. Josephson the next morning, so she accompanied her mother as promised on a shopping trip. Her father joined them on July Fourth as planned, and since Elizabeth still hadn't heard from Mrs. Josephson, they all went to the world's fair. The Ferris Wheel was everything people said it was. It was a little crowded with sixty people in each box, but that was the only thorn of the day. The view from that height laid out the Midway Plaisance outside the gates of the Exposition, the Exposition grounds with all the lakes and bridges, and the city — all like a magical carpet that they swooped up from and back down to. The two suffragette speakers drew huzzahs from the crowd, and her father even stayed to listen, taking notes for a future newspaper article. He took so many notes during his almost three days at the fair that he had to buy another notebook. She saw her mother and father laughing together as they rarely did at home, and suddenly they weren't old beyond their time but rather two fine-looking people who appeared urbane enough to be from any big city and of far more wealth than they really were. Bands played, orators expounded, flags flew from posts and walls, but the fireworks reflecting in lakes and ponds drew more oohs and ahs than anything else. They talked to each other on the newfangled telephones, saw the Buffalo Bill Wild West

Show outside the Exposition grounds, and came back to the hotel worn out but still laughing.

When her father went home, Elizabeth began to lose hope that she would get to meet with Dr. Morganstein.

"Perhaps I should just pay a cabby to take me to the hospital and drop me off at the front door. Surely nothing could happen in broad daylight." Speaking to the young woman in the mirror who nodded in a most encouraging manner made it all sound eminently sensible.

Until her mother asked where she was going, and she could not lie.

"I think not." The queen of England could not have spoken more imperiously.

"But, Mother, I —" Elizabeth closed the door and leaned against it. "What do you suggest?"

"Wait."

"But surely Mrs. Josephson has forgotten or . . ."

"Women like her do *not* forget. Rest assured that she has been unable to arrange your visit. You have no idea what extenuating circumstances there may be."

"I know." The sigh came clear from the soles of her slippers. "But we leave so soon."

"I am aware of that." Annabelle turned

from where she was folding garments and packing used things in their trunk. "I should have allowed for more room. I forget how many things would come home with us from shopping in Chicago."

"One shopping trip would have been sufficient."

"Not the three?" Annabelle arched an eyebrow and returned to her task.

"I think I shall go down and ask Mr. McKnight —"

"I think not."

Elizabeth closed her eyes and clenched her teeth. Just because she'd given in earlier did not mean she'd given up. *Father God, please, you know the main reason I wanted to come here was to visit Mrs. Morganstein's hospital.*

"Shall I ring for dinner to be served up here, or would you rather go down?"

"Either. It makes no difference to me."

A discreet knock on the door that echoed in the middle of her back made Elizabeth start. She turned to open the door, her heart leaping with hope.

A uniformed young man offered her an envelope on a silver tray.

"Thank you." Closing the door, she made sure the envelope was addressed to her and slid a fingernail under the flap to lift it open.

She read the precise handwriting that first apologized for the delay and then invited her to accompany Mrs. Josephson to the Alfred Morganstein Hospital for Women at two o'clock that afternoon. They would leave from the main entrance to the hotel, and her mother was invited along if she so desired.

Elizabeth took a deep breath to calm her racing heart and read the missive aloud.

"Send her a message back with my regrets but thank her in my name and say I have too much to accomplish yet to join you." Annabelle held up a hat she had purchased at a special millinery shop. "I do hope this looks good with that watered silk, or I shall have to have a new frock made to go with the hat."

"Yes, Mother." Elizabeth penned the note on hotel stationery and rang for the young man to deliver it. When their noon meal was delivered a few minutes later, she had a hard time concentrating enough to finish hers. Half an hour in advance of the appropriate time, she pinned her hat in place, unfurled her parasol to make sure it worked, furled it again, checked her reticule, and made a final trip to the necessary.

"Elizabeth Marie Rogers, stop fidgeting. You are driving me mad."

"I'm not . . ." Elizabeth had the grace to stop. She crossed to the window and stood watching the people rushing by three floors below. A carriage pulled by a matched team of bay horses arrived under the portico.

I wonder if those — no, surely not. People living in a hotel wouldn't keep horses and a carriage like that. Not when other conveyances were so available.

Elizabeth crossed to drop a kiss on her mother's cheek. "I'm not sure when I shall return. Don't wait tea for me."

"I won't." Annabelle turned, hands on hips. "Do you think I should order another trunk?"

Elizabeth slipped out the door before an answer would be required.

"And have you enjoyed your visit to Chicago?" Mrs. Josephson asked when they were settled in the carriage Elizabeth had seen brought round.

"Most certainly. I believe my mother would stay another week if my father and I would agree to it."

"And why would you not agree?"

"Dr. Gaskin needs me and so does my father. I help run the offices for both of them. I'm concerned about my doctor. He is having a hard time recovering from the loss of his wife."

"I'm sorry to hear that."

"He believes I will take over his practice when I finish medical school."

"I hear a doubt in your voice."

Elizabeth nodded. How could she be so honest with this woman? It was as if she peered right into her soul. She felt as though she'd known her for years, not just a matter of days.

"If I remain in Northfield, my mother will continue to parade eligible young men before me and expect me to live at home until I marry. Since I believe I will be married to being a doctor, I do not plan on matrimony."

"Ah, then you will miss out on some of the greatest joys of life. Perhaps your mother sees where you're headed and does not want that for you."

"But how can I manage both and do my best at either?"

"Why do you try to live the future now and not let the day's own troubles be sufficient for the day? If you believe God is sovereign, which I think you do, can you not trust Him with your future?"

Elizabeth looked up to see such compassion on the face of the older woman that she caught her breath. "Why . . . why are you doing this for me?"

"Because I feel God has given me a second chance in you."

The confusion on her face must have been evident, for Mrs. Josephson patted her hand. "Someday I will tell you a long story, but for now let us go visit with my friend. She is looking forward to meeting you."

"And I her. I cannot begin to tell you how grateful I am for this opportunity."

"Who knows what God has in mind."

The carriage stopped in front of a brick building with the door and frame painted white. Red geraniums filled the window boxes as well as two urns on either side of the door. The building glowed like a rosebush in the middle of a thorn field. The tenement buildings lining both sides of the street burgeoned with despair, their broken windows leaking the miasma of hopelessness. Flies rose in a blue cloud from the body of a cat lying in the gutter. Tin cans and other garbage were piled by a broken tree trunk, where once a bit of green had lived. A baby squalled, shut off by the sound of a slap and a curse.

Hand in hand two little girls watched the open carriage with round eyes.

Elizabeth wanted to take them back to the hotel for a bath and a good meal, buy them each a dress and a doll, and never bring them back to such filth.

"Come." Mrs. Josephson took her arm, and they mounted the steps to enter a room filled with women and children like the two outside. Crying babies, children too tired to cry, and mothers with eyes as vacant as the derelict windows on the street outside were everywhere. Elizabeth stopped to take it all in.

"Come," Mrs. Josephson said again and led her down the hall. Walls painted white, floor waxed to a shine, gas fixtures lighting the way, windows in the rooms off the hall with glass that sparkled in the sun — this oasis of cleanliness and order resided in a desert of degradation.

They stopped in front of a polished oak door and knocked.

"Come in."

"We have come." Mrs. Josephson opened the door and motioned Elizabeth to go before her. "I have brought her to you, as I promised. Dr. Morganstein, may I present Miss Elizabeth Rogers of Northfield, Minnesota, which is not far from Minneapolis."

"Thank you, dear Issy." Hand extended, a six-foot-tall woman with pince-nez on the end of an extraordinary nose came around the desk to grasp Elizabeth's hand. Her gray hair in a haphazard bun with a pencil stuck in it and her stethoscope looped in the pocket of her all-encompassing white apron, Dr. Morganstein would have intimidated a big man, let alone a young college student — until Elizabeth looked into her eyes. If God lived on earth, His eyes would be like the doctor's, Elizabeth decided. Or rather this woman had eyes like Jesus surely had. Dark, fringed with long lashes, brows thick but quick to arch, and a gaze so full of love that Elizabeth felt her throat tighten. *Oh, God, please let me work with this woman.* The prayer went heavenward even as her hand met the doctor's.

Dr. Morganstein covered Elizabeth's hand with her other and, nodding, looked deep into her eyes. "Yes, yes."

The slight sibilance on the *s* made Elizabeth think English was not this woman's native tongue.

"Sit down, my dears, please sit. I have half an hour before I must be in surgery, and I want to know all about you."

"Know about me?" Elizabeth's voice squeaked on the last word.

"Yes, and then I shall have my head nurse, Mrs. Korsheski, show you around. I was hoping for more time together, but this case that came in is close to an emergency."

At the end of the half hour Elizabeth felt as if she'd been interrogated rather than interviewed, but in a pleasing way.

"She'll do." Dr. Morganstein tapped her knuckles on a stack of papers on her chart-buried desk and rose to leave the room. "Thank you, dear Issy, for finding her for us."

"Th-thank you for the time." Elizabeth stood and shook the doctor's hand again. How she would love to turn that desk into the same kind of order she had done for Dr. Gaskin and for her father. Perhaps she could work here next summer. The thought darted through like a swallow on a bug hunt.

The tour, led by a tiny human dynamo, led her upstairs and down, through wards and nurseries, surgeries and storage. By the time she returned to Mrs. Josephson, who had remained in the doctor's office bringing some order to the chaotic desk, Elizabeth felt as though she'd been racing. She thanked her guide, who rushed off when someone called her, and turned to Mrs. Josephson, shaking her head. "I cannot believe this place."

"It is amazing, is it not, and what you don't realize is how much is accomplished here with minimal funds. Althea is a wonder. That is for sure. Come now, we will have tea at the hotel. If your mother would like to join us . . ."

Elizabeth took a deep breath. "Thank you beyond words. I will ask her if she would like to."

Looking back a few days later as the train chugged westward, Elizabeth thought the visit to the hospital to be far beyond her wildest hopes. It was more like a turning point in her life, if that were possible. While she'd gone to Chicago hoping to meet the doctor, she was returning home with two new friends, and from what she could gather, friends in high places.

Would getting into medical school really be as easy as Mrs. Josephson had said?

CHAPTER
TWENTY-THREE:
BLESSING, NORTH
DAKOTA
AUGUST 1893

"Manda, I'll be leaving in the mornin'," said Zeb MacCallister, leaning against the fence.

"I want to come along." Manda kept her gaze on the horse she had trotting around the corral on the end of a long light rope. She clucked and flicked the rope to signal an increase in speed.

"No. I'm sorry, but Montana is no place for a young woman."

"You say your ranch is so beautiful. Who keeps your ranch house for you, cooks and cleans while you do the chores?"

"No one. My ranch house, as you call it, is nothing more than a log shack. I have a half-breed Sioux who helps me with the horses. Besides, we're not at the homestead much. We travel with the herd to find grazin'."

Manda tugged on the rope, and the horse turned willingly toward her. "The ones you brought weren't even broken, least not all of them. I could do that for you there, well as here." She kept her concentration on the horse, her body loose but for chewing on her lower lip.

Zeb leaned his chin on his arms crossed on the top rail of the corral. "I know you could. But what about Deborah? She'd be heartbroken if you left. She's had too many people leave her already."

"She'd understand. She has Thomas and Johnny now. She likes being the big sister." She looked to the man she'd learned to call Pa. "I don't belong here. She does."

"What do you mean? You . . ." He stopped when she gestured to her pants and boots. "Skirts, pants, has nothin' to do with who you are."

Manda leveled him a look that clearly said she believed otherwise.

"I live a rough life."

"And our dugout wasn't?"

"Manda, Zeb, breakfast." Mary Martha waved to them from the long front porch of the house. While others in the valley had built two-story houses, this one hugged the ground, growing out sideways as they needed more room. The porch that used to front the entire house was now bracketed by rooms at either end like arms wide open in welcome.

"Be right there." Manda took the rope under the horse's chin and rubbed his ears. "Good horse." She untied the knot and let the gelding go, then coiled her rope and left it hanging on a corral post before she and Zeb strode on up to the house.

As soon as they washed up and sat down at the table, Deborah filled her father's cup with coffee. "You want some?" she asked Manda, then tongue between her compressed lips, she carefully poured that one too.

"Thank you very kindly," Zeb said with a smile. "You're growin' up faster than pokeweed."

"What's pokeweed?" Deborah took the chair beside him.

"Down south where I come from, pokeweed is one of the first spring greens. Grows so fast that if you blink, it's taller'n you." He looked up to see Manda studying his face. "We called it poke, is all."

"I'm growing fast as pokeweed too." Johnny pointed at his bare chest, earning a smile from his uncle.

"Pa-a-a." But Deborah looked at him out of the corner of her eye, as if not sure if he was teasing.

Manda snorted. "Pigweed grows just as fast." *I'm going to Montana with you or trailing*

309

behind you, but I'm going.

Mary Martha set a platter of pancakes in the center of the table. "Let's have grace. Manda, would you please?"

Manda swallowed a huff. "Dear Lord, bless this food and us. Amen."

"My, that was short and sweet." Mary Martha set a platter of sliced ham on Zeb's right. "Please start the passin'." When she returned with another platter of fried eggs all sunny-side up, she took her seat with a sigh. "I thought that cloud cover from last night might cool us off, but don't reckon it will."

"How long since it rained?" Zeb dished up an egg for Thomas sitting on a box on a chair to his left.

"First of May. Drought was real bad for two years before last. How was it in Montana?"

"Dry, but we had some rain."

Manda filled her plate and refilled her mouth as fast as she could chew and swallow. The conversation swirled around her, but all she could think was that he'd turned her down. Her pa didn't want her along. All this time she'd been planning and dreaming of moving to Montana. Even thought about just heading west to see if she could find him. Some father. If he hadn't wanted them, why'd he go and adopt them both?

But she knew the answer as well as she knew her horses. Everything had changed when Katy died. She raised her eyes to glare at the man across from her who laughed with Deborah like he had all of a lifetime to spend with them. Instead, he was leaving.

As if feeling Manda's anger, he looked up, puzzlement wrinkling his forehead.

She stared down at her now empty plate. "May I be excused, please?"

"Of course." Mary Martha looked from Manda to Zeb and back again, her mouth pursing as her head nodded slightly.

"Ma?" Thomas held up his empty plate. "More?"

In the break of attention, Manda slipped from the table and out the door more quietly than any wild thing. Once outside, she dogtrotted to the small pasture where her horse, Cheyenne, grazed. She whistled, a three-tone whistle she used only for Cheyenne. The filly trotted over to the fence and blew in Manda's face, a soft whuffle that combined both nicker and snort. Manda slipped her latigo around the bright sorrel neck and flipped a loop over the animal's nose. Leading her out of the gate, Manda pulled the bars back in place and swung aboard without even grasping the mane. She kept the high-stepping horse to a jog until they were far enough from the house that they couldn't be heard, then she leaned forward and tightened her legs. The filly leveled out in a mane-whipping gallop, her hooves staccato against the hard dirt road.

Manda rode south to bypass the Bjorklund farms, then north along the river. Baptiste had said he would be fishing today since Metiz wanted to dry fish for the winter. Knowing where most of his favorite fishing holes were, she only slowed to make sure he wasn't sitting on the bank with a pole or setting his trotlines. When she saw him, she dismounted and tied the filly to a willow branch.

"You're in a hurry." He turned to watch her approach, reading her face as only he knew how. "What's wrong?"

Manda plunked down beside him. "Zeb is leaving in the morning."

"Alone?"

She nodded. "I tried to talk him into taking me along, but he said no."

Baptiste watched a leaf drift by on a slow swirl. "You think Montana is better than here?"

"I think in Montana we could be together." There, she'd said it — the words that had been drumming at her waking and sleeping. She knew he'd never be more than her friend if they stayed here. But Montana . . .

Baptiste nodded.

Manda pulled a stem of grass and nibbled on the tender end. At least here along the riverbank grass still grew.

"I would have to leave Grand-mère."

What could she say? The truth of it could not be argued.

"We cannot go without marriage."

Manda sent him a sideways glance. *And who would marry us?* He'd said the word. Marry. Her insides turned to mush, mush cooking on a slow stove. The warmth spread to her fingertips. He really had been thinking some of the same things as she.

Manda settled back on her elbows, the woods' duff an aromatic cushion. Her horse stamped, tail swatting the flies. A black fly settled on her arm and bit. No wonder horses and cows swished at flies. She smacked her arm so fast the fly had no chance. She flicked it off her skin with one finger and returned to studying the river.

"Flies make good bait."

"Sorry."

He turned and his shoulder brushed hers. Shocks ran clear to her toes. "I want to go

313

to Montana, but I must talk with Grand-mère first."

"She will tell you to go."

"I know." His sigh matched her own.

"Ingeborg and Haakan will take care of her."

"Does she let anyone take care of her?" He shook his head, his long braid dividing his back. "Not even me."

The urge to touch his braid, his back, brought Manda's hand up in the air, only to drop to her thigh again — unrequited.

Baptiste returned to his fishing, jerking the rod when the tip twitched. A fat perch flew through the air and landed splat behind them. Hands grasping the string, he pulled the flopping fish toward him.

Manda watched his hands. Long fingers, sinews taut on the backs, sunbaked to a deep copper. Deftly he removed the hook from the fish's lip, threaded a forked stick through gill and mouth, and poked it like the others back in the river mud. This way the fish would stay cool in the water. With a worm from the oldest part of the manure pile at the back of the Bjorklund barn wrapped back on the hook, he tossed the string, weighted by a small rock, out into the current.

"Not biting much today?" His hands, how

would they feel on hers? Her face grew hot at the thought.

"Should have set trotlines instead."

With mosquitoes zinging around their heads for background music, Manda returned to her propped-elbow position. She needed to get home. They'd be missing her and wondering where she went. Not that her taking off was an unusual occurrence. She rode the horses she trained for miles, getting them used to all kinds of terrain until they became fluid in obeying her commands. The horses she trained to harness, she drove instead of riding. Anyone who bought a horse from Manda MacCallister knew the animal would be dependable.

She slapped a mosquito and wiped away the spot of blood. Had he sucked hers and Baptiste's? The thought of their blood mingling, even inside a mosquito, re-ignited the warmth within. "I need to be going."

Baptiste leaned forward and jerked the line of fish from the river. He handed her the stick. "Tell your Ma this is from me."

Manda nodded. She knew he would catch more for Metiz, but the generosity of this man always caught her unawares. She who tended to hoard was learning through him to give. She stood, the desire to touch him making her shake.

"I'll come by tonight."

"All right." She trailed her hand along his shoulder. He bent his head to trap it with his cheek. A moment only, but one her fingers, let alone her heart, would always remember.

"Good thing you knew the way home," she murmured to the filly as she slid off at the corral gate. Had they galloped? Loped? Her horse wasn't blowing, so they must have taken it easy. How could she have been so lost in her head that she'd not paid attention? She propped the fish stick against the corral post, slid back the bars, and led her horse into the field bordering the corral. She wouldn't be needing her again today. She had others to work.

"Manda, where did you go? Pa has been looking for you." Deborah came walking toward her as she neared the house.

"Baptiste sent us fish for supper." She hoisted the stick for Deborah to see, as if that had been the point of the ride.

"You could've taken me to play with Astrid." Deborah plunked herself down on the steps to the porch.

"I didn't go see Astrid."

"I know. You went to see Baptiste."

Manda sat down beside her sister. Deborah laid her cheek on her calico-clad knees, facing away.

"I wasn't gone that long."

"Yes, you were. I looked all over for you, but then when I saw Cheyenne was gone, I knew."

"Sorry. I should have told you, but I was in a hurry."

"You're going to Montana, ain't you?"

"Don't say ain't." Manda jiggled the fish stick. "I got to get these in water. What did you want?"

"Nothin'."

Manda felt like groaning. Instead, she laid a hand on her sister's head. "Look at me." When Deborah turned tear-filled blue eyes her direction, Manda fought a lump in her throat. How could she leave this little sister, the only true relation she had in the whole world? And yet she couldn't take her along either. "Why are you crying?"

"I ain't." Deborah used her skirt hem to wipe her eyes. "Got smoke in my eyes. That's all."

"Don't say ain't." Manda sighed and sat up straight, her hands dangling between her knees. If she told anyone what she was thinking, they'd tell her no. If she didn't tell them, she was being a cheat. Nothing she hated worse than a liar and a cheat. Lying came by not telling, much as by telling. She thought back to when their pa never returned from getting supplies. One moment she feared he'd left them, the next she knew he hadn't. Something had happened to him.

She shook her head and stood. "I got to take care of the fish. You want to help me or keep on playing guessing games?"

Deborah peeked up. "Can I scale 'em?"

"Sure, why not?" Manda tugged on her sister's braid instead of hugging her close as she wanted to.

"You all right?" Mary Martha looked up from the bread she was kneading as the girls came into the kitchen. She swiped a wisp of hair from her eyes with the back of her hand, leaving a floury trail on her forehead.

Manda held up the fish. "Baptiste sent us these."

"Oh, fish for supper. How nice." Mary Martha studied Manda before returning to her dough. "Anytime you figure on needing to talk, I'm here."

"Yes'm. I know."

"I can't just cut and run. I can't sneak out and not tell anyone. I just can't." Manda used the horse she was training for a sounding board. The gelding flicked his ears and kept to the even lope she demanded. They

318

circled back toward the barn, but when he tried to pick up speed, she tightened the reins. Even pace, minding the rider, that's all she demanded from the horses. And got.

She dismounted at the gate and, unlacing the cinch strap, pulled the saddle off with both hands. Turning, she slipped the head-stall over the horse's ears and let him loose. This was the last one of the day.

"We have buyers comin' tomorrow."

She jerked around at the sound of Zeb's voice. "Why'd you sneak up on a body like that? Scared me half to death."

"Sorry, I thought you saw me comin'." Zeb slipped through the bars and picked up the saddle, then slung it up onto the top rail. "I'll give them all a good brushin' in the mornin'. Should get top dollar."

"Not with the drought here. Be lucky to get half."

"You watch. Got some fellows comin' up from Grand Forks. They want two teams and some riding horses."

"Umm." Manda looped the braided reins over her arm. "You best ask for gold. Paper money might not be good in Montana."

"It's not the end of the world, you know. It became a state in '89, just like North Dakota."

"But you're still homesteading."

319

"Manda, you can still homestead in western North Dakota, though it's nothing like this rich valley."

"If it's so rich, why don't you stay here?"

"I can't."

She watched him shaking his head, shoulders curving in as if fending off a blow.

"We — Deborah and me and all the others — loved her too, and we had to stay here." The words tripped over each other in their haste to be heard.

"You're too young to understand. That's all." He spun away and headed for the far corral.

"That's right. Run away. Runnin's always easier than stayin'." Her mutter carried no farther than the fence. Hoisting her saddle off the rail, she took it into the barn to hang on its tree. *Now he'll probably never speak to me again. Manda MacCallister, when your mouth gets to goin', you sure don't have no way of stoppin' it.*

CHAPTER
TWENTY-FOUR

At the knock on the door Manda glanced up from the rawhide she was braiding. Who could it be this late in the evening?

"You want to get that?" Mary Martha called from the kitchen.

"All right." Manda untangled herself from the lengths of latigo and went to the door. "Baptiste!"

"May we come in?" At his *we* she realized Thorliff was with him.

"Ah . . . a'course." *Ma would wonder where my manners went. But he's never come to the door like this before. I usually just go out my window when he whistles.* Her thoughts must have registered on her face because Baptiste motioned to the door again.

"Sorry." Manda held the door open for them to enter. "Is . . . is anything wrong?" *Someone hurt? What? Tell me what?*

"Is Pastor here?"

"In the other room."

Thorliff shifted from one foot to the other.

Something was wrong, Manda knew for certain. Both of them acted like cats on a hot stove. None of the normal laughing and funny pokes.

"Could you get him please?" Now it was Thorliff sounding all polite.

"What's wrong?" Manda kept her voice low.

Baptiste shook his head so slightly she'd have missed it if she hadn't been studying him.

"Who was it?" Mary Martha followed her bulging apron into the room. "Why, Baptiste, Thorliff, how good to see you. Is something wrong?"

"No, ma'am. I — we'd like to speak with Pastor, and Mr. MacCallister too, if you don't mind."

"Of course. Manda, your pa is out to the barn. John is . . ." She started to leave, then turned back, gesturing toward the sofa and chairs. "Please, make yourselves to home."

"What is going on?" The words came out hissed because Manda couldn't get her teeth to unclench.

"Just wait." Baptiste's voice wore the tone of command he used when they were out hunting and he'd seen the quarry long before she had.

Manda crossed to the chair where she had all her supplies and gathered up the yards of rawhide strips and the already braided latigo. "I was trying to get a new lariat done for Pa before he leaves in the mornin'. Thought he could use an extra."

Both young men nodded.

Talk to me! What in tarnation is going on?

"Good evening. Sorry, I didn't hear you come in." John Solberg gestured toward the chairs. "Sit down. The coffee will be hot in a few minutes, or would you rather have something cold?" Pastor Solberg's entire face smiled.

"Neither right now, sir." Baptiste glanced from the pastor to Manda. "Please go get your pa."

"Well, of all the —" While Manda rarely flounced, this time she managed with aplomb. The screen door closed behind her with a satisfactory clap. She leaped off the porch and charged down to the barn, where Zeb was checking the shoes on his horse and the two pack animals.

"They want you up to the house."

He released the front hoof and straightened. "Who?"

"Thorliff and Baptiste." She knew she sounded abrupt even for her, but by now she wanted to skin her two best friends. Flay them head to foot.

"Okay, but . . ." At her shrug, he headed for the house, then stopped. "Are you coming?"

"Don't know why. No one ever tells me nothin'."

"Quit pouting and come on along. Perhaps we can have some more of that raspberry swizzle you made. It was right good."

"We drank it all."

Zeb sighed. "It's not like you couldn't make more."

Manda left off digging a hole to China with her boot toe and, at the crooking of his finger, walked beside him to the friendly lit windows and open door.

"This house sure does cast a welcome, don't it?"

Then why don't you stay here? But this time she kept her words to herself. At least he was speaking to her again.

Zeb paused just inside the door. "Good evenin'. This looks to be a mighty important meetin'."

"Yes, sir." Thorliff nodded. Baptiste did the same.

Pastor Solberg motioned toward a chair. "Have a seat. Manda, you want to help your ma get the refreshments ready?"

No, I'd far rather stay here and find out

what's going on. But with only the slightest flaring of her nostrils, she did as requested. Until she got around the door. She held her breath so she could hear better. When Mary Martha frowned at her, Manda shook her head. *Please don't make me come help.*

"So, boys, what can we do for you?" Pastor Solberg's voice could be easily heard.

"Not for me, Pastor, but for Baptiste here." Thorliff was speaking.

"You know, Mr. MacCallister, that Manda wants to go to Montana with you." Baptiste could be heard easily, his voice carrying a new tone of assurance that she'd not heard before.

"Yes, I know that. I told her no." Zeb sounded puzzled.

Puzzled didn't begin to cover what Manda felt. But at the same time a thrill of pride for Baptiste made her shiver.

"Well . . ."

A slight pause. Manda wet her lips.

"Manda and I would like to be married and go with you, sir." The words came in a rush.

Manda felt as if she'd just been poleaxed. She leaned against the wall, fighting to regain her breath.

The silence in the other room thundered in her ears.

"I see." Pastor Solberg finally said. "You love Manda, son?"

"Always have — since the day Thorliff drug her to school."

Manda shivered again, this time with the thrill of his words. He'd never said "I love you" to her. *He loves me. He really does.* She clasped both hands over her heart. Surely they could hear it thundering. She turned at the hand on her shoulder to see Mary Martha smiling at her. Manda went into her ma's arms like a lost child coming home.

"You know that some folks around here wouldn't take kindly to this union," they heard from the other room.

"I know. But no one will care in Montana. If we can't go with you, Zeb, we will go on our own. Maybe even on to Wyoming. I can provide for her. You know that."

And I have my hundred dollars. Surely that would go some to buy land or to pay off a homestead.

Mary Martha stroked her daughter's hair. Manda felt a drop of moisture on her hand and took her ma's hand in her own. "Don't cry," she whispered. "Please don't cry."

Mary Martha sniffed. "I'm trying not to, but you know tears are for joy too."

Manda turned back to listening.

"Will you marry us?"

Manda could feel the looks going between Zeb and the pastor.

"You'd best ask her pa first, son."

"Mr. MacCallister, could I please marry Manda? We do want your blessing."

Manda could hear Zeb's sigh. She leaned into her ma's arms.

"Baptiste, I reckon I have no trouble with tellin' you yes. Are you sure that is what Manda wants?"

"Yes, but I knew I had to ask you first."

Of course that's what I want. I been waitin' forever. Manda gripped Mary Martha's hand and clenched her bottom lip between her teeth.

"Then, if you all agree, I must say that I will be happy to perform this marriage. You best go ask your intended, but I have a feeling she and my wife are hiding right behind that door and didn't miss a thing."

Manda and Mary Martha looked at each other, unable to stopper the giggles that burst forth like the bubbles on apple cider kept a mite too long.

"You go on out back with that man of yours, and I'll serve the others." Mary Martha gave the girl a push.

Her face feeling as if she'd been toasting in front of a roaring fire, Manda accepted the hand Baptiste held out to her, and together they walked past the others and let the screen door slam behind them.

Mary Martha picked up the tray and carried the glasses of raspberry swizzle, along with cookies, into the other room.

Manda and Baptiste sank down on the rear porch that pretty much matched the front one. He took her shaking hands in his and leaned forward.

"Do you want to marry me, Manda?"

"You know I do. We been over that already. What made you change your mind?"

"Thorliff and Grand-mère. They both said I was two kinds of fool to let you get away." His eyes glimmered like sunstruck obsidian.

Manda waited for words she'd been longing to hear. "Well?"

"Well what?"

"Ain't you got something else to say to me?"

Baptiste wrinkled his forehead. "You're going to marry me." He thought. "When?"

She shook her head. For as smart as he was, he sure needed leading. "You told Pastor and Pa that you loved me. Don't you s'pose you oughta tell me?"

Laughter burst from Baptiste as though she'd just told a world-class joke.

Manda tried to withdraw her hands, but

he only clenched them more firmly.

"Not funny."

"Yes, it is. All right. Manda MacCallister, I love you. There now, how's that?" He waited. "Well?"

"Well, what now?"

"Don't you have to say the same?"

"Oh." Manda swallowed a snicker. She leaned her head into his shoulder. "I love you, Baptiste LeCrue, now and always."

"Now that's taken care of, we need to go ask your pa again if we can go with him. And if he would give us a couple of days to get married and get ready."

"I can be ready in an hour or so."

"Don't you want to say good-bye to people here?"

Yes, but if they make remarks about you, I might have to bust 'em one. "Not too many."

"Ah." He leaned forward and kissed her forehead first, then her nose, and finally her mouth.

"Hmm," Manda whispered when he pulled back. "I like that."

"Me too." He stood and pulled her up with him. "Come on, squirt, let's get on with this."

"Name's Manda." She playfully punched him on the shoulder. "You big brave."

She wanted to hold a finger to her lips to

keep the warmth of the kiss in place but followed him back into the kitchen instead.

"We are gathered here in the presence of God and this company to celebrate the marriage of Baptiste LeCrue and Manda Norton MacCallister." Pastor John Solberg's strong voice rang clear and true.

Manda's knees were shaking so bad she thought everyone clear to Grand Forks could hear them rattle. No matter how many times she tried to swallow, her mouth only dried up more. If she hadn't been hanging on to Baptiste's arm, she knew for certain she would've melted down into a puddle right in front of the altar. But when he covered her hand with his, strength flowed back into her backbone, and she straightened right up.

Behind her feet shuffled and a throat was cleared. Not that there were very many people in attendance. She hadn't wanted any more. Just the Bjorklunds and Metiz. Thorliff was standing up for Baptiste, and Deborah, who hadn't quit crying since they told her the news, stood beside her.

"Marriage is a holy institution."

Thank you, God, we didn't just run off like I wanted. But this dress sure itches. I don't never want to wear anything starched again.

She glanced down at the yellow lawn skirt. She'd never worn anything so pretty in all her life. *Maybe if it just wasn't starched . . .*

Baptiste squeezed her hand, and his smile set her stomach to fluttering. Did he go from boy to man overnight, or did she miss out on something?

Where had her mind gone? Surely she ought to be paying attention. After all, this was her wedding day. The thought made her shiver. Was she ready for this?

The amen drew her back from her rolling thoughts. She glanced up to see Pastor Solberg gazing at her and then at Baptiste. *Was his mind going like hers? Was he wishing he could run to the river or ride off on a horse?*

Pastor's smile held all the reassurance of the noonday sun. He turned to Baptiste. "Do you, Baptiste LeCrue, take this woman to be your wedded wife?"

Baptiste's "I do" rang with total conviction.

She drowned in the look he gave her. With each word either of them spoke, she grew more certain. This surely was the way life was supposed to be. *God, you know I don't ask for much. I told you once that if you'd not bother me, I'd leave you alone too. If you remember, could you now forget I said that? If it would be all right, that is. I'm sorry for doubt-*

ing you, and I sure have enough to be grateful for now. Thank you for Baptiste and . . . and this. Her amen that sang with the others carried all the commitment she could surrender.

When Baptiste turned her toward him to kiss her, her neck and face burned like a prairie fire blown by a hard west wind.

But the kiss — ah, the meeting of lips, hearts, and souls — lasted an eternity, but the seconds were far too short.

She laid her hand on her chest to suck in enough breath to live. The look she gave Baptiste made chuckles pass over the gathering that sounded like a mother hen tucking her chicks under her for the night.

Baptiste pulled her hand through the crook of his arm, and they walked down the church aisle to the music of Uncle Olaf's guitar.

"You're crying." Baptiste touched her cheek.

"No, I ain't." Manda sniffed but didn't dare wipe her eyes. "It was just so pretty and all." A sigh caught her unaware.

"What?"

"Leaving is going to be far harder than I thought."

"Manda, you look so pretty." Deborah put both arms around her sister's waist. The "I don't want you to go" was muffled in the ruffles down the front of Manda's dress, loaned to her by Anji.

Manda wrapped her arms around Deborah's shaking shoulders. "I know. But I will come back to visit, and when you get bigger, you can come to Montana too."

"I already am bigger," Deborah said, wiping her eyes.

Manda kept one arm around Deborah and turned toward Pastor Solberg, who was trying to get everyone's attention.

"Folks, Haakan and Ingeborg have invited us all to their house for dinner, so I suggest we get in the wagons and head right on over." Pastor Solberg made shooing motions with his hands to the laughter of all.

Manda felt she'd never been hugged so many times in her life by the time the tables were cleared again. Everyone seemed to be standing around waiting for something. She and Baptiste looked at each other, both wondering the same.

When a wagon turned into the lane, Andrew threw his hat in the air. "Here it comes."

"What comes?" Manda looked to her father, who appeared as confused as she. It was his two packhorses pulling a prairie schooner with white canvas stretched over hoops to create their new home.

"Well, I'll be a . . ." Zeb took off his hat and smoothed back his hair before settling the flat-brimmed hat back in place with both hands. "I was glad to say you could come along, but I didn't expect a wagon."

"Something to get used to, all right, but you know women. When they get a bee in their bonnet, you never can tell what's going to happen." Haakan pushed back his hat with one finger.

"This is all we could manage in such a short time." Ingeborg came to stand beside Manda and Baptiste.

"But . . . but, I thought . . . I mean Pa was all loaded. What more did we need?"

"There are blankets and a quilt in the trunk, pots and pans, flour, beans, and other basic supplies. I fixed you a medicine kit. Everyone donated what they could."

Metiz stood on the other side of Baptiste. "Furs and skins too. I put in a knife for each of you."

"There's a cutting from that rosebush by the porch. It should root easily." Ingeborg gave Manda another quick hug. "We weren't sure if you were going to have your own house or live with Zeb, but either way, I'm sure you'll have use for all these things."

"We can never say enough thanks." Baptiste turned to Thorliff. "You knew?"

"Ja. Spent half the night helping Hjelmer set the hoops. That canvas has been patched some, but it should keep things dry for you."

"I'm so sorry we didn't have time to make a wedding ring quilt for you like we have the others." Ingeborg shook her head. "But you can pick it up when you bring the horses back next summer."

"Sure." *How do I thank you for all of this?*

"We thought you and Baptiste might like to start out in the wagon this afternoon. Zeb will catch up with you tomorrow."

"That would be good." Baptiste let out a breath and nodded.

"All your things are packed." Mary Martha came to give Manda another hug and to peel Deborah away from her sister's side.

As Baptiste helped Manda up over the wagon wheel, ignoring her snort, he whispered something in her ear.

She nearly choked, sat herself on the seat, and turned to wave at those surrounding them. "Thank you all for . . . for everything." She smoothed the skirt of the dress she still wore. Anji had said it was hers, another present. And if the look Baptiste gave her as they pulled out had anything to do with

anything, perhaps she'd wear it again sometime.

"Where's my hat?" She shaded her eyes
against the westering sun.

Baptiste reached behind the seat and
pulled up a sunbonnet, also yellow and
trimmed with daisies. "This one?"

"No. My . . . perhaps so." The wide brim
did indeed shade her eyes. Who knew how
life was going to change if her wearing a
sunbonnet was any indication?

CHAPTER
TWENTY-FIVE

Dawn had yet to ribbon the horizon.

Thorliff slung his bag into the chest at the rear of the cook shack and slammed the lid. While he wouldn't be along with the threshing crew for the entire harvest, he'd help out with a good part of it. That was his and Mor's plan. Haakan still insisted that Thorliff didn't need more schooling. Not that so many hands were needed, since the drought made the harvest both early and slim. They'd finished their own acres and those right around Blessing in little better than a week.

Mrs. Sam turned from storing flour and beans, her dark face nearly disappearing into the shadows. "You gonna drive de team, or me?"

"I will." He leaped to the ground, ignoring the step that folded up when they traveled.

"Breakfast is ready," Ingeborg called from

the kitchen door.

"Tell her we already et." Mrs. Sam leaned her head out the door, referring to herself and her daughter, Lily Mae. Between the two of them they would cook for the traveling crew. Haakan and Lars had built the compact house on wagon wheels several years earlier so that they could have good food all the time. Some of the places they'd set up the threshing machine as they traveled from farm to farm had fed them so poorly, their stomachs rebelled.

Haakan finished the blessing as Thorliff slid into his place. He'd hardly slept between spending a late evening walking along the river with Anji, then going to bed and dreaming of never finding home again. He filled his plate with sliced ham, fried eggs, and biscuits dripping with butter and strawberry jam. He licked the jam from his fingers and caught his mother's gaze.

"Sure is good." He took another bite. "No one makes biscuits good as you."

"Astrid made these."

He glanced at his sister, who stuck her tongue out at him. "Oh, I guess you're getting to be a good cook too, but only because you have a good teacher."

"All right, Thorliff, what is it you want?" Ingeborg poured her husband another cup

338

of coffee.

Thorliff flinched. *How did she know?* "I . . . I was just wondering if you could invite Anji over once in a while. She'll get lonesome with me gone."

"Ha." Astrid wrinkled her nose. "We're all too busy to miss anyone."

"I sure hope that's not true." Haakan looked up at his wife.

"W-e-ll." Ingeborg appeared to consider both sides, then laughed as Haakan shook his finger at her. "Letters would be nice, on a regular basis I mean, not onc a season."

"Last year I sent you two telegrams."

"Ja and scared the life near to out of me with them. I thought sure someone had been hurt or killed or something."

Haakan shoved back from the table, shaking his head. "A man can't win."

"I put paper, pencil, and envelopes, already addressed, in your kit. Just as a hint, mind you." Ingeborg handed her husband a tow sack.

"What's this?"

"Something special for the journey."

"For me?"

"If you don't want to share."

"Um. I don't share very good."

"Thorliff, you saw the sack." She turned to wink at her eldest. He grinned and stretched his arms above his head, then stood and pushed his chair back in place.

"Come on, Far, we got miles to go."

Lars had the boiler nearing the pressure for them to leave. Ever since they had bought the new steam tractor and put the separator up on wheels, they'd needed fewer horses and men to keep in business. Traveling around the countryside, the machine looked like some gigantic monster, belching steam and smoke with a racket to be heard for miles. The rear wheels on the tractor were nearly as tall as Thorliff and the cab perched above that.

"Go with God," Ingeborg yelled above the engine noise.

Haakan and Lars waved from the iron-roofed cab and shifted gears, and the beast lumbered forward, the treads in the wheels gouging holes in the road as it passed. Thorliff waved from the seat of the cook wagon, and Hamre drove the wagon that carried barrels for water and other supplies.

Hanging back enough to miss most of the dust, Thorliff let his mind wander. *Anji.* He was already missing her, and it wasn't like he saw her every day anyway. He thought back to the night before, his last visit with her. . . .

■ ■ ■ ■

"I'm going tomorrow, and when I get home, I leave right away again for school," he said, taking her hands in his and facing her in the brilliant moonlight. He wanted to touch her face, her hair. Her lips, parted on a soft breath, smiled in that special way she had just for him.

"I know, but that is the way life is." Anji sighed and leaned her forehead against his chest.

His heart thudded as if he'd been running five miles. He dropped her hands and cupped his palms along her jawline, lifting her chin so she had to look up at him. "I . . . I love you, Anji Baard." There, he'd said the words that had been drumming in his heart and mind for months. Her smile made him want to run and jump and shout for joy.

"And I you. I have loved you ever since I first saw you, back when our wagon was heading west."

"And my far invited all of you to homestead here. We were so little then." His thumbs caressed the curve of her cheeks. Her skin felt soft as pussy willows in the spring. His eyes memorized her face — the slightly tipped nose, eyebrows that could say more with one arch than a page in a book, eyes that looked at him with such love he could feel his heart clench.

"Can you — will you wait for me?"

"Yes. Four years is nothing. Besides, I can't leave my mother."

"I know. Someday though, I pray you will go to school to become the teacher God meant for you to be."

"Someday."

Her breath teased his lips. He leaned forward. Their lips met in a trembling kiss that whispered of love and yearning and . . .

"Thorliff, you sleepin' up dere?" Mrs. Sam rapped on the wall behind the seat.

He jerked upright. "No, not at all." But when he looked ahead, the distance between him and the metal monsters had widened to nearly half a mile. The horses pulling the wagon had slowed to a shuffle. He flipped the lines, and they picked up their feet to a slow but jingling trot. He could feel the heat creep up his neck, and it wasn't from sunburn.

They pulled into the first farm just in time to set up to serve dinner, which Mrs. Sam and Lily Mae had been preparing as they traveled. Since they couldn't light the fire, they had laid out sandwiches and potato salad, which Ingeborg had helped prepare the long night before. The threshing crew ate quickly so they could get started to work.

As soon as they had the steam engine up to pressure, had checked all the belts one last time, and Hamre had filled all the places needing oil, Haakan released the lever, and the long belt began to turn. Thorliff waited for the signal and threw the lever for the bed of the threshing machine to pull sheaves of wheat into the maw of the dragon. Within minutes golden wheat streamed into the gunnysack hooked under the chute.

Each wagon pulled up to the carrying belt, the men forked sheaves, and straw blew out the arched spout into a growing stack. Wheat spears snuck inside shirt necks and under overall straps. Sweat poured from the bodies as the sun burned down. Besides taking care of the oiling, Hamre kept water in a covered barrel for the men to drink.

Always on the watch for sparks, they kept buckets of water near all sides of the machinery. Sparks could fly from the smokestack of the steam engine in spite of the metal roof on top.

By dusk, when the last wagon left empty, the threshing crew collapsed in the shade of the monolith called steam engine.

Mrs. Sam brought cold drinks around for all of them. "Supper ready soon as you wash up."

Thorliff groaned. What would it hurt to eat dirty for a change? He slapped his hat against his bent knee and watched the dust fly.

Haakan finished checking over the machinery and dumped a bucket of water over his head so that it sluiced down his whole body.

"Good thing we's near de river yet and can refill de barrels. Dat man say some wells be dryin' up," Mrs. Sam said.

"You're right. Bad enough the harvest is so light, but to go without water too . . ." He shook his head, water drops splattering the thirsty earth, rock hard from lack of moisture.

Thorliff watched his father joke with the others, but when it came to him, the silence ached. All because he wanted to go to school. He thought back to the worst fight he'd seen in his family. Usually if Haakan and Ingeborg had a disagreement, they went to the bedroom or out for a walk. Not this time. . . .

"Where will you be when Thorliff needs to come home?" Ingeborg poured another cup of coffee for her husband, her hand resting on his shoulder.

"Thorliff will come home with the rest of us."

"Then you think you will be done by September tenth? Is the harvest that bad?"

"I hope to heaven not." Haakan shook his head and twisted to see his wife's face. "You aren't going to back down on this, are you?"

She shook her head. "No. This is too important. Thorliff must have this chance."

"And it doesn't matter that we sweat our blood for him to have this farm?" Haakan lowered his voice with great effort.

Thorliff wanted to slide right under the table. Veins corded on his father's neck. The handle snapped on his coffee cup, and he threw it toward the woodbox, but it pinged off the side of the stove. When Thorliff started to get it, Haakan roared. "Leave it be. Why isn't this farm enough for you? Are you better than the rest of us?"

Thorliff straightened his spine and looked straight into his father's eyes. "Not better, no, never that, but different. Andrew is in love with this farm, not me."

"You hate this good life of tilling God's good earth?"

"No, Far, that's not it at all. I love the land and all of you. I just want something else, that's all. Something else."

"Haakan, never have I gone against your will. . . ." Ingeborg paused for a moment, obviously thinking back to the time she'd been working the fields against his express wishes and lost a baby due to an accident. Then taking a deep breath, hands strangling her apron, she continued. "But this is what is right. Our children must be given every opportunity that we can give them. Not everyone in this great land will be a farmer; we need teachers and writers and doctors and . . ." She let her hands drop to her side. "Please, don't make him go against your wishes."

Haakan shoved back from the table and headed for the door. "You will do what you must, but I cannot give my blessing. I cannot."

Thorliff fought the tears that burned at the back of his throat and watched his mother dry her eyes on her apron.

"Mor, I cannot go then."

"Yes, you will go. He will come around. Just give him time."

But they were running out of time, and each farm they left brought that time that much closer. Sometimes if he let himself think of it, rage simmered low in his belly. Why did this have to be so difficult? Why did his father have to be so stubborn?

CHAPTER
TWENTY-SIX

"We need to go." Metiz stood in the door-way several days after the threshing crew left.

"Where?" Ingeborg turned from the jars of string beans cooking in the copper boiler. She wiped her forehead with the back of her hand. "Whew, this is hot."

"To Agnes."

Ingeborg untied her apron. "Did someone come for you?"

Metiz shook her head. "Just know."

Oh, God, please let this be a false alarm. Please, Lord, don't take Agnes. And yet as she tied on a clean apron and her sunbon-net, she knew she didn't want Agnes suffer-ing any longer. Each time she'd seen her, she'd looked more of another world than of this one.

"Let me send Astrid over to Kaaren's." Outside, she shaded her eyes with her hand. The oxen were plodding back from the river, drawing the wagon bearing the barrels of water that kept the garden producing. Andrew and his helpers were laughing as they came. No matter how hard they worked, they always seemed to find something to laugh about.

"I'll get the buggy hitched." Ingeborg went to the fence and whistled. The grazing horses raised their heads, and when she whistled again, they ambled toward the barn. By the time she had a rope around one neck, Metiz had swung the gate open, then closed it as they passed through. Within minutes Ingeborg had the horse harnessed and backed into the shafts of the two-wheeled buggy Haakan had purchased at an auction south of town. Due to the drought, there'd been too many auctions, and always Haakan came home with items they didn't need as much as the seller had needed the money.

She buckled the shafts to the belly band and threaded the lines back to wrap around the whip stock.

"Where you going?" Astrid came running across the yard.

"Metiz said we are needed at the Baards'. Watch the clock. The beans will be ready to come off at ten."

"All right. You want me to finish dinner?"

349

"Most likely. Go tell Tante Kaaren what has happened."

Andrew ran up in time to hear the last instructions. "We'll take care of things here, Mor. You needn't worry about us."

"Thank you, son." Ingeborg stepped up into the buggy on one side, Metiz on the other. "I will send someone to let you know." She clucked the horse forward and into a fast trot.

They turned into the Baard lane as young Gus came trotting out. "I was just coming to get you. Ma is asking for you." Tears streaked his tanned cheeks.

"Jump in." Ingeborg had stopped the horse to talk.

Metiz scooted over, and Gus climbed in. Before he sat all the way down, Ingeborg had the horse moving again.

"Tell me what's happening."

Gus sniffed and scrubbed under his nose with the back of his hand. Shirtless, he wore his overalls with one strap unhooked. "She . . . she woke up so weak she could hardly talk. Anji tried to get her to eat, but she wouldn't. Not even drink her coffee. After she slept again, she asked for you." He hiccupped and looked out over the wheat stubble. "Is . . . is she going to die?"

"Only God knows that. We will do what

we can."

He leaped to the ground when they stopped at the gate to the yard. "I'll take care of your horse."

"Thank you." Ingeborg and Metiz hurried into the house.

"She's in the bedroom." Anji, red eyed and sniffling, led them across the kitchen.

"How is she?"

"Sleeping."

They stepped into the room to see Agnes still in her nightdress and lying so still Ingeborg caught her breath. Was she already gone? But moving closer, she could see the sheet move just slightly with the woman's breathing. The thing that grew inside her mounded the sheet enough to look as if she were about to give birth.

"Can I get you anything?" Anji looked from Ingeborg to Metiz. "Hot water, cold water, coffee, anything?" Her voice cracked.

Ingeborg laid her hand on Anji's arm. "Where is Joseph?"

"Out at the barn. He was here until a few minutes ago. The boys were too."

"Let me listen. Is she running a fever?"

Anji shook her head.

Metiz sat on one side of the bed and Ingeborg the other. Taking Agnes's hand, Ingeborg pressed gently.

Agnes's eyes fluttered open. "You . . . are . . . here."

"Ja, Metiz said you needed us."

"Good." The word faded on a sigh so faint that Ingeborg leaned closer. She looked to Metiz, who shook her head so imperceptibly that had Ingeborg not been watching, she'd have missed it.

"I . . . I am . . . going home."

"Ja. Our Lord is waiting for you." Ingeborg heard Anji sob behind her.

"Please, the psalm."

"Ja." Ingeborg turned and whispered to Anji. "Call the others quickly."

"S-so hard . . ." A pause, each one longer than the last. "For them."

"Ja. I shall miss you so, dear friend."

Agnes squeezed Ingeborg's fingers butterfly light.

One by one the men filed in, Knute and Swen following behind their father, eyes red. Joseph took Metiz' place at her motion. "She's in no pain?" Joseph asked.

Metiz shook her head. "Beyond pain."

Ingeborg laid her other hand over Agnes's. " 'The Lord is my shepherd. . . .' "

"Ja." Her eyes opened halfway. A smile touched the corners of her mouth. "Ja."

" 'I shall not want.' " The others joined in, faltering one at a time. " 'He maketh me to lie down in green pastures: he leadeth me beside the still waters.' " Gus turned his head into his arm. Becky sobbed on Anji's shoulder.

Ingeborg felt the hand go limp as if life hovered on a breath. The lines smoothed out on her friend's face. The smile deepened slightly.

" 'Yea, though I walk through the valley of the shadow of death, I will fear no evil. . . .' " The words trailed off as each realized what had happened.

Joseph choked on a sob but kept going. " 'Surely goodness and mercy shall follow me all the days of my life: and I will dwell in the house of the Lord forever.' "

Becky ran to her father and threw herself in his arms. He hugged her close and reached for the others. Together they stood, arms around each other, tears streaming down their faces.

"She is with God." Joseph took out his handkerchief and wiped his face. "I'll go tell Pastor."

"I will, Pa. Let me." Knute patted his father's shoulder and left the room.

"I didn't think she'd go so soon." Joseph sat back down on the bed and picked up his wife's hand, stroking her fingers with the tips of his own. "She was the best wife any man could have."

"The best friend too." Ingeborg wiped her eyes again. "She stood beside me through everything. After Roald died, she took me to task about forgiving and letting go and getting on with life. She told me my sons needed me. She said I was trying to kill myself with work, but that wasn't God's way. It took a lot for her to say all that to me."

"Had a healthy dose of gumption, she did."

Ingeborg looked around to see the others had left without her knowing. "So now we comfort the grieving and rejoice that she was here with us for as long as she was." A sob caught her, and she sniffed again. "I know that's the Christian way, but some things are almost harder than a body can bear."

Joseph blew his nose and wiped his eyes. "Until this thing took her over, I always thought God would take me first, me being older and all." He laid Agnes's hand across her chest. "I thank you for coming like you did."

"You are most welcome." Ingeborg rose. "I'll leave you alone with her." At the door she paused and looked back. Beauty bathed her friend, making her look young again.

Peace filled the room like a shimmering rainbow.

Anji stood looking out the kitchen window, hands cupping her elbows. She turned when she heard Ingeborg's step and, without a word, headed straight for her arms. Ingeborg held the young woman, resting her cheek on Anji's head, stroking and murmuring gentleness.

"Where is Becky?" Ingeborg asked when the weeping storm had abated.

"Sh-she went out with Swen."

"And Gus?"

Anji shrugged. "Same." She drew back enough to pick up her apron to wipe her eyes. "I wish Thorliff were here."

"I know."

"I . . . I don't want to put Ma in the ground."

Ingeborg fought the tears and again lost the battle. She sighed. "Neither do I."

"She told me yesterday she wanted me to go to school."

"She told me that too. She doesn't want you to stay home and raise the younger ones."

"Who will, then?"

"God will work something out. No need to make any decisions right now."

Joseph stood in the doorway to the bedroom. "I'm going out to finish the box."

"Someone else can do that."

"I know, but I want to. It's the last thing I can do for her." He set his hat on his head. "She who did all she could for me."

Another wagon drove up, and Kaaren climbed over the wheel as soon as it stopped turning. "Am I too late?"

"Ja, she slipped away so quick." Ingeborg wiped her eyes again. "You can go see her."

Kaaren nodded, her eyes streaming as she mounted the stairs, one arm around Anji's shaking shoulders.

Before Metiz, Kaaren, and Ingeborg left, they washed, dressed, and laid Agnes out in the parlor, her bed a door over two saw-horses and padded by one of the quilts she'd sewn. Pastor and Mary Martha drove up as they were leaving.

"The burying will be tomorrow. I've already sent Sam out with the message." Pastor Solberg took out his handkerchief to wipe his forehead and at the same time his eyes. "Sure is hot, and not a breath of air stirring." He sighed. "This one is harder than most."

"I know." Ingeborg climbed up in the buggy. "What time?"

"Eleven. Then we can have dinner for everyone."

"We'll take care of the food," Ingeborg said.

The west wind blew hot across the plains as the people of Blessing gathered to pay their last respects to Agnes, a favorite of all. It blew hats to tumbling and skirts whipping as if angry to witness the grief played out before it. Tears dried before they were born, and no one had enough moisture to moisten their quivering lips.

How I wish Haakan were here, something to lean against other than that wind. Ingeborg fought the sobs that tore at her throat. *Father, I know Agnes is with you, but I miss her so. We all do.* She looked over to the Baard family gathered together without their center. Joseph looked to be a shell with all the heart and soul sucked out. Becky sat close to Anji and lay against her sister's shoulder, her face pale as skimmed milk.

"Dearly beloved . . ."

Pastor Solberg had said those words at a wedding such a short time ago, and now for this. She could scarcely say the word *funeral.* So many they'd had in Blessing, but surely this was the worst. She barely remembered the one for Roald and Carl and the two little ones.

The wind snatched at the pages of Pastor's

Bible, so he closed it and held it in front of him with both hands like a shield against the enemy.

"Today we bury our sister in Christ, Agnes — mother, wife, friend. She has had a place in all our hearts, and her solid common sense made a difference in many lives. Agnes Baard truly lived what she believed. She loved our Lord with all her heart, strength, soul, and mind, and her neighbors as herself. Our Lord is right now saying, 'Well done, thou good and faithful servant . . . enter thou into the joy of thy lord.' She is in that place He prepared especially for her.

"We are left to grieve, but not for Agnes — we rejoice for her — but for ourselves, for we miss her so." He paused to blow his nose and wipe his eyes.

"Friends, I have studied much on heaven lately, and I no longer believe it is far away but rather very close. The Bible says we are separated but by a veil, and those already gone to be with our Lord can see through the veil or across the chasm. All the saints are there rejoicing in a new one come home and grieving with us in our sorrow. Christ himself is grieving with us. He knows our sorrows. He felt the worst of all when his

Father left Him to hang on that tree. For us."

Ingeborg felt an arm go around her waist and then another as her two children did what they could to comfort her.

"If any of you would like to say something . . ." Pastor waved a welcoming hand.

Only the sound of the wind could be heard until Metiz stepped forward. "Agnes Baard was my friend. She say I must believe in the man named Jesus, son of Great Spirit. I ask why. She say so I live with all my friends in home of Great Spirit. I ask why. She say because God loves me and wants me there too." She swept her arm to include everyone. "I believe. I know I see Agnes again."

A song sparrow trilled as if rejoicing in the good news.

"Agnes made sure we had enough to eat one winter," said one man.

"Agnes helped me laugh again after my baby went on home to heaven. Bet she is holding my baby right now. Agnes loved babies so."

The litany continued of the good deeds Agnes had done on this earth.

Ingeborg finally stepped forward. "Agnes grabbed me by the back of my neck and led me to believe again after Roald died. She snatched me back from the black pit of despair that threatened to devour me. I owe Agnes my life. Thank you, God, for a friend like her."

Pastor Solberg waited a few moments, then recited the age-old words with great feeling. "Dust to dust. Ashes to ashes. Lord, we commend this body to the earth from which we come, knowing that her spirit is with you and that on the Last Day, with a trumpet blast, you will raise all who have died, and we who believe in you will rejoice forever in the mansions you have prepared for us." He leaned over and picked up a handful of dirt, drizzling the sign of the cross on the box Joseph had so lovingly made.

Solberg nodded for any others who wanted to do the same, then raised his hands. "Into your hands, Father, we commend our dear Agnes, in the name of the Father and the Son and the Holy Ghost, amen." He blew his nose again and announced that dinner would be at the Baard home as soon as the food could be set out.

Ingeborg wrapped an arm about Anji, and together they turned to the wagons.

Knute and Swen took the shovels that had been stabbed into the pile of dirt. Four men lowered the box into the grave, and the filling in began.

Becky clapped her hands over her ears. "I don't want them to cover up my ma."

"Me neither." Anji held her clinging little sister. "Hush now. We must serve dinner to all these folks. I need you to help me."

Ingeborg smiled down at Astrid, who still hung on to her hand. Together they walked to the wagon.

"Wish Pa and Thorliff were here," Astrid said.

"Me too," Ingeborg replied, giving the girl's hand a squeeze.

By the time the meal was served and everything cleaned up again, Ingeborg looked around the empty kitchen, empty because only the cat sat in Agnes's chair. Becky and Anji had gone to lie down, and the men had taken Gus with them to repair machinery in the machine shed.

"Oh, Father, bless this house and those who dwell herein. Comfort them as only you can do." Ingeborg picked up her last pan and let the screen door close gently behind her.

The funeral might be over, but the grieving had only just begun.

That evening the Bjorklund family gathered at the boardinghouse after the chores were finished. Bridget had made ice cream for dessert, so the twins and Astrid were sitting on the back step licking their bowls clean.

The boys had started a baseball game, the thwack of the bat Uncle Olaf had turned for them sounding clear in the gloaming.

Ingeborg joined the girls, taking a seat beside Grace, who leaned into her aunt.

Sophie shook her head. "Sure was a sad day. Wish Pa was here."

"Me too." Astrid set her bowl down. "I'm going to play ball. You coming?"

"No."

Ingeborg laid a hand on Sophie's forehead. No, she wasn't running a fever.

"I'm too sad. Poor Becky and Gus don't have a ma anymore. It ain't fair."

"Sophie, don't say ain't." Kaaren sat down on the other side of the girls.

"Still not fair."

"No, it's not." Kaaren agreed with her daughter.

"Ah, I miss her so, and it's not like I saw her every day, but the knowing she was here, that was comfort for sure." Ingeborg turned to look up to see Hjelmer and Bridget behind them.

The bat cracked a resounding hit, and cheers went up on the ball field.

"Run, Trygve, run!" Andrew never worried so much about winning as having a good time. Yelling was part of it.

"You tell 'em, Andrew," Penny called, smoothing her apron over her rounding middle as she sat down beside Grace.

"Sure wish those clouds would bring rain instead of heat lightning." Hjelmer sat down in one of the rockers and motioned for his mother to take the other.

"Ja, that would be good." Bridget sat and fanned herself with her apron. "The wind is so hot and mean today, and now, when we could use a breeze, nothing stirs. The air is still as a stick." She looked up when her husband, Henry, laid his hands on her shoulders.

"Agnes will be missed, all right. She always made me feel right to home."

Thunder rumbled in the distance. Lightning flickered and danced across the black clouds.

Ingeborg swatted a mosquito. Fireflies twinkled in the grass.

"I think it must be time to go home. The boys can no longer see the ball." They all stood, stretching and yawning.

"Some day this has been."

"One I'd just as soon not repeat for a good long time." Kaaren put her arms around her girls. "Come, let's start walking, and

363

Trygve will catch up with us."

"I can hitch up the wagon if you like." Hjelmer rose and smoothed back his hair, dark blond now rather than the near white of his youth.

"No thanks. Walking will be good."

The church bell ringing brought Ingeborg out of a deep sleep. Two rings and a pause. Two rings and . . .

"Fire! There's a fire someplace! Andrew!"

CHAPTER
TWENTY-SEVEN:
WITH THE
THRESHING CREW

"Make sure those barrels are full of water."

"I did." Thorliff waved as he hollered back to his father up on the tractor. While they used the water mostly for the steam boiler, they also kept the barrels full in case of fire. He'd put out a small fire at the last stop. In spite of the spark shield, it only took one spark to start a fire with the land as dry as it was. Besides the barrels, he now kept a bucket close at hand too.

"They had a fire a couple farms over, a lightning strike." Lars finished tightening the long belt from the tractor to the separator. He waved at Haakan and engaged the pulley. "Today I want you as the grease boy."

"All right." Thorliff reached in the tool chest for the oilcan. He checked to make sure it was full again. Haakan and Lars always made sure everything was greased, all the belts checked for wear, and everything tightened down before beginning the day's work.

Wagons loaded with sheaves of wheat were already lined up. At Lars's signal they pitched the first load onto the conveyer, and the day's work began. Besides the greasing, Thorliff made sure there was fresh water for the hands to drink. Cruel hot and humid as it was, they'd had one man pass out the day before. Most of them had taken to wearing wet bandannas tied around their necks and to soaking their hats and shirts.

Hot as it was on the ground, Thorliff knew it was much worse up in the tractor cab keeping that fire going to produce the steam up in the boiler. At one point Haakan poured the bucket of water right over himself and Lars.

Mrs. Sam rang the dinner bell, and with sighs of relief they all watched the machinery shut down. They lined up at the long window that opened onto a ledge and helped themselves to the bacon beans and corn bread, finding whatever shade they could to sit and eat. Thorliff shoveled his food in, hardly taking time to swallow. He had to grease all the machinery joints again before the rig could be started up. Back on his feet, he dunked his hat and bandanna in one of the barrels, wishing he could dunk his whole body. What a relief a dip in a river would be. Thoughts of home crashed through the barrier he had built up during the day. How were they all? Especially Anji. Had she written? He'd soon find out. They were close enough to Devil's Lake to get mail this evening. If there was any to be had.

That evening Thorliff took out the journal he'd brought along and, after reviewing the last two pages, continued writing his latest story.

"Another week and you leave?" Haakan leaned back against the wagon box. He chewed on a piece of dried venison, too hot and weary to do more.

"Five days." Thorliff looked up in surprise. This was the first time his far had spoken to him, other than giving direct orders, since the argument at home. He waited for a response, then bent his head to write again. Too often he was too tired at night to write more than a paragraph, but he persisted. Fireflies dotted the darkness while moths and mosquitoes buzzed the lamplight. "How much longer do you think you'll be?"

"Another couple weeks is all. Sure thought there'd be a letter from your ma there."

"Tante Kaaren likes Lars better." Thorliff bit his lip. He shouldn't be teasing Haakan, should he?

Haakan snorted. "Just because he's gotten more letters don't mean more than Kaaren likes to write and your ma doesn't. Anji said anything more about how their family is doing?"

"Just that she feels lost, and so do the others. Good thing Joseph Baard didn't come along on the crew this year."

"He wouldn't leave Agnes. We all knew it was coming. A blessing really. She'd faded away right before our eyes."

Thorliff considered what he'd written. *Seems to me that dying is easier than living. The pain is gone, and believers go to heaven while those who have to go on living feel sorrow drag them down and into despair if they are not careful.* He remembered the days when his ma and Tante Kaaren had suffered after their husbands died. He'd tried so hard to help with the chores and even the fieldwork. *The soddy was so dark in the winter. And cold. Sometimes I thought we were never going to get warm enough. But when spring came, I never wanted to go back inside. I'd rather have slept outside too if the mosquitoes would have left me alone.*

Thorliff looked over at his father sitting at the rim of the lamplight. "Can I ask you a question?" His heart thumped against his ribs.

"Of course."

"About my going away to college." His throat dried up like a wind just blew through. "Do . . . do you think you could possibly . . . ah . . ."

The silence stretched. *Why didn't I just keep my mouth shut? Now I did it.*

Haakan hawked and spat off to the side. "I'd rather not talk about it now. I'm just too tired."

Thorliff heard not only the weariness in his father's voice but also a sadness, or was it resentment? Why, oh, why had he brought it up? Now there'd be a cloud, or even worse, over the remaining days — if Haakan talked to him at all. Thorliff closed his journal and spread his bedroll under the cook wagon, not that there was much dew to worry about. He watched the heat light dancing in the distance and fell asleep with a *Please, God* on his heart.

Two days later, when they finished the last of the farms in the area that had contacted them, Haakan shut down the tractor and climbed down to the ground. "Thorliff, go hitch up that wagon. Mrs. Sam, is your rig ready to roll?"

"Yes, suh. But we need to stop in town for supplies."

"Be that as it may. Right now we're going to the lake. All of us. Bring soap and towels. Lars, you got any fishhooks and line?"

"Just let me dig them out. You s'pose that lake has any periwinkles in it?"

"If not, we can use grasshoppers. There's plenty of them around. Surely the fish there eat grasshoppers."

"I got bread and bacon grease. Lily Mae can fry up some leftover beans if'n you don' catch no fish."

"We'll catch fish if we have to swim after them."

Thorliff and Hamre had the wagon hitched up in record time. Everyone tossed in their gear, and they were off.

"How far to the lake?" Hamre yelled over the noise of the horses and the wheels.

"About two miles. See it out there?" They crested a slight rise and saw the lake shimmering like a mirage.

"Look, there's smoke." Thorliff pointed off to the north.

Haakan looked to some tall grass along the road bending before the wind. "East wind is blowing it away from us. Too far away for us to help."

They soon pulled close to the lake, bulrushes lining the shore. "Over there looks to be a good place. You all go on and get cleaned up, and I'll go this way to fish." Lars nodded toward the swampy area off to the right where blackbirds sang. "Looks to be a creek flowing in there."

"You sure?" Haakan wrapped the lines around the brake handle. "We're not in any particular hurry, you know."

"I'd rather fish than swim any day."

Hamre leaped from the back of the wagon. "I'll catch grasshoppers." Soon he returned with a handkerchief clenched in his fist, the hoppers pushing against the cotton, a foot or two making its way through the creases. Hamre raised his other hand. "Look, they spit all over me." Stains of yellow and tan freckled his skin.

"You'd spit too if some giant grabbed you up and stuffed you in a pouch like that." Lars reached for the handkerchief, pulled the ends up tight, and held them fast with a bit of twine he pulled from his pocket. "There now. That'll keep 'em." He glanced around the group. "Anyone else want to come? I got another hook or two."

"Later." Thorliff finished pulling his boots off and grabbed one of the horses by the halter. "Come on, Nellie, you need a drink." Hamre took the other horse, and after kicking off his boots, they waded out knee deep. The horses drank, nosed the water, and

371

drank again. Prince, the dark gelding, buckled at the knees and, before Hamre could stop him, flopped on his side, legs thrashing the water, and rolled. When the horse surged to his feet, Nellie took her turn. Already drenched from the horses' brief swim, Thorliff and Hamre dove into the water and came up blowing like porpoises.

Dragging their lead lines, the horses ambled out onto the bank and put their heads down to graze. For a change they had real green grass, not the dried-up pasture they'd grazed elsewhere.

"Let 'em be," Haakan said when Thorliff started to follow them. "Throw us the soap." He waved at Mrs. Sam. They all soaped their clothes and rinsed them by diving and swimming.

Thorliff surfaced after rolling around to rinse his clothes and set his feet down on the sandy bottom. He sat back, his shoulders under the water. Lily Mae and Mrs. Sam were dipping and rinsing. As if attached by a pull line, Thorliff stared at Lily Mae's slim figure, her clothes molded to a body that had begun to assume its female shape. He gulped and felt the water sizzle as he ducked under.

Anji, I miss you so. If I were staying home

instead of going away to college, we could get married. Far would give us some land, and we'd build a house.

He stayed under until his lungs screamed for air. When his head broke the surface, he was turned the other way, the lowering sun shining a golden path across the water. He kept his eyes wide open, for every time he closed them, he saw Anji, dressed in her yellow graduation dress, as if etched onto his mind for all eternity. Sadness sat like a buffalo robe on his shoulders. Stiff, heavy, cumbersome. Breathing took an effort.

He removed his shirt and, twisting it with his hands, wrung out what water he could. He climbed out of the lake, sat down, and pulled on his boots. "I'm going to help Lars catch our supper," he announced and left without a backward glance.

"Don' stop with supper. Breakfast be a good time for fried fish too."

He stumbled along the bank, his mind screaming "what if's" all the while. What if he were making the wrong decision? What if something happened to Anji? What if . . . ? When he located Lars, he took the pole he was handed.

"Thanks."

"Right out there beyond that log is where I been getting most of them." Lars pulled his forked stick out of the water. "I'll take these so we can scale them for supper." He stopped for a moment, studying the younger man. "Are you all right?"

Thorliff nodded. "Sure." But he knew if he looked Lars in the eye, all his sad and terrified thoughts would be seen. Here he was supposed to be a man, and he felt like blubbering like a little boy. When a fish hit his hook, he jerked it with a vengeance, then had to search for his catch in the reeds.

He could feel the others glancing at him that evening around the campfire. Bellies full, they lounged on the grass, no one wanting to leave the coolness and sounds of the lake. Loons called, their song a haunting plea. But soon the mosquitoes drove them back to the wagon and to the shadowy monstrosities they served.

Thorliff flipped from one side to the other, plagued by every worry he'd ever suffered.

Before dawn they pulled out, the clanking and groaning fitting right in with his state of mind. Rather than driving the cook wagon, he motioned for Hamre to take the lines, and he took a place on the tailgate of the wagon carrying the barrels. One of the hired men cocked an eyebrow, but no one said anything.

That night Haakan drew him aside. "Since

we are close to the train line here, how about you head on home in the morning?"

Thorliff nodded, his boot toe making circles in the dirt. Even his father didn't want him along. Sadness must be contagious.

"See you when we gets home." The next morning Mrs. Sam handed him a tow sack with sandwiches, some venison jerky, and a jug of water.

"No, I'll be gone then." *If I go. How can I not go? Because my father doesn't want me to, that's why.*

He wanted to scream at the voices fighting in his head.

"Oh, dat's right. Well, you take care of yourself in that big school, you hear?"

"I will."

"Dey better feed you right."

"Thank you, Mrs. Sam. You took good care of us out here."

He turned and climbed into a wagon going into town. No one was even taking him to the train. He just begged a ride with a stranger. With his bedroll tied over his shoulder, his journal and extra clothing inside, and his food sack in his hand, he knew this was the best way, but somehow his insides didn't agree.

"So how's the harvesting been in other places?" the driver asked.

"Same as here. Bad."

"You been with that rig long?"

Thorliff shook his head. Did three years constitute long?

The man took the hint and didn't ask anything else, taking to whistling between his teeth instead, a two-tone hiss that repeated as often as the horses' hooves clopped.

Thorliff shifted on the seat. He clasped and unclasped his hands, then dropped his head forward. He tried to picture Anji's face. Forced himself to think what he needed to pack to take to college.

Why bother? You aren't going anyway!

Shut up! Clamping his hands over his ears under the guise of scratching his head didn't even help.

"You always whistle like that?" He couldn't believe the words coming from his mouth.

"Well, ex-*cuse* me." The whistling stopped, but now Thorliff had something else to feel guilty over. Why would he treat another like that? His mor would box his ears for being so impolite. Cruel, in fact.

Never had he felt such relief at seeing the train station. "Thank you for the ride."

The man grunted and clucked the horses forward.

When he asked what time the train left, the man behind the window shook his head. "You just missed it by no more'n half an hour. Not another one going east until tomorrow morning."

Thorliff groaned. He heaved a sigh and shrugged. "Guess I'll have to wait."

" 'Bout all you can do."

"Can I throw my bedroll down here at the station?"

"Don't know why not. Can't offer much in the way of comfort, but you're welcome to the floor."

"Thanks." Thorliff spent most of the day wandering the dirt streets of Devil's Lake.

When he returned to the train station, he took out his journal and, recalling every Bible verse he'd learned about honoring one's parents and living peaceably, wrote them out. Sure that if he went to St. Olaf he was going straight to hell, he curled up on top of his bedroll and let the mosquitoes have a feast.

CHAPTER TWENTY-EIGHT: NORTHFIELD, MINNESOTA LATE AUGUST

"Don't forget we are having company for supper tonight," Elizabeth's mother said, meeting her as soon as she arrived home after finishing the bookwork at her father's printshop.

Elizabeth sighed. "Yes, Mother." She hated to ask the next question.

"And I want you to wear something nice."

Elizabeth skipped the next question, as it had already been answered. "And who is this surprise person of the male persuasion that I am to dress nice for?" Why couldn't her mother just give up? She hated to count the number of *nice,* meaning eligible, young men who had been invited for dinner or supper or the theater or . . . The list went on.

"His name is Thornton Wickersham, and he is a nephew to Pastor Mueller. Mr. Wickersham plans to attend Carleton College this fall and is coming to town a bit early to get settled."

Thornton Wickersham? Elizabeth did all she could to keep from laughing out loud. With a name like that he must be a dandy of the first order. "So" — she swallowed her chuckle — "are the Muellers coming too?"

"Yes, of course. And Dr. Gaskin. I think it's about time he began to mingle with his friends again."

Elizabeth closed her eyes and counted. When she could speak without biting off her mother's head, she continued. "Mother, first of all, you and father are not necessarily friends of the doctor, and secondly, it's only been two months since Helen died." Thinking of the doctor brought a vision of eyes that no longer twinkled and a mouth that drooped like his mustache. In spite of the ministrations of his capable and caring housekeeper and amiable and able nurse, the lines seemed deeper on his face and his hair whiter by the time Elizabeth arrived at the office every morning. He left more of the initial exams up to her and came in to make sure her diagnoses were accurate.

While he referred to her as his doctor-in-training, Elizabeth knew he was too tired to carry the load he used to, or too hung over, depending on the time of day. She'd caught him sneaking a drink from a bottle kept in a locked drawer in his desk.

"For medicinal use only," Dr. Gaskin had said to her before capping the bottle and putting it back. "I've had such a backache lately that this seems to be the only thing that helps."

"Not meaning to be funny, but have you seen a doctor?"

"That young whippersnapper thinks he knows everything, but he knows nothing."

Having developed great respect for the new doctor, Elizabeth just shook her head. "And how much of your *medicine* do you take before retiring?"

He glared at her over his half glasses. "That is none of your business, young lady." But even his voice had lost its power.

Elizabeth left her thoughts on the doctor and looked back at her mother. "Perhaps inviting the doctor is a good idea. Just please ask Father to go easy on the before-supper cocktails."

Her mother looked over her shoulder. "Are you saying what I think you are saying?"

Elizabeth nodded.

"Hmm. I shall have to resort to tampering then." Mrs. Rogers beckoned her daughter with one finger. "Follow me."

Elizabeth did as told, curiosity bubbling

as she kept pace. Her mother stopped at the tea cart that served as a repository for cut glass bottles of various shapes, all containing the liquor served in their house. Her mother took a pitcher from the under shelf and, removing the stopper, poured about a third of the liquid out of the bottle. Then taking another pitcher, this one full of water, refilled the decanter and set it back in its place. She then took the pitcher with bourbon in it to the kitchen where she poured it into a bottle kept far back in the cupboard.

"We have solved his problem, at least for this evening." Annabelle dusted her hands as if finishing a less than nice job. She smiled at her daughter, the kind of smile that two women exchange when they are outmaneuvering the men in their lives. Especially when it is for the good of the men in question.

"Mother, if you dislike drinking so much, why do you keep these here?" Elizabeth motioned toward the bottles.

"Because your father insists." Annabelle sighed. "And because my father insisted too. So I do what I can to see that drunkenness is prohibited."

Elizabeth nodded. "I see."

Arms linked, they left the parlor and climbed the stairs to their rooms.

"Now, you take a nice cool bath and have a lie-down so that those circles I see under your eyes disappear and you are able to enjoy our evening. I shall do the same. Thank God for Cook."

Elizabeth laid her head against her mother's shoulder. "In spite of your trying to marry me off, I do love you." The tender kiss on her forehead returned the compliment. She chose the lie-down first, the breeze entering her room through the shade of the mulberry tree cooling her skin. She poured water into the basin on the nightstand from the pitcher of water and dipped a cloth in it to wipe off her face and neck. Sighing with the pleasure of it, she lay down on her bed and fell instantly asleep.

"Ah, my dear," her father said, meeting her at the foot of the stairs some time later, "is this the same girl I sent home because she looked so tired?"

"Yes, Father. Sometimes I think the smell of the ink is what gives me a headache."

"Or perhaps the pounding of the press." He took her hand and pulled it through the crook in his arm. "Come, I have someone for you to meet."

"Thornton Wickersham?" She kept her voice to a whisper.

"Yes, but I think you shall like him in spite of your mother's finagling. For a change, I do."

"That's something." Elizabeth's droll smile made her father chuckle.

They paused in the arched doorway, surveying the room that glowed with fresh flowers and the evening sun slanting through the lace-curtained windows. The French doors leading to the backyard framed beds of brilliant three-foot zinnias and marigolds fronted by rioting petunias. Pinks, reds, whites, golds, and oranges — the hues blended into a symphony of color.

"Oh, here you are, dear." Annabelle beckoned from the settee. "Let me introduce you, and then I promised Dr. Gaskin that you would play for him."

Elizabeth nodded, but her father intervened. "I'll do the introducing while you make sure everyone has a glass of lemonade." His slight twist on the word gave his opinion of their liquid refreshment. Elizabeth pinched her father's arm but kept a slight smile in place. *Wait until he finds out his whiskey isn't what he thinks it is.*

Dr. Gaskin started to stand when they reached him, but Elizabeth waved him back. "You've been on your feet enough today. You just sit there and let us wait on you."

She peered at his glass. "Can I refill that for you?"

Doctor looked up at her father, glanced at the glass, and raised his eyebrows.

"I take it you have enough?" Her smile said she knew well enough what he was asking for. She caught her father mouthing "later" and tugged the teeniest bit on his arm. Pastor Mueller stood beside his wife, who looked to be in the family way again. While some women bloomed in their pregnancies, Mrs. Mueller faded like a blossom spent and too tired to hold its head up any longer. The doctor had warned her of the dangers of another baby, but . . .

Elizabeth drew her thoughts back from things medical and shook hands with her pastor. "So good to have you here." What she'd like to have said was *"Why don't you leave your wife here to rest and you go home and take care of those four boys?"* But she kept her smile in place and patted Mrs. Mueller's hand.

"I have someone I'd like you to meet." Pastor took Elizabeth's hand and led her toward a young man who stood waiting to meet her. "My nephew, Thornton Wickersham, my sister's oldest boy. Thornton, this is Elizabeth, whom we've told you so much about."

Elizabeth extended her hand to shake his and, by the look on his tanned face, had caught him by surprise. He shook it and smiled back at her, regaining his composure in an eye blink.

"I'm pleased to meet you. Living up to their enthusiasm would be difficult, but you more than accomplish that."

Oh, bother. A smooth talker. That's all I need. Elizabeth quickly catalogued his appearance — dark curly hair cut short, twinkling amber eyes flecked with gold, squared chin balanced by a broad forehead, and shoulders that well filled his jacket. "And you." *But what is my father impressed with? Not looks, that's for sure.*

"I'm looking forward to getting to know you and hope that you will introduce me to some of the young people in town. I'll be a senior at Carleton. I'm coming here so I can study under Dr. Wahlberg."

And every girl on campus will make sure you know her name. "I'll be happy to do just that. And now excuse me. My mother insisted that I provide music before supper."

"You minx." Her father's whisper tickled her ear.

"Anything special you would like to hear?" she asked the doctor on her way to the ebony Steinway.

"Something light. Debussy, Mozart, perhaps a bit of Beethoven."

"At your service, sir." She sketched a curtsy before sliding onto the piano bench, and after loosening her arms and hands, she spread her fingers over the keys. Closing her eyes, she stroked the keys, rippling arpeggios, and flowing from measure to measure of liquid joy.

When supper was announced, she returned from the land of dreams to find Thornton Wickersham leaning against the concert grand piano, his eyes on hers as if waiting for her to awaken.

"That was magnificent."

"Thank you." Her fingers found notes of their own, not needing sheet music or even concentration.

"I've heard some of the world-class pianists, but you excel even the best. Why are you not on a concert tour?"

"Because she wants to be a doctor." Phillip Rogers took the young man by the arm. "Come. Supper is waiting."

"You do?" His gaze had never left hers.

"Yes." Elizabeth hit a final lingering note, and her hands drifted down to her lap, hands once again, no longer instruments of music.

"I see."

I doubt that you do, but at least you are not so obsequious you squeak. She stood and walked beside him into the dining room, now lit with two candelabras, one at either end of the twelve-foot table.

All through a delicious meal of roasted capon, she studied him, trying to pick out something to dislike. He made Mrs. Mueller smile with a funny joke, complimented her mother on the food, asked her father about an editorial he had run the day before, and still managed to inquire at length about her dream of medicine. All with the carefree ease of a diplomat with years of experience. And he was nice. Not husband material, but nice.

An idea pecked at the shell enclosing it like a chick on the way to hatching. What if . . . ? She didn't dare look at her mother for fear the scheme was written all over her face.

CHAPTER
TWENTY-NINE:
BLESSING, NORTH
DAKOTA
SEPTEMBER 1893

"Thorliff, you're home!" Anji threw herself into his arms.

He let her cry on his shoulder, smoothing her hair with one hand and stroking her back with the other. Sobs shook her body and burrowed into his soul.

"I'm so sorry I wasn't here." His whisper only made her cry harder.

"I . . . I miss her so. Every day I wake up thinking I'll tell Ma something, and she's not here. Her chair sits empty. I can't hear her singing. Thorliff, I want to hear her sing just one more time. That's all I ask." She wiped her eyes with her fingertips, then dug in her apron pocket for a handkerchief. She held it up for him to notice the neatly embroidered *A* bordered by two tiny blue forget-me-nots. "No matter what I do, there is some part of her with me."

What if it were my mother? The thought brought a lump to Thorliff's throat like a piece of coal. He sniffed back the tears An-ji's drew forth and took the handkerchief from her hand. Gently, tenderly, he wiped her eyes and the tear tracks down her cheeks. All the while, he poured his love into her eyes to soothe her soul.

"Th-thank you." She tucked her handker-chief back in her pocket. "Sorry to greet you like this. I figured I could handle it by now, but the sight of you . . ." She sighed. "She loved you, you know."

"She's been nearly a mother to me too, through all these years. If I wanted advice, I just had to ask, and sometimes I got it even when I didn't ask."

"Or didn't want it. I know. Ma had a gift for seeing inside of folks and finding the best." Together they sat on the steps of the back porch so they could be in the shade.

"Have you been home yet?"

"No, I came straight here. Far sent me home early since we were near a train sta-tion." He slid his fingers between hers so their palms lay together and rested them on his knee. "How's your Pa?"

"Not good. He wanders around like a lost soul. Swen's been in charge in a way, telling Pa that such and such needs doing, then Pa goes and does it. The younger ones don't know what to make of it, not that I do. But

I feel kind of the same. Guess it's different for women though. People got to be fed, clothes washed, the garden put by. With Ma so sick, most of it fell to me, so I just keep on doing what I been doing."

"Penny said a farm burned south of here."

"Uh-huh. A young couple's place. Your ma helped birth their baby, so they're staying over to your house in the soddy." She swiped at a stubborn tear.

"Could they come help out here?"

"I don't know. I can manage. All of us are pitching in, that's all."

Thorliff lifted their hands and kissed the tips of her fingers. "I need to get on home and surprise Ma before someone tells her I got off the train."

"Thorliff, you are such a good man." She leaned her head against his shoulder. "I am the luckiest girl in the world."

Oh no. I just hope you never learn how sad and scared I am inside. I'll try to be who you think I am. Truly I will. He surged to his feet, pulling her up with him. "I'll be back later." He dropped a kiss on her forehead and nearly ran out the yard, picking up his bedroll at the gate. He waved once and took off toward home.

Paws stood at the gate of the yard, barking to announce a visitor. When he heard

Thorliff call his name, he tore out to meet him, yipping and grinning his embarrassed doggy grin.

"You're forgiven." Thorliff rubbed the dog's ears and head, leaning down for a quick lick on the cheek. Paws wriggled and whined, trying to make up for his gaff. "That's okay. You didn't know it was me. You were just doing your job. Good dog." He adjusted his pack and picked up his trot again. Home had never looked so good. But where was everyone?

Surely they had heard Paws barking.

He dropped his bedroll on the front porch and looked over to Aunt Kaaren's. Glancing up, he saw the sun stood directly overhead. Dinner should be on the table, but no good smells teased him from the kitchen. He headed for the cheese house. Perhaps they were all working in there. But when he opened that door, all that greeted him was the smell of ripening cheese and the slightly sour smell of whey dripping from the presses into buckets for the pigs.

"Where are they, Paws?"

The dog looked over his shoulder to the other big house, then yipped and started off, now looking over his shoulder to make sure Thorliff was following.

"You better not be leading me on a wild

goose chase." Paws yipped again, tongue lolling from the side of his mouth.

"Halloo. Anyone home?" He leaped up the porch steps and went in the front door. Following the sound of voices, he wound his way back to the school wing.

"Thorliff!" Astrid saw him first and ran to throw her arms around his waist. "You're early."

Grace and Sophie followed Astrid, and by the time he'd greeted them all, his mother stood in front of him, waiting her turn.

"Are you all right?"

"Ja. Pa just sent me home early because we were near a train station yesterday. The train had just left though, so I slept at the station last night."

"Have you had anything to eat?"

"Leave it to a mother." Aunt Kaaren came to give Thorliff a hug too. "Good to have you home. Welcome to pandemonium alley." She indicated the room that usually wore a comfortable look with sofas and table and chairs for games and studying. With no furniture, no curtains, and strips of wallpaper on some walls and not others, it was obviously refurbishing time.

"We wanted to have it all done before the threshing crew returned." Ingeborg wiped wallpaper paste from her hand. "Having someone as tall as you will surely make this job easier."

"You can have my job," Ilse called from the top of a ladder where she was smoothing a strip of paper in place with a damp cloth.

"Where's Andrew?"

"He went with the Mendohlsons to see if they could salvage anything from their burned place."

"Tante Penny told me about that. Lightning start it?"

"Ja, and they hadn't plowed a fire break around the buildings. There have been so many fires, but they've stayed mostly in the fields. Thank God we haven't had a real prairie fire."

"There was one north of Devil's Lake. We saw it burning one night and still some the next morning. But it was far away from where we were."

"You didn't answer me. Are you hungry?"

"Starved. Mrs. Sam sent food with me, but I ate the last of it early this morning."

"Good. Astrid, you go set the table."

"Can't we eat outside?"

Kaaren nodded. "That would be fine. A picnic under the cottonwood tree."

Within minutes they had taken plates full of venison stew with dumplings outside and found places on benches or the dry grass. Trygve said grace at his mother's insistence, and amid chatter and laughter, they caught Thorliff up on all the news. There were two new calves. A letter had arrived from Manda saying that they were at the ranch and they loved it. There were three new registrants for the deaf school, one a man of twenty-three, and one of the cats had a new batch of kittens in the barn. The last piece of information was signed by Grace, who always knew when baby animals of any kind were being born. If there were bummer lambs or piglets in need of bottle feeding, she took care of them. Andrew had trained her well.

Thorliff told of the adventures of the threshing crew, not that there were many funny stories to tell this year. The drought was all anyone talked about, or so it seemed. "Far said he should be home in two weeks or so unless someone new comes to get him."

"Thank the good Lord there were no accidents this year." Kaaren leaned against the tree trunk. "And we'll keep praying for their safety."

Ilse brought out a plate of molasses cookies and passed them around. "You want I should mix up more paste for the wallpaper?"

"Yes, please. Maybe with Thorliff helping we can be finished by suppertime." Kaaren arched her back, pushing her shoulders into the tree. "I'd rather plant a garden or do the wash any day. Two more weeks, and we'll have students arriving. Where does the time go?"

"Only one week and Thorliff leaves." Astrid leaned against her big brother and looked up at him with sad eyes. "I really don't want you to go away."

He swallowed a lump in his throat. "Me neither."

"Thorliff, you're not having second thoughts again, are you?" Ingeborg stopped folding the blanket she'd been sitting on and stared at him.

"No, no second thoughts, only third and fourth and . . ." He sighed and shook his head at the same time. "I just keep thinking maybe I should wait and go next year." He didn't mention that Haakan had refused to even talk about it.

"Ja, well, you cannot back out now. Kaaren and I finished your new suit, and Bestemor knit you two new sweaters, one a vest and the other long sleeved with a V neck. Your trunk is nearly full."

"I hemmed you six new handkerchiefs." Astrid grinned when he tugged on her braids. "Stop that. And I did them on the sewing machine."

"She's going to be a good seamstress. You just watch."

"Astrid is good at whatever she does." Sophie both signed and spoke at the same time so that Grace could be sure what they were saying, although Grace had learned to read lips to go with signing.

"I made you a pi-ow." Grace spoke slowly and precisely, her eyes dancing at the look of astonishment on her cousin's face.

"Grace, you can talk!" Thorliff leaped to his feet and, grabbing Grace's hands, swung her around and around, her skirts flying and her laughter rising like soap bubbles on a breeze.

"We've been working very hard all summer, but she wanted to keep it a secret and surprise you." Kaaren blinked several times before she continued. "Grace wanted to talk so desperately."

Thorliff stopped swinging her and dropped to his knees so he could see her eye to eye. "Grace Knutson, I am so proud of you I could . . . I could . . ." Bereft of words, he hugged her to him. When she patted his cheeks and threw her arms around his neck, he glanced up to see tears streaming down his mother's face. Likewise his aunt's.

He pulled back enough to look Grace straight on so she could read his lips. "Grace, if you can do something so wonderful as this, you are an example to all of us." She smiled the kind of smile that makes angels sing, let alone humans. He cleared his throat, tried to say something else, then hugged her again instead. *Ah, Gracie, if you can do this, I can surely go to school and do well. Someday I am going to write your story.* He looked up at his aunt. *And yours.*

The days before he was to leave disappeared in a heartbeat. Each day he looked for a letter from Haakan, a telegram, anything that would give his blessing. He spent part of each evening with Anji. When he choked up telling her about Grace's speaking, the tears rolled down her cheeks also.

"She is the most precious child. I watch her at church and did so when we were in school. She is always looking out for someone less fortunate and sharing something she has without letting anyone know."

"God knows."

"She and Andrew are much alike."

"Ja, but he fixes things with his fists."

Thorliff shook his head.

"He is a boy."

"Who thinks he's a man."

Anji chuckled at the look he gave her. "Ah, my Thorliff, how often I watched you keep him out of trouble. He and the woodpile have gotten to be pretty good acquaintances at times."

"But you know, he never fights for himself but always for someone else. I know Pastor sees that, but often I didn't think it fair that Andrew was punished."

"We did have plenty of chopped wood for the stove." She laid her head on his shoulder so naturally she might have been doing it for years. "Woodpiles are good for discipline. One has a lot of time to think when chopping wood."

"A lot of anger gets worked off there."

She looked up to his face. "Don't tell me *you* ever had to do that?"

"Fine, I won't tell you." Her lips invited his kiss, pleaded for one. He obliged, and their lips lingered together. When he lifted his head, he put a hand to her cheek. "I must go."

"I know. I will see you in the morning at the train."

"Ja." His throat closed. Tomorrow was indeed the day. And he hadn't heard from his father.

It seemed half the countryside had gathered at the train station in the morning to see Thorliff off. No one from Blessing had ever gone away to school like this before.

"You don't look as happy as I thought you would." Ingeborg leaned close so others didn't hear her.

"I know." Thorliff sighed. "This is a big thing."

"True. A gift from God."

Thorliff chewed on the inside of his cheek and looked up the track. He could see the smoke from the stack in the distance. He really was going off to college, something he'd thought on and dreamed about for years. Why couldn't he get more excited?

Kaaren hugged him and slipped something into his pocket. "For a rainy day."

"Must be going to be a lot of rain. You aren't the first one." Her chuckle at his sally made him smile in return. He turned to look down at Anji, who clung to his left arm. "Just think, your turn will be next."

A slight shake of her head said what she thought about that.

Thorliff turned to his aunt Penny. "You make sure of that, will you please? There must be some way Anji can go to school to be a teacher."

"I will." Penny and Hjelmer smiled at each other and then at Thorliff. "You can trust us."

The train puffed into the Blessing station, metal screeching against metal as it braked to a stop. The conductor stepped off.

"Mercy, I don't have room for all these folks."

"We aren't going, only Thorliff." Sophie pointed to her cousin. "He's going to college."

"Well, can you beat that." He took a gold pocket watch out of his vest pocket. "If he's going on this train, he better get to moving."

Amid hugs and handshakes and more "rainy day" gifts, Thorliff picked up his carpetbag of food and books and last minute things. He took in a shoulder-lifting breath and let it out. He turned to Anji. "I will write to you every day." His eyes promised truth to his words.

Anji nodded, her smile trembling but still radiant.

Turning to his mother, he said, "Thank you, Mor. Tell Far . . . tell him . . ." He rolled his lower lip between his teeth and let out a breath. He reached for the handlebar with one hand and swung his bag up with the other.

"Thorliff!" A call echoed across the prairie.

CHAPTER THIRTY: NORTHFIELD, MINNESOTA SEPTEMBER 1893

Elizabeth set her foot atop the wooden ball and swung back her mallet.

"Stop. Stop. That's not fair." Thornton Wickersham strode toward her.

"Of course it is. House rules." She swung her mallet again.

"Not by the book." He withdrew a roll of paper from his back pocket and held it for her to see.

"And your point, Mr. Wickersham?" Elizabeth set her foot back on the ground and relaxed her grip on the mallet handle, setting the head on the ground and leaning lightly on the handle.

"But the book says . . ."

"Rule number four according to Phillip Rogers: One can use one's foot to hold his or her own ball in place while he or she smacks his or her opponent's ball into the lilacs. Personally, in this case I'd go for the pond, but" — she glanced at his white pants and shoes — "I'll take pity on your spiffy attire and go for the lilacs. Hate to have you mess up your white shoes retrieving your ball from the pond. They do float however." She indicated the two balls lying side by side on the close-clipped grass.

"I still say —"

"I know. It's not fair. But, my dear sir, rule number six, according to . . ."

"According to Phillip Rogers." He rolled his eyes, his grin spoiling any seriousness he tried to affect.

"Splendid. You're catching on." She assumed a schoolmarmish expression. "Rule number six: All is fair in war and croquet."

"Sure hope I never have to go to war with your father. Hit the ball so we can finish this round." His sigh lifted both shoulders and drooped his face.

With one tap she sent his ball rolling toward the lilacs, and then while he groaned, she knocked her ball through the last two wickets to hit the post. "That's three to one. Care to go again?"

"No, thank you. I don't think my male ego can handle another trouncing like this." He gathered the balls and mallets, setting them into their places on the croquet cart. "I suppose you are equally adept at chess." One eyebrow quirked at the question.

"I played on the St. Olaf chess team last year."

Thornton groaned again. "I suppose our two colleges are arch rivals?"

"Something like that." She tucked her hand into his arm. "Come, I see Cook is bringing out refreshments. She rather likes you, you know."

"I imagine she would give me a drubbing in croquet too." His mournful look sent her laughter pealing through the leaves of the sycamore that spread a bounty of shade over the white-painted iron chairs and table. A platter of cookies and iced glasses of lemonade awaited them.

He seated her first before taking his own chair and leaning back with a sigh. "What a pleasant afternoon. Thank you for taking time from your busy schedule to entertain me."

"My pleasure." She passed the plate of cookies and nodded for him to choose a glass. Did she dare tell him, or rather ask him, about the plan she'd been concocting? In the three times they'd seen each other since the first supper, she'd grown to enjoy him more and more. She hadn't taken much time to keep friendships alive, so laughing and teasing with him was fun. In her mind one of the advantages was that she felt no romantic attraction to him at all, so they could be friends.

He'd inhaled three cookies before she got up the nerve to speak. "Thornton, I have a big favor to ask."

He set his glass down. "Ask away. I'll do whatever I can."

"This is a really strange request."

He cocked an eyebrow.

She took a deep breath and with a slight nod began. "Please don't take this wrong."

Both his eyebrows rose. "Just say what you mean. Life is much easier that way."

"All right. My mother would much rather I lived an active social life, and that includes seeking a . . . a . . ."

"Mate?" His eyes danced.

She could feel the heat begin at her collarbone. "I wasn't going to be quite so blunt, but . . ." She looked up from drawing rings on the tabletop with her glass to find him stifling laughter. "You're enjoying this."

"Very much. I like seeing the perfectly controlled Miss Rogers having trouble with her words. A bit of vindication for the sport?" He nodded toward the croquet cart.

Elizabeth shook her head. *Men!* She sighed again and dove in. "My mother is disappointed that I am choosing a single life with medicine as my goal. So in order to keep her happy, I wondered . . . ah . . ." This is where it got sticky. "I wondered if perhaps we . . . I could . . . ah . . ." Another sigh.

"Yes?" He glanced upward as if conversing with someone in the tree, or above it, with God perhaps. "She stutters and stammers. Am I so difficult to communicate with that she fears what I will say?"

"Mr. Wickersham, you are teasing again."

"I know. You are such a delight to tease." He leaned forward and tapped her hand, the hand that had gone back to moving the glass around. "Elizabeth, just say it."

"Would you please pretend with me that we are interested in each other, even though we are not, so that my mother will give up all her matchmaking schemes and let me build the life I want and feel God wants me to have, and if this is all right with you I will be eternally grateful and never ask a favor again." She drew in a deep breath, wishing she had a fan.

"Don't go that far."

"What far?" She glanced at him from under her lashes.

"That you will never ask a favor of me again."

"Oh."

He rolled his lips together, slightly nodding at the same time. "Let me understand this correctly."

It was her turn to nod.

"You want to use me as an escort and possible marriage candidate, all as an act so that your mother will cease her motherly duties."

She eyed him with questions burning on her tongue. *Will you? Won't you? Don't torture me!* At that she chuckled. Of course, that was exactly what he was doing.

"If I take on this role, for which, by the way, I am eminently suited, as I have no interest in matrimony myself for some years, what will I receive in return?"

"Hmm." Elizabeth rubbed the point of her chin with one finger. "This is only fair, I suppose."

"Seems so to me."

"Am I to understand that you are considering going along with my charade?"

"I am considering it."

Elizabeth eyed the cookie platter, now empty, although she had only nibbled on one. "Would frequent gifts of cookies be a consideration?"

"That is a good place to start."

She remembered the rapt enjoyment on his face when she played the piano. "How about dinner invitations that include personal concerts?"

"Ah yes. May I make a suggestion?"

"Of course."

"When there is an event at Carleton at which I need a companion, you will fulfill that role so that I do not have to fend off the young ladies."

"You are insufferable. Do they throw themselves at you with abandon?"

"Frequently. It keeps me from studying." He assumed a pained look, as if living a life of travail or perhaps his shoes pinched.

Elizabeth threw back her head, the suppressed laughter no longer obeying her restrictions. "The stage is missing a great leading man. Have you thought of that as a career?"

"No. I fear I am destined for the ministry."

She laughed harder. "I th-think not." When their laughter subsided to intermittent chuckles, she leaned forward. "So we are in agreement?"

"That we are." He held out his hand. "A gentleman and gentlewoman's agreement?"

They shook hands and turned at the sound of her mother clearing her throat. "I thought to join you for refreshment, but if I am intruding . . . ?"

"Not at all, Mother. Sit down. I'll ask Cook to bring out refills." *Ah, she must surely have all manner of designs after catch-*

408

ing that little scene. It took all Elizabeth's willpower not to rub her hands together in Machiavellian glee.

To find a man she could be so comfortable with, like a pair of well-worn shoes, and not have to worry about offending him with her forthright tongue and opinions, one who liked so many of the same things she did, yet had no more romantic interest in her than she in him — what a priceless gift. *Thank you, God.*

So what will school bring? Elizabeth wondered later. After seeing Thornton off, she had gone down to the newspaper office to work on her father's books. Still seated at the desk with a ledger open before her, she locked her hands and stretched them over her head. If nothing else, it should be interesting. And challenging. She sighed. *And Mother will be happy, so my life will be much easier.*

CHAPTER
THIRTY-ONE:
NORTHFIELD,
MINNESOTA

Thorliff felt as if he'd been on the train forever and was being transported into a new life.

"You going to school in Northfield?" The conductor stopped beside his seat.

"Yes, sir."

"Which one?" At Thorliff's confused look, the man added, "Carleton or St. Olaf?"

"St. Olaf."

"Ah, good school. Of course they both are. Your first time away from home?"

"By myself, yes. I came from Norway when I was five."

"Where's home now?"

"Blessing, North Dakota. We farm there." At the mention of home the ache that had been growing burst into bloom. Home. What had made him leave?

"What's that near?"

"North of Grand Forks in the Red River Valley."

"Good land there. I used to run from Minneapolis to Fargo. Now I do this route to Northfield." He leaned down a bit to glance out the window. "Another fifteen minutes and we'll be at the station. Lord bless your year."

"Thank you." As the man continued on, Thorliff half stood. "Ah, sir?"

The conductor turned and swayed back. "Yes?"

"Can you tell me how I get my trunk to the school?"

"There will be wagons at the station that say St. Olaf. Just load yours on one and climb on yourself, or you can walk up to the campus. Not far."

Thorliff thanked him again and resumed his seat. The mention of home made him remember back to his getting on the train in Blessing. . . .

"Thorliff, wait!" The shout came from the western side of town.

Thorliff stepped back off the metal stool. Surely that was his father's voice. Everyone turned at the sound of galloping horse's hooves. He glanced over to see tears brightening his mother's eyes and knew his must be the same. He cleared his throat and turned to look at Anji, who slipped her arm

411

back in his.

Horse and rider galloped around the station and slid to a stop as the rider hauled on the reins. Andrew let out a holler, and others called greetings as Haakan swung off the horse and dogtrotted up to his son.

"I couldn't let you go without saying goodbye."

Thorliff's heart felt near to jumping out of his chest, then it settled back to its normal thrumming. He tried to speak, but no words passed the lump in his throat. *He came. Far came!*

Haakan clapped his hands on Thorliff's upper arms and looked into his eyes. "I'm proud of you, son. Go with God. We're sure going to miss you." He started to say something else but choked. He reached for Thorliff's hand to shake it, then pulled him into his chest and hugged him close. "You have my blessing, whatever it is good for." These words were meant for Thorliff's ears alone and were branded on his heart.

"Mange takk." Ingeborg put her arms around both her tall men.

"All aboard!"

"Remember we are praying for you." Ingeborg patted his cheek. Haakan squeezed his son's hand one more time.

The train huffed and whistled and with a

squeal inched forward.

Thorliff waved at Anji, his smile wavering as much as hers. He waved at all the others and grabbed onto the bar by the door.

"Get on!" Andrew yelled, waving his hat.

"I will." Thorliff jogged two steps and hopped up on the step where his satchel still sat waiting for him. He leaned out, waving his hat until Blessing station disappeared in the shimmering heat. . . .

"Northfield. Next stop, Northfield," the conductor called from the end of the car, bringing Thorliff's thoughts back to the present.

Thorliff watched as the houses grew closer together. When he saw streetlights, he knew he was in town. Though he saw mostly the backs of brick buildings, he studied everything with curious eyes. While small compared to Minneapolis and St. Paul, Northfield made Blessing look like a dot on the prairie. He saw churches with spires, three-story buildings, a park, the river winding through the town, a creamery that looked to be exceedingly prosperous, schools, and shops of all kinds. Tall trees lined some of the streets, and there was green grass in many yards. Was the drought not so bad here? The farms along the way had looked about the same as those at home, dry and tired.

His stomach rumbled. He'd run out of food except for some cheese, and he hated spending his money on the outrageously priced sandwiches he'd seen. And a cup of coffee? He'd chosen to drink water from the cooler on the train, which tasted terrible.

"Northfield. All bound for Northfield."

As the train screeched and hissed to a stop, Thorliff tucked his book back into his bag and shrugged into his jacket.

How could Blessing and home seem so far away? Sure, he'd ridden miles of track, but it wasn't another world, was it? Once he'd seen a telescope that, when you looked in one end, brought distant things up close. Then he'd looked in the other end. That's the way he felt now, small and almost invisible.

He swung his carpetbag to the brick walk and looked down the train to see men unloading trunks, boxes, and crates. Surely his was among those. He looked out to the street where wagons were lined up, and sure enough, two of them had "St. Olaf College" lettered on the side. Several other young people looked as lost as he felt there at the train station, while others were being greeted by people they knew.

He headed for one of the St. Olaf wagons. At least he was doing something besides standing there feeling that he was the least member on earth.

"Sir, my name is Thorliff Bjorklund, and I am starting school at St. Olaf. Is your wagon available to carry my trunk?"

"Of course, young fellow, and you too." The driver swung to the ground. "Let's go get your luggage. How much do you have?"

"This" — Thorliff lifted his carpetbag — "and one trunk."

"You don't have that trunk plumb full of books, now, do you?"

"No, sir." *I don't even own that many books.*

"Good. They do weight up." The man barely came to Thorliff's shoulder, yet had even broader shoulders and a head that seemed to sit right on them. Legs bowed as if he rode a barrel instead of a wagon seat, he still set a pace that made Thorliff stretch out. When Thorliff pointed to his trunk that was lined up with the others, the man grabbed the leather handle and half hoisted it to his shoulder.

"Let me get the other end." *My goodness, he's strong as a draft horse.* Together they hauled the trunk to the wagon and slid it in the back.

A young woman with a quivering chin waited by the curb. "Could I please ask you to fetch my things also, if this is indeed a conveyance to St. Olaf?"

"It is, miss." Mr. Muscles tipped his hat. "Come on, young feller, perhaps you can help me again." They hauled two trunks and a wooden box back to the wagon in as many trips. "The ladies always bring twice as much as the gents," Muscles whispered to Thorliff as they shoved the last box in.

"Really." He wiped his forehead with the back of his hand.

"Anyone else here need a ride to St. Olaf?" When no one answered, Muscles helped the young woman up onto the wagon seat. "You'll have to ride in the back there, young feller."

"Good." Thorliff slammed the endgate shut and climbed over the back to sit on the wooden box.

That night, having registered, paid his money, been assigned a room, and found the dining room, Thorliff sat in his dormitory room gazing at the empty bed across from his. His roommate would be arriving on the morrow. But this night he felt more alone than ever in his life. He could hear others laughing down the hallway, and two were talking in the next room. He'd already put away his things and made his bed, so all that remained was to read his Bible and write a letter home. Two letters, to be exact.

He glanced up at the gas lamp that shed more light than three kerosene lamps. How could he afford to stay here and still have enough money to last the year? Surely there were places in town that were less expensive. Perhaps he could find one where he could exchange work for his bed and board. Or maybe he could stay with a farmer nearby. He'd seen plenty of cows that would need to be milked.

"But, Thorliff, I want you to have time to study and not work all the time." He could hear his mother's voice plain as if she were in the room. This seemed to be a night for sighing. He flopped back on his bed and locked his hands behind his head. Someone overhead was moving furniture. *Lord, how will I stand this? I know you said you would be with me. Why, then, do I feel so alone?*

Quit feeling sorry for yourself, you big lug. He swung his feet back to the floor and rose to cross to the desk. Sitting down, he took out a sheet of paper and an ink bottle.

Dear Far and Mor,
    You would love it here. The view from

this hill is amazing. I haven't seen such a high place since we left Norway. My room and all the buildings have gaslights like we saw in Minneapolis that time we went there. Of course they have gaslights in Grand Forks too, but here I can see my paper nearly as well as in the day-light.

My train trip was uneventful, but I didn't read much. I was too busy watching the scenery. There are more hills and trees here, and the town is huge.

He chewed on the end of the pen. How to separate the things he was feeling from the things he would put on the paper? He went on to describe his room and the dining hall.

Tomorrow I will go look for my class-rooms and perhaps meet the teachers. I haven't met many students yet. There is a meeting tomorrow for those of us just arriving. That is all for now. Thank you for giving me this opportunity. I promise to do my best. Give my love to everyone.

Your faithful son,
Thorliff

Without reading it over, he blew on the last words, folded the paper, and slid it into an envelope. He said much the same to Anji, only asking her how things were at her home and if they'd thought any more about getting someone in to help. He signed it, "Yours faithfully, Thorliff."

After addressing the envelopes, he set them against the wall, then undressed and hung his clothes on the pegs provided. He took his Bible to bed with him and, head propped on one hand, turned to Psalms and Proverbs, where he read a chapter in each. He understood how King David felt. Sometimes it seemed that God had closed the door and left him alone.

CHAPTER
THIRTY-TWO:
ST. OLAF COLLEGE

One week at college and Elizabeth already felt as though she'd never had a summer vacation.

She sat in the St. Olaf library with her advanced chemistry book open in front of her. For some reason she was having trouble concentrating. *Just read it again and again until you understand it,* she ordered herself. Instead, her gaze strayed to the young man sitting across the table and down a chair.

When he looked up and met her glance, she caught her breath. He had the most incredible blue eyes she'd ever seen. Deep clear blue like the sky straight above on a perfect summer day just before the sun breaks the horizon. She smiled and nodded. He did the same and returned to his book.

Hmm. Was he shy? She was sure he was a freshman. She'd never seen him before, and he looked too young to be an upperclassman. She forced herself back to chemistry.

When she looked up again, he was gone.

Her curiosity made her shake her head at herself. What was there about him, besides the eyes, that held her attention? She catalogued his face from memory. Handsome in a way, square jaw, straight nose, would most likely fill out more. He was thin now but wore an air of strength. So what was it?

She glanced out the window to see the sun setting. Time to get on home. Her mother hated her walking home after dark. She slid her books into her satchel and smiled at the librarian as she passed. Halfway down the stairs, she stopped.

"I know. It's the sadness." Someone bumped into her from behind and gave her a strange look as he passed her. "Sorry. Talking to myself again." It was him, the one with the blue eyes, the sad eyes. She watched him clatter down the stairs ahead of her.

She inhaled the fragrance of fresh wax, disinfectant, and books. A library had a smell all its own, and she loved it. If she weren't going to be a doctor or a concert pianist, then she would study to be a librarian. There were many worse friends in life than books, although her mother would tend to disagree with her. Annabelle Rogers would rather do needlepoint or some other needlework than read any day.

Strange, here she was thinking about her mother in the library, of all places. She pushed the heavy door open and stepped outside to breathe in the dying day. Leaves had already begun to fall, due to the drought. Someone was burning them somewhere. The trace of leaf smoke could not be confused with anything else. It was one of the hallmark scents of fall, her favorite season, other than spring of course. She waved to an acquaintance and headed for the path leading down the hill, the path taken by most of the townees. While she walked, she reviewed the bones and cartilage of the knee, then the ankle. While her anatomy professor admitted to being uncomfortable with women in his class, he expected even more out of them than the men. Right now they were reviewing bones, but the part she was looking forward to was the study of the vascular system and then the nervous system. Life would be so much easier if she could take all of her courses at St. Olaf instead of going to Carleton for her sciences.

How intricate we are. She'd been impressed with the fetal pig she'd dissected the year before, but the human body was so much more exciting. She'd assisted Dr. Gaskin when he had operated on a badly broken hand, putting bits of bone back in place like a jigsaw puzzle.

"It will all grow back," he had assured her. "And since the tendons aren't severed, he will most likely have full use of his hand."

"If we can keep the infection out."

"Right. And thanks to carbolic acid, we have a good chance of that. You have to remember to boil your instruments and scrub your hands in carbolic acid also. Much has been learned about putrefaction since the war. And while years ago we might have amputated his hand, now we will pray for perfect healing instead. The human body has been given remarkable abilities to heal itself. That is why the first rule of a physician is —"

"To do no harm." She finished suturing and bandaging the hand under his watchful eye. Once the chloroform cone was removed, their patient began to stir within minutes. His nurse stuck her head in the door. "Patient in room two is getting impatient."

Dr. Gaskin exchanged smiles with Elizabeth. "Thank you, my dear. I will be on my rounds, or Nurse will be flailing me about the head and shoulders with excess verbiage."

Elizabeth shook her head. "You know you

love it. You're looking better than I've seen you in some time."

"Oh, pshaw." But the light in his eyes told her he knew and appreciated her concern.

Now forcing her wandering mind to match her feet and go forward once she reached the bottom of the hill and came out from under the trees, Elizabeth set a brisk pace for home. She'd promised her father some time at the paper tonight.

The two of them walked back to the office after supper. Lights glowed in windows and threw square outlines onto the lawns. Arm in arm, father and daughter watched the streetlights come on as the lamplighter took his long pole from post to post.

"Summer is indeed past when they start lighting the lamps before seven." Mr. Rogers checked his pocket watch to be certain. He couldn't have read it had it not been for the streetlight. "I have set something in motion that I must tell you about."

"Oh? You sound serious."

"Yes. I have let young Hans go." Rogers shook his head. "He was never going to make a newspaperman. In the two years he's been with me, his writing hasn't improved a mouse's whisker, and he and the printing press are mortal enemies."

"Um." She knew he'd been having difficulties for some time, so why the switch now?

"I heard him calling my press Bessie the . . ." He hawked and spat. "Well, I would never use such words around ladies, and I fear that he might have where you are concerned. Is that true?"

If he knew she'd fended off Hans's groping hands, he would have not only fired the youth but run him out of town as well. On a rail or worse. She'd heard more contemptible terms in her travels with the doctor, but she'd never let on. Like blood, you got used to it.

"But, Father, he learned that from you." She kept an innocent tone in her voice to match the look on her face. When she peeked out the corner of her eye, she saw him scowling.

"You minx. You just like to tease your old father."

"What else have you been hatching without telling me?"

"I've hired a new man. I decided that since there has been some money missing, I would rather someone stayed at the office through the night. Just a precaution, mind you."

"Of course." She had an idea that with

Hans gone the change drawer would not be losing any more change. But she couldn't prove it and hadn't wanted to smear the young man's character. "So?"

"So I want you to look at that back room and see what needs to be done to turn it into living quarters. The young man I hired attends St. Olaf, so I thought perhaps he could walk you to school in the mornings as dawn comes later and later." At her snort, he clamped his arm closer to his side, squeezing her hand in the process. "Now don't you go arguing with me on this. You are too precious to me to take any chances. Besides, the world needs a doctor of your caliber."

"Father." She reached up and kissed his cheek. "I'm not a doctor yet." *And it sounds like he is finally in agreement with me.*

"But you will be and a blessedly good one too." He pushed open the door, setting the bell to tinkling. "Let's look at that room."

"Fixing a room up is more in Mother's domain than mine."

"I know that, but I'd rather present this to her as a *fait accompli.*" He turned on the gaslights as they made their way down the hall. The back room had become the catch-all for anything out of use that still had pos-sibilities. Not that any of the things stored

426

there were ever brought back into use, but her father hated to throw anything away. A furnace down in the basement heated the entire building, including the attic if they opened the vents.

Elizabeth stopped in the doorway. "Needs a massive cleaning out. Can that young man come help do that?"

"What a good idea. And isn't there a bed and dresser up in the attic at home? I thought to give him a desk too, so he can study here under the gaslight."

"It would help to put up a partition, then you would still have a storage room here."

"We could do that later. I shall ask him if he can come on Saturday. Then perhaps he could start the first of next week."

"What will he cook on?"

"Oh, can't he eat at the college?"

"Not if you promised him room and board."

"Did I say he's already been published and plans on being a writer? Perhaps we can turn him into a journalist."

"Father, you are changing the subject." Elizabeth fetched a pad of paper and, with a pencil, began making notes. "He will need a rug. I know there's one at home that would work. Some kitchen things. Perhaps Cook would make extra, and he could pick up his supper on the way home at night."

"I knew you would think what's best to do." Her father turned back to his office. "I'll leave you to that while I finish my editorial for this week. Have you written that article on the incoming freshmen at both Carleton and St. Olaf?"

"It's almost finished." She crossed to the window and looked out. "How dreary. We'll need curtains for sure, but mostly it needs a good scrubbing." She sniffed. "I sure hope he doesn't mind the smell of ink. If he lives here, it will permeate his very pores." She wandered out to the desk in the front of the shop where she did the accounts and sat down to finish her article. *I wonder if I've seen him on campus.*

CHAPTER
THIRTY-THREE:
BLESSING, NORTH
DAKOTA
OCTOBER 1893

"Mor, I miss Thorliff something dreadful."

"I know, Astrid, me too." Ingeborg gave the cookie dough one last rolling. "You want to cut these out?"

"I guess." Astrid took the cookie cutter and placed it precisely on the edge of the dough so as to use every scrap. "Have you seen Andrew yet?"

Ingeborg turned at the careless tone of her daughter's voice. She knew that tone. It meant Astrid was hiding something. "No. Why?"

"Oh, nothing. I just wondered." Astrid waited while her mother slid the pancake turner under the cut dough and lifted it off the floured board. "Shall I sprinkle sugar on them?"

"Or you could make faces with the dried currants."

"Or both?" Her blue eyes reminded her mother so much of Thorliff that her heart turned over. "I think we shall box up some of these and send them to a certain person away at college."

"Can I put in that muffler I knit for him?"

"I thought that was for Christmas."

"Well, it froze here last night. He might get cold there."

"Ah, Astrid, you surely may. I'll put in a jar of rhubarb jam too. If he is doing his own cooking, he will like that."

Astrid cut some more cookies, then cocked her head. "Does Thorliff know how to cook?"

"He won't starve." Ingeborg slid the flat cookie sheet into the oven. "We need some more wood."

"That's Andrew's — I'll get it."

Ingeborg looked after her daughter as she darted out the back door. *All right, now what is going on? Andrew either isn't home from school, or he doesn't want to come in, fresh cookies or no. Lord, what is it? You know I trust them into your care, but not knowing sometimes makes it hard to leave them there. Do I go looking for him, or do I wait?*

Astrid returned with an armload of wood and dumped it into the woodbox beside the stove.

"Is there something you want to tell me?"

The little girl shook her head and raced

430

out the back door again.

Wait seemed to fill the kitchen. The orange cat asleep on a rug behind the stove mewed and arched her back, stretching every limb and hair the way only cats can do. She strolled over and rubbed against Ingeborg's leg.

"Ja, I know. You want to be petted, but my hands are full of cookie dough. Ask Astrid."

When Astrid came in and dumped another load, the cat twined about her legs, purring loud enough to be heard past the barn. She picked up the cat and held her under her chin. The purr volume upped, if that were possible. "It wasn't Andrew's fault. That mean Toby Valders pulled Ellie's braids, pulled 'em real hard so Ellie had tears in her eyes, and she's so much littler than him."

Ingeborg rolled more cookie dough.

"Pastor made Toby chop wood, and he had to apologize, but he didn't do so good." She looked up from petting the cat. "Toby is just plain old mud-ugly mean."

"Astrid, what a thing to say."

"Well, he is. Andrew had to sweep the schoolroom and some other stuff. But you won't tell him I told you, will you? Please, Ma. Andrew didn't hurt him bad."

"No, I won't." *But I'll get the truth out of*

him. Andrew never lies.

Ingeborg took the first pan of cookies from the oven and, one by one, lifted them onto the towel she'd spread on the table for just that purpose. "Go upstairs in the closet under the eaves and bring me that cardboard box the boots came in. That should be just the right size for the cookies and jam."

"And the muffler."

"That too." Ingeborg turned her head at the sound of Paws barking. Most likely that was Andrew. She knew for certain when the tone changed from warning to ecstasy. If only it were as easy for her to do the same. Sometimes she wished she didn't know when one of her children misbehaved out of her sight, but God always managed to bring it to her attention.

"You're home late." She smiled at her son when he entered the kitchen and handed him a cookie, still warm from the pan.

"I know." Andrew took the cookie in one hand and dumped a book on the chair with the other. The thundercloud that rode him like Manda rode horses said he hadn't worked off the anger by a long shot. "Do you know what that Toby Valders did today? He made Ellie cry! He . . . he laughed. Until I hit him. Then he quit laughing."

"I expect he did."

"He wasn't laughing when he was chopping wood either. He was lucky I didn't hit him with a log." Andrew stomped across the room and back. "Mor, he can't go on picking on other people like that. He thinks it is funny, but it's not. Pastor makes him chop lots of wood, but that doesn't do any good."

"Maybe it all depends on how much he has to chop. Hard work takes the mean out of some people." Ingeborg rolled another circle of cookie dough. "The Bible says to forgive those who hurt you."

"I know." He slumped in a chair. "But I forgave him lots of times, and what good has it done? He keeps on doing the same old mean things."

Lord, give me wisdom, and I need it right now. "Andrew, you can't go on letting your fists take over for your mind."

"I tried not to."

"And maybe Toby tried not to tease."

"No, he didn't." Pure disgust painted his words.

"How do you know that? Could you see in his heart?"

"Mor, only God can do that." Andrew reached for another cookie. "I'm going to the springhouse for a glass of milk. You want

433

the pitcher brought in?"

"Yes, please. And some eggs too. I thought a cake might be good for supper."

That night when Ingeborg checked on Andrew after he'd gone to bed, she found him writing by the lamplight. She sat beside him on the bed and waited.

"I'm writing Thorliff a letter. This room seems so empty without him here."

"We could have Hamre bring his things in here."

"Maybe." Andrew returned to his writing, then put his pencil and paper on the stand that held the kerosene lamp. "You know when I came home from school and was so mad?"

"Oh ja, I know."

He glanced up with a sunbeam smile and went back to studying the calluses on his fingers. "Pastor made me look up some Bible verses. One said that unless I forgive someone, God doesn't forgive me."

"Forgive others as we have been forgiven?"

"Uh-huh. Another said that a soft answer turns away wrath."

"I know. But that's not easy to do."

"So does that mean I should tease Toby back instead of hitting him?"

"You ask hard questions." Ingeborg

watched the flame flicker in the glass chimney. "Are you nice to Toby ever?"

Andrew tipped his head to the side. "I don't talk to him much 'cause I don't like him."

"So what do you think God wants you to do in this instance?"

"Do I gotta love him?" Sheer horror made his mouth drop open.

"What does the Bible say?"

He traced circles on the sheet covering his lap. "To love your enemies and be kind to those who persecute you." Silence stretched as the circles continued. He looked up at his mother. "God asks hard things, huh?"

"That he does. But He also says He will deliver us from evil, and I believe that includes evil thoughts and evil actions."

"And punching someone is evil." It wasn't a question, but the words carried a heavy load.

"Do you want to pray about this?"

"I will." He slid down to lie prone. "I got to think on it some more first."

"All right. Since God loves us and hears us all the time, He can help with our thoughts too." She leaned over and kissed his cheek. "I'm proud of you, Andrew Bjorklund."

" 'Cause I hit Toby Valders?" His eyes lit up.

She ruffled his hair with a loving hand. "Good night, Andrew."

"So do I need to go talk to Pastor about this fighting son of ours?" Haakan sat against the bed pillows, his Bible in his lap.

"No. At least not now." She slid into bed beside him and laid her head on his chest. "Did he tell you?"

"Ja, when we were milking."

"And what did you tell him?"

"I told him to make sure the first punch was hard as he could throw so the other guy didn't get up and come back to hurt him."

"Haakan Bjorklund, what a thing to say." She stared at her husband, then thumped him on the shoulder when she realized he was teasing her.

He cupped her head with one hand and laid his other on the Bible. "I told him the answers are in this book, and if he could find them and put them to work, he was a better man than his pa."

"Did you really?" At his nod, she laid one arm over his chest and hugged him. "He'd have to go a long way to be a better man than his pa." Some time passed before they fell asleep.

■ ■ ■ ■

She was dreaming of someone pounding nails when she finally woke enough to realize someone was banging on the door.

"Ingeborg!" Hurrying footsteps crossed the kitchen.

"Ja? Who comes in the middle of the night?" Haakan reared up and threw back the covers, but Ingeborg was already pulling on her wrapper.

"Hjelmer?"

"Ja. Penny is having the baby."

"Ah, good. It's about time." While she talked, Ingeborg changed from nightdress to day clothes, tying on an apron as she entered the kitchen where Hjelmer paced from one side to the other. "How long ago did the pains start?" She lit a lamp and went for her bag.

"Forever ago." Hjelmer wiped his forehead with the back of his hand. "She says there is no rush, but you know Penny. She's so stubborn she'd —"

"Easy. First babies usually take longer." Ingeborg made sure everything was in its place and snapped the brown leather bag shut. "I'm ready. Did you go for Metiz?"

"Do you need her?"

437

"No, but I know she would love to be there when this baby is born."

"I'll bring Metiz." Haakan finished tying his boots. "You go on before Hjelmer here keels over with a heart attack."

Hjelmer usually had plenty to say, but this night he flicked the horses into a fast trot and said not a word.

"Hjelmer, Penny is healthy and has been so all along. There is nothing to worry about." The specter of Katy dying in childbirth hung over them all.

"Ja, I know."

But Ingeborg knew he was only mouthing polite words. *Oh, God, please let me be right this time. Give her strength and an easy birth.*

Penny met them at the door, ready to toss a bucket of soapy water out on her roses.

"What were you doing?" Hjelmer stared at his wife, fear, shock, and horror chasing each other across his face.

"I scrubbed the floor." Penny clamped her jaw and waited for the pain to pass. "I thought I might as well get some of the housework done while I am waiting."

Ingeborg broke out in laughter. "Ah, Hjelmer, you are a wise man to have married such a woman as this."

"Well, you said to walk, and that seemed a waste of time, so I scrubbed instead.

Think I'll work on blacking the stove next."

"Ingeborg, is she touched in the head?"

"No. Not at all." She set her bag down by the door. "Now you go out in the blacksmith or something. We'll call you when we need you."

"Penny?" Hjelmer took a step toward his wife, but she shook her head.

"This here's woman's work. You go on now."

"What would you like to do next?" Ingeborg looked around the immaculate kitchen. " 'Pears to me, you been keeping right busy the last few hours."

"Ja, I let Hjelmer sleep. No sense the both of us pacing the floor. Time passes much easier when you're busy." She doubled over, her arms clasped around her belly.

"How far apart?"

"Too far. It's going to be some time yet."

"Why don't you lie down and let me see how far along you are. Has your water broken?"

"No. You think beating the rugs on the line will help this along?"

"Can't hurt, unless you'd rather scrub the stairs. Kneeling is a good position. It takes the pressure off the baby."

"Scrubbing it is. You could go on back to sleep in our bed until I need you."

439

Ingeborg laughed. "Thanks, but I'd rather start some bread for you."

The two women worked away, trading gossip and snippets of news. When the contractions came, Penny grew quiet but then picked up right where they'd left off as if nothing had happened.

"Oh, oh. Bring a rag and a bucket."

"Water?"

"Mm-hmm. Uff da. That one was a doozy."

Ingeborg brought the bucket and mopped up the floor. "Okay, from now on we walk together. Don't want you collapsing on me, then I'd have to call Hjelmer, and he dithers enough for ten men."

"Funny, isn't it, how men . . ." Another one hit.

"I think we'll go upstairs now." One stopped them midway.

Ingeborg settled Penny on the bed with her back propped against the headboard, one carved by Uncle Olaf with oak leaves at the height of the curve. "Now remember, shouting with the contractions helps release them, so don't go all brave on me. Let's just get this baby born with the least amount of work on your part."

"She near?" Metiz climbed the stairs and joined them. "Haakan, go stay with

440

Hjelmer."

"Good. I haven't heard any hammering from the smithy."

"He's probably groomed all the hair right off that new horse." Penny arched and groaned, panting her way through.

"Not long now." Metiz laid a wrinkled hand on Penny's belly and kept it there through another contraction.

Ingeborg checked the progress. "We have a crown. Not much longer now. You push whenever you need to."

Penny groaned again and pushed, her body convulsing, her teeth clamped so hard her jaw was white.

Ingeborg guided the baby out, gently turning the shoulders to cause the least tearing. "Penny, my dear, you are made for having babies."

The baby let out a squall, his face all screwed up as if he were telling them exactly what he thought of the indignity he'd just been through.

"Oh, oh. A Bjorklund through and through," Ingeborg said, tears streaming down her cheeks, as always was the case at the beauty of birthing a baby. She laid the baby on his mother's chest and turned to Metiz.

"He gift to many." She nodded, her eyes

seeing far into the distance.

"We're naming him Gustaf after Hjelmer's far and Joseph after my uncle. That's a lot of name to live up to, little one." She cupped his head with her hand. "Your pa will be so proud of you."

"Oh, I have to go get Hjelmer." Ingeborg dried her eyes. "You finish here, Metiz?"

The old woman nodded. "You go."

Not finding the men in the smithy, Ingeborg leaned her head into the barn and announced, "You have a baby boy."

Hjelmer ran by her as if wolves were chasing him, not bothering to say a word.

Haakan picked up the brush Hjelmer dropped and, after putting the brushes away, shut the door behind him and put an arm around his wife's waist. "That was fast."

"Ja, she was born for having babies. Easier time I haven't seen. And he is beautiful. Started telling the whole world what he thought of leaving his safe home and coming into this one. He'll be a talker, that one." She leaned her head against his shoulder. "The sun's coming up."

"I better get back for chores. You want me to come for you later?"

"No, Metiz can stay. I'll come now." She turned and reached up to wrap her arms around his neck. "Though God seems to have decided we will have no more children, I sure do appreciate His allowing me to help others' babies into the world. There is nothing this side of heaven more wondrous."

Haakan kissed her and held her close, knowing that tears always came after such great joy.

A week later came another cry for help. Knute Baard galloped up to the house before breakfast. "Please, come quick. Pa fell out of the haymow."

CHAPTER
THIRTY-FOUR:
NORTHFIELD,
MINNESOTA

Thorliff stared at the grade on his paper.

"You look like you lost your last friend." Benjamin, the student who sat behind him in English, tapped him on the shoulder.

"Ah." Thorliff felt as if he'd come from a far land. The large C in red ink stared back at him. He'd never gotten a C on a paper or test in his entire life. And this had been review material. It must be a sign. As he'd been suspecting, he was not supposed to be in college.

"Got a C, eh? Not bad. The highest mark was a B. Ingermanson doesn't believe in giving A's, at least not at the beginning of the year."

"How do you know that?"

"My brother had him for two years. Said he is a fine teacher but rough on the freshmen."

But maybe your brother didn't dream of being a writer. Maybe he . . . Thorliff shook his head. He'd thought this would be one of his easier classes, but so far nothing was easy.

"My brother said you can always go talk to the man. He really does want to help his students think and write clearly."

"Ah ja. Thank you."

"All right, class. We'll begin for today." Mr. Ingermanson strode to the front of the room. "I know many of you are surprised — perhaps shocked is a better word — at your grades."

Thorliff felt that the teacher was looking right at him. Horrified was more like how he felt. He kept his gaze on his paper, fearing anyone could read his thoughts in his eyes.

"You have one week to rewrite this assignment, using my comments as guides. I will add one more question tomorrow. You will find it on the blackboard when you come to class." He looked around the room. "Any questions?"

Someone behind Thorliff asked, "Can we bring our grades up that way?"

"Yes, one grade level. But I am not guaranteeing that. Anyone else? Good, then let us begin the lesson for today."

When he left class, Thorliff wasn't sure he had heard a word the teacher said. The notes he'd taken said differently, but his mind refused to concentrate. After his last class he headed to the newspaper office to help clean up his future quarters. Perhaps he would be able to study better without all the distractions of the dormitory.

The tinkle of the bell over the door announced his entrance.

"How can I help you?" The woman behind the desk pushed her glasses back up on her nose with one finger.

"I . . . I'm Thorliff Bjorklund, I . . ."

"Ah, the new boy. You go right on back through that door. They are waiting for you. By the way, I'm Mrs. Freeland. I help out here some."

Thorliff did as told, sniffing the smell of printer's ink as he went. Smelled almost as good as books.

"Ah, there you are." Mr. Rogers stepped out of his office to meet Thorliff in the hall. "Come with me. Elizabeth is anxious to get started. There's a wagon outside the back door to load those things we're getting rid of."

"Yes, sir." Thorliff followed the man to the end of the hall.

"That's the press in there, affectionately called Bessie when she is running right, and I have a few other names for her when she isn't." Phillip indicated the machine in a room to the left. "And this will be your quarters. I think we will partition off half this room for storage."

A young woman, a handkerchief covering her hair, stepped from behind a bookcase.

"This is my daughter, Elizabeth. Thorliff Bjorklund, my dear."

"Oh, it's you." Elizabeth whipped the handkerchief off her head. "From the library, I mean."

"Ja." *What do I do? Shake hands?* "I-I'm pleased to meet you." He ducked his head.

"You know each other?" Mr. Rogers looked from one to the other.

"We've not met," said Elizabeth. "I am very happy to meet you, Mr. Bjorklund, and welcome to Northfield and St. Olaf. I know you are going to love it here."

He kept his face blank. Love it here? All he could think of was going home. "Thank you." *Dolt, can't you think of anything more to say than that?*

"You are welcome." She gave him a quizzical glance. "Then let us begin. I've asked Old Tom to bring his wagon and help us." Hands on hips, she stared around the room filled with boxes and old machinery, furniture, and a broken picture frame hanging askew on the wall. A coat of dust grayed everything and made the windows opaque.

447

"I think I have some things to finish at my desk." Phillip gestured toward the other room.

"You don't mind what I throw out?"

"Ah . . ." He stared around at the mess, shaking his head. "I trust your judgment." He beat a less than dignified retreat.

Elizabeth shook her head. "Okay, let's move enough to sweep that end of the room, which will be used for storage. I'll look in boxes to see what we can toss." A knock at the door admitted a basset-faced man who, after being introduced to Thorliff, looked around the room, his head moving like a pendulum.

"Might just carry it all out to m' wagon. Be easier."

"As I said, we'll clean at that end and move what needs to be saved down there."

Tom scrunched his mouth from side to side. "If you say so."

Thorliff moved enough to sweep out a corner, then began stacking the boxes Elizabeth pointed to in that area. She had Tom cart out the throwaways. By the time they'd reduced the mess to half, Thorliff was longing for open fields and threshing dust rather than inside dirt.

"Here, I brought you refreshments." Phillip stood in the doorway with a pot of coffee and a plate of sandwiches. At Elizabeth's raised eyebrow, he added, "Cook sent them over. I made the coffee."

She groaned. "Not your usual."

"No, fresh and only half the grounds."

She turned to Thorliff. "We can be grateful for that."

Since his stomach had been rumbling for the last hour, he fell to, as did Tom, so the conversation was mainly between Elizabeth and her father and mostly regarding the stuff left in the room.

They went back to work, now scrubbing walls, ceiling, windows, and the floor of the area she'd decreed his new quarters. The smell of soap and wet rags filled the room, but the walls turned into white plaster, the floor wore a coat of paint, albeit dark brown, and the gas jets on the wall worked after Tom tinkered with them a bit.

While Elizabeth asked him questions, Thorliff answered with as few words as possible. *She gives orders like a sergeant,* he thought more than once. But since this was her place, he did as told, relieved when she finally announced they were finished for the day.

Elizabeth sat down on the only chair and looked around. "Once we get that other end partitioned off, this should be fine."

"More than fine." Thorliff leaned against the now clean wall. His end of the long room, about ten by fifteen feet, included a window, an outside door on one wall, and a door into the hallway of the offices on the opposite. A square grate allowed heat from the furnace below to warm the room in winter. Once he had a bed and perhaps a table and chair for a desk, he would be fine. The thought of an indoor privy and running water in the bathroom seemed like found wealth. He'd nail up a board with pegs for his clothes and be right at home.

"What a difference." Mr. Rogers brought a tray with coffee mugs into the room.

"I could build that partition over the weekend if you want." Thorliff nodded toward the other side.

"Can you hang a door?"

"Ja. My pa can build anything, and I always helped him."

"Good. I will get the materials first thing in the morning." He handed a cup to Thorliff. "Drink up, son. You can spend the night here if you like. Tom will bring a bed over from the house."

"I think I'll go back up the hill for tonight, thank you."

"Do you have much to bring down?"

"A trunk and a box." His belongings had

grown with the purchase of textbooks.

"I'll send a wagon up, then. Let's go on home."

The three walked as far as the Rogerses' home, and Thorliff bid them good-night. He caught himself whistling on his way up the path. At least he now had a job and a free place to live. The cloud that had been smothering him seemed to lift somewhat.

He fell into bed without writing on his letter to Anji. To save on stamps, he wrote to her each night but mailed the letter once a week. The same with the letter for the family at home.

Over the weekend he did as he'd said, sawing and hammering until a wall, complete with door, blocked off the storage area. He painted it with the whitewash provided and fell into bed that night too tired to do more than mutter the most perfunctory of prayers.

Monday afternoon when he returned from school, Mr. Rogers set about teaching him to set type. Phillip showed his new assistant the cases of different kinds and sizes of type, arranged with capital letters in the upper cases and the smaller letters in the lower cases. He set up a slug line and explained spacing and sizing, the inches required for the newspaper columns, and the setup of the press.

"You always have to remember your images are backwards, so you'd best follow the old saying, Mind your p's and q's, because they look so alike."

Thorliff nodded, trying to take it all in.

"Here, I'll set a line of type, and then you do the same."

"Okay." But watching his mentor pick the slugs and set them, his fingers moving fast enough to blur, made Thorliff's mouth go dry. Surely he'd never reach that speed.

"I should have Elizabeth teach you this. She's an expert at it."

"Really?" Thorliff leaned down to pick up another slug that he'd dropped. Picking type was difficult with five thumbs on each hand.

"The hardest part is remembering where all the letters are boxed. Then after the paper is printed, we return it all to the correct sections in the cases. That will always be your job on Fridays. The paper comes out on Thursday. I print it late Wednesday." Phillip looked up to Thorliff. "Remind me sometime. I have a funny story about running out of type."

"Ja — er, yes." Thorliff bent down to find another piece he'd dropped. The letters had a life of their own, jumping out of the line with the least provocation.

■ ■ ■ ■

The old building creaked and talked as it settled each night. The wind whistled at the window. Thorliff tried to study, but where the dormitory had been too noisy, now the quiet set his teeth on edge. What was happening at home? He'd not had a letter yet this week.

Lord, I want to go home. I can't see far enough here. Too many buildings. Too many people. I always thought I was a good student. Pastor said so many things, good things, and I guess I believed him. But here I'm just not good enough. I can't even get the type back in the right cases, and I'd begun to think I might want to be a newspaper man.

How can it be so dark even during the day when the sun is shining? He finished with his prayers for those at home and crawled into his lonely bed. How was Andrew doing? Ever since he was born, they'd shared a bed. *Lord, help me know what to do.*

When he stopped by the mail room at the school and pulled a letter from his box, his step felt lighter. He waited until he was on the path down the hill to open his letter from Anji.

Dearest Thorliff,

I am so glad you are doing well at school. Things are hard here right now. Pa fell out of the haymow and must have broken something in his back. The pain is something fierce. Your ma is taking care of him, as we all are. He sleeps on a padded board and tries not to move any more than necessary.

Other than that, I miss you and pray for you every day.

She continued on with news of the family, but the tone of her letter said far more than the words, and Thorliff knew he must go home.

Tucking the letter into his shirt pocket, Thorliff trotted down the hill and toward the train station. He jingled the change in his pants pocket. Surely it would be enough to pay for a telegram.

Rushing into the station, he headed over to the telegraph desk and gave the operator his message, panting with each word given. "Anji Stop Coming home tomorrow Stop Tell Mor Stop Love Thorliff"

"That will be twenty-five cents." The telegraph operator looked across the counter. "You must have had bad news, son."

"Ja, I did." Thorliff counted out the change and dropped it in the man's hand. "What time does the train leave for St. Paul tomorrow?"

Back at the newspaper office, he knocked on Mr. Rogers' office door.

"Come in, Thorliff." Phillip Rogers set his pen down and leaned back in his chair, stretching his hands over his head. "Good to see you." He turned his head slightly sideways. "I have a feeling I'm about to hear bad news. What is it?"

"I have to go home. I'm leaving on the train in the morning."

"Some emergency, I take it?"

"I'm needed there."

Mr. Rogers waited, obviously hoping Thorliff would say more. "When will you be back?"

Thorliff shrugged. Was he coming back? Could he tell this man such news out of the blue like this? "I-I'm not sure."

"Will you be back?"

Thorliff ignored the question. "Is it all right if I leave my things here?"

"Yes. This is your home and your place of work. I-I hate to lose you, boy."

"Thank you."

"Of course. But . . ." Rogers paused.

"You'll let me know right away?"

That night the hours passed slower than a sick centipede. Long before daylight Thorliff gave up and rose. He turned on the gas lamp and set three ads, not noticing that his fingers had indeed grown more nimble. All he could see was that he only got three done and there was a stack yet to do.

Anji, I'm coming. His thoughts ran far faster than his fingers. He packed his valise and headed for the train station before Mr. Rogers arrived. If he was going home, he should be happy, right? But instead he felt that he was standing still, waiting for lightning to strike.

He entered the station and headed for the ticket desk.

"Hey, young man, you're Thorliff Bjorklund, aren't you?" the telegraph agent called across the room.

"Ja." Thorliff turned and headed the other way. What could be the problem?

"Here. This came for you early this morning." He handed him an envelope.

"Thank you." Thorliff turned away, ripping the envelope in his haste.

"Dearest Thorliff Stop Do not come home Stop I forbid it Stop I will not speak to you ever again if you do Stop Anji"

Thorliff grunted as if a horse had kicked him right in the belly. He read the words again. They didn't change. Anji didn't want his help.

He sank down on one of the polished oak benches, slumping against the curved back. Surely if he went, she would relent.

Anji, how could you write such a thing? I thought that you loved me, needed me. The thoughts pounded so hard his head ached. Elbows propped on his knees, he held his head in his hands. Blessing seemed as far away as the Big Dipper in the night sky. What? Why? How was Joseph? Who was helping Anji? And so soon after her mother died.

Anji, why have you turned me away?

He read the telegram again, then crumpled it in his fist. *If she really loved me, she wouldn't write such a thing.* He smoothed the paper against his thigh, pressing out the wrinkles. *What kind of a man am I that I — God, help me!*

A burn started in his belly. *Fine, if she no longer needs me . . .* He stared at the brief words again, folded the paper in half and then in half again. On his way out the door, he dropped the paper in the wastebasket.

He strode out of the station, marched to the newspaper office, and entering by the back door, threw his satchel onto the bed. *If there is someone else, why didn't you tell me?* The burn flared brighter. Thinking words he knew his mother would not approve of and he didn't either, he left again and, taking the river track, jogged until he was out of town, then broke into a run. He ran past dry fields with cows grazing on what they could find. He pounded past cornfields that rattled in the dry wind. He ran on and on, trying to outrun the cacophony in his mind. He ran until his lungs screamed for air and the spear in his side doubled him over. When he could breathe again, he sat down against a tree, hugged his knees, and let the tears flow, soaking his pant legs. Finally the storm passed.

He stared out over his bent knees, upon which rested his chin. *So now what?* "God," he said, looking up, "if all this comes from your hands, you must have a plan." He sniffed and blew his nose on a handkerchief that wore an ink blot.

"I can't go home. Or won't go. . . ." His words trailed off. *Ah, Anji . . .*

Putting his handkerchief back in his pocket, he continued his prayer. "Mor and so many others gave so I could come." He looked up through the turning leaves. "So I stay." His hands clenched to fists. "And you will take care of Anji and" — his voice cracked — "those at home." A sigh let his shoulders slump. "So be it." He picked himself up and started the long walk back to town.

A church bell chimed the hour. The green haze of the trees of Northfield floated like a gossamer blanket over the town. Up on the hill Old Main, with its clock and bell tower, rose like a medieval fortress above the trees. The dream to come here was real, no longer just a dream or a wish. Now all he had to do was continue to follow the dream God had given him.

That's all.

He shoved his hands into his pockets, his long strides eating up the miles back to town.

ABOUT THE AUTHOR

Lauraine Snelling is an award-winning author of over forty books, fiction and nonfiction, for adults and young adults. Besides writing both books and articles, she teaches at writers' conferences across the country. She and her husband, Wayne, have two grown sons and four granddogs, and they make their home in California.

The employees of Thorndike Press hope you have enjoyed this Large Print book. All our Thorndike and Wheeler Large Print titles are designed for easy reading, and all our books are made to last. Other Thorndike Press Large Print books are available at your library, through selected bookstores, or directly from us.

For information about titles, please call:
  (800) 223-1244

or visit our Web site at:
  http://gale.cengage.com/thorndike

To share your comments, please write:
  Publisher
  Thorndike Press
  295 Kennedy Memorial Drive
  Waterville, ME 04901

LP FIC SNELLING
Snelling, Lauraine.
A dream to follow

8-08   ML